Riverside Serenade by Elizabe...
A man on a mission, Joshua She... ...oth-
er's fiancé is sneaking around with. When a chance ... ...n the
Riverwalk dumps Joshua into the river, it's love at first sight until
he finds out who Ecko Lewis really is. Can Ecko overcome Joshua's
suspicions and accusations? Will Christmas on the Riverwalk bring
them to embrace love?

Key to Her Heart by Martha Rogers
Valerie Murray is in the process of saving her business on the
Riverwalk when Colt Jamison returns to San Antonio. He offers
to help her with publicity, but Val doesn't trust him. When Valerie
realizes he is her only hope for getting the store out of the red, she
reluctantly accepts. Despite Colt's success, she still hesitates to open
her heart out of fear he will leave her once again.

Lights of Love by Lynette Sowell
When her mother catches the flu, Gabriela Hernandez is stuck at
home during her family's kitchen renovation. If only her father would
let her run their Riverwalk restaurant. Seeing contractor Miguel
Rivera every day makes Gabriela remember why she once loved him.
Miguel has overcome many regrets, except for breaking Gabriela's
heart. Will Miguel and Gabriela discover a future together, even
when the past won't stay dead at Christmastime?

Remember the Alamo by Kathleen Y'Barbo
When the role of a lifetime—in a remake of *The Alamo*—comes his
way, Joe Ramirez calls it an answered prayer. To keep her job, Sienna
Montalvo, aspiring filmmaker and assistant to the director, must
entertain the star during the holiday hiatus. Will Christmas with the
Montalvos be a losing battle, or will Joe forever *Remember the Alamo*
and the love he finds at Christmas in San Antonio?

A RIVERWALK CHRISTMAS

FOUR-IN-ONE COLLECTION

FOUR COUPLES FIND LOVE IN
ROMANTIC SAN ANTONIO

ELIZABETH GODDARD
MARTHA ROGERS
LYNETTE SOWELL
KATHLEEN Y'BARBO

BARBOUR
PUBLISHING

ISBN 978-1-60260-967-9

Cover design: Kirk DouPonce, DogEared Design

Published by Barbour Publishing, Inc., P.O. Box 719, Uhrichsville, OH 44683, www.barbourbooks.com

Our mission is to publish and distribute inspirational products offering exceptional value and biblical encouragement to the masses.

 Member of the
Evangelical Christian
Publishers Association

Printed in the United States of America.

RIVERSIDE SERENADE

by Elizabeth Goddard

Dedication

For my husband, Dan—
one look in your eyes and I *knew*.

Chapter 1

Suddenly a great company of the heavenly host appeared with the angel,
praising God and saying, "Glory to God in the highest, and on earth
peace to men on whom his favor rests."

LUKE 2:13–14 NIV

My flight was delayed, Daddy." Holding her cell against her ear, Ecko Lewis rolled her carry-on luggage behind her through the San Antonio International Airport. "I missed my appointment." She didn't want to tell Daddy it was an interview. Not yet.

"Oh, baby. I'm sorry to hear that. Are we still on for lunch?"

"That's what I'm calling about." Ecko stepped onto the down escalator and tugged her luggage to an upright position on the step behind her. "The person my appointment was with had a full schedule and could only make time for me at lunch."

And if she didn't hurry, she'd be late for that, as well. She'd taken an early-morning flight that should easily have gotten her from Kansas City to San Antonio in time for her ten-thirty appointment.

"I had hoped to see you. You're heading back to Kansas today, I presume?"

When she stepped from the escalator, Ecko caught a glimpse of her reflection and tugged the top of her short-cropped blond hair. "I'm here for a few days on assignment."

And that was true—she'd assigned herself the task of finding a job that would allow her to live near her father. Her college years followed by working to establish her career hadn't provided much in the way of family time. Since Mom's death over a year ago, Ecko regretted not having spent more time with her. And, after Ecko broke off her engagement six months ago, Daddy was all she had left.

God, please let me get this job.

"That's great. Why didn't you tell me? I could have cleaned the place for you," Daddy laughed.

"Oh, no. That's all right. I'll be working. A friend agreed to let me stay in her apartment while she's out of town." Ecko winced. The truth? The newspaper she'd worked for in Kansas City canceled her gossip column.

Still, she considered it a blessing. Now she had more time to search for a serious job in journalism like she'd wanted all along, and hopefully she'd find it in San Antonio. If she wanted to surprise Daddy, staying with him wouldn't work.

"I understand. You probably don't need any distractions."

"I want to focus on this and get it right. But don't worry, Daddy, I plan to make time for you, too." She hoped Daddy would be happy when he heard the news that she'd gotten a job in San Antonio. Her heart raced a little. It scared her to think how much she had riding on this interview. Ecko rounded a corner and spotted the rental-car booths.

"Good," he said. "Because—Ecko, I've got some news for you. I'd planned to share it at lunch."

Ecko had never heard this much enthusiasm in his voice. Puzzled, she got in line at the rental counter and absently stared at the large red letters. "What is it?" *Don't tell me he got a job somewhere else.*

"I wanted to tell you in person," he said, then covered the mouthpiece of his phone as he spoke to someone.

"Please, tell me now. What if we don't connect?" Doubtful, but Ecko wanted to know what Daddy was so anxious to tell her.

He released a sigh. "All right. We can always celebrate later."

Celebrate? Though she should be excited Daddy had news worth celebrating, panic swelled inside. She was almost to the counter and would need to end her call. People who conducted business while talking on a cell phone with someone else annoyed her.

"What's the news?" she asked.

"I'm engaged to be married."

Engaged? The man in front of her finished his business and stepped away from the counter, leaving room for Ecko. Frozen, she squeezed the phone, allowing Daddy's words to sink in. They reverberated through her head as she stepped to the counter. A young woman with long dark hair stared at her, waiting, but Ecko's mind had gone blank with Daddy's news.

"Can I help you?" the employee asked.

Ecko tugged her credit card from the slot in her wallet and slid it forward. "I reserved a car."

"Baby, did you hear what I said?"

"Yes, Daddy. I'll call you right back." She flipped the phone shut.

❄

"I don't trust him." Feet anchored wide apart, Joshua Sheppard stood in the opulent living room of his mother's mansion.

"Watch your mouth, Joshua. I'll not have you ruin this for me." Arranging a vase of crimson roses, his mother gave him a warning glance. In her late fifties, she still bore some of the youthful beauty that had generated her career as the famous top model, Giselle Honors. When she retired, she'd changed her name to dodge the media hounds and fortune seekers, but the ruse hadn't lasted long.

"You've known him less than a month. What makes you think he's different from the others?" Joshua continued to press the matter, knowing he would hurt her, but better Joshua now, than a wayward husband later. The last two prospective husbands were not in love with her, but wanted their hands on her fortune. Joshua had proven that to her, at least.

Why couldn't she see Tom Lewis was no different?

Appearing to consider his words, his mother tucked one last rose into the vase then peered at the arrangement from different angles. Finally, she walked around the table and took Joshua's hands in hers. "I'm in love with him, Joshua. I can't explain it other than to say it was love at first sight."

"Love at first sight? There's no such thing." Joshua held back his scoffing tone, but a person needed time to know if someone was right for them.

"I appreciate that you saved me from marrying the wrong man before. But this time, I want you to back off. You might not trust Tom, but I'm asking you to trust me."

As Joshua looked into his mother's eyes, he saw the love she had for Tom there. Truthfully, he'd not seen that before. He wished this man returned her affection. But the information he'd overheard Tom saying to a woman not his mother burned in his pocket. He'd written down the exact words. What should he do? Showing his mother wouldn't be enough proof. She'd simply state he was misinterpreting the words. No, he'd have to prove without a doubt that Tom was cheating on her before he'd even married her.

"I don't want to see you hurt, or your reputation smeared through the media again." Silently, he vowed to discover the truth about Tom.

"I understand, but if you interfere, this time *you* will be the one to hurt me."

Under her stern gaze, Joshua felt himself shrink as if he were a small child. Memories flooded his thoughts—his mother sitting on the edge of the bed in tears because of his father's indiscretions. Thankfully, the man had disappeared from their lives years ago.

No, he would never allow that to happen again. He would do what was necessary to stop the approaching nuptials.

✵

Slow, shallow breaths. Ecko wished she had a paper bag to keep her from hyperventilating. She'd decided to find a parking spot near the Riverwalk before she called Daddy back. But how was she supposed to arrange her jumbled thoughts for an interview when all she could think about were her father's words?

Sitting in her parked rental car, she tugged the cell from her purse and dialed.

"Baby," Daddy answered. "I was beginning to worry about you."

She heard the pain in his voice. "Sorry, I had to get to the Riverwalk where my lunch appointment is. I don't want to be late again." *Deep breath.* "I want to congratulate you, Daddy, but—"

"I know. It's a bit of a shock, isn't it?"

To say the least. "You know I want you to be happy. But who are you engaged to? Is it that woman you told me about over Thanksgiving? You met her a few weeks ago." Ecko grabbed her briefcase and stepped from the car.

"Yes."

"Isn't that fast? You've only known her a month." And Mom had only been gone a year—a pang squeezed Ecko's heart.

"Baby. . ." Daddy sighed. "I know what it looks like, but I'm a grown man. I'm capable of making a decision like this."

With or without your approval. Though Daddy didn't say it, she could hear it in his voice. And yet, she knew he wanted her approval. How could she convince him to wait? "I know what it's like to rush into an engagement and discover later that you made the wrong decision. I'm just thankful I didn't find out too late."

"You can't compare this to what you had with Brennan." He sighed, again. "Listen, this is why I wanted to tell you in person."

He wanted to gauge her reaction, she knew, but Ecko didn't think it would have made a difference. Oh, how she hated being at odds with Daddy.

Rushing through the hotel decorated for the Christmas holidays, she headed across the lobby where she found an exit that led to the Riverwalk. Stepping out into the open air, Ecko was wrapped in the aroma of Tex-Mex wafting from nearby restaurants. Her stomach growled.

"Okay, Daddy. Congratulations. I couldn't be happier that you're engaged. What's the date? June or July? It'll be a summer wedding, right?" Six months would give him time to change his mind.

"That's just it, Ecko. I'm hoping you can take an extended holiday. We're getting married the day after Christmas. With our busy schedules, it was the only time."

Ecko stopped mid-stride, causing a woman behind her to shove her forward. The woman apologized and moved around Ecko, who barely noticed. *Breathe, just breathe.*

With a well-paying stable job as an industrial engineer, Daddy was a good catch. All the more reason to be concerned. "Daddy, I'm sorry I have to say this, but I think your fiancée is pressuring you to move too fast."

Daddy didn't answer. A glance at Ecko's watch told her she had five minutes to find the restaurant for her interview and compose herself.

Had Ecko lost the connection? "Daddy, you still there?"

"Yes, I'm still here." He released another heavy sigh. "Ecko, this was my idea."

❇

Joshua hurried through the crowded sidewalk, thankful the

weather wasn't inclement. Sometimes, he'd give anything to have the snowy white Christmas scene on Christmas cards and in movies here in San Antonio. But then again, he wouldn't be able to shovel his way through traffic quickly enough, and he had to hurry if he were to catch Tom and his girlfriend eating at the Paloma Riverwalk restaurant. He imagined them sitting together at the riverside, though chilly, under a large magnolia tree. Anger nearly blinded him.

A crowd gathered around a group of schoolchildren, singing Christmas carols. They blocked his way. Excusing himself, he squeezed in front of proud mothers, fathers, and tourists to the other side while the children's choir sang "The First Noel," then "Feliz Navidad."

Finally, Joshua shoved free, ending up at the edge of the river. He shook his head. There should be another venue for such activities. He heard someone behind him, making the same excuses. For some reason, he turned to glance behind before moving on. Blond hair flashed in his vision as a body surged from the crowd and slammed into him.

His feet on the edge of the sidewalk, Joshua teetered backward, hovering inches from the river.

Chapter 2

The blond woman stared at him, her silver-gray eyes widening as her mouth dropped open. She reached toward Joshua.

He could feel himself falling back—just out of her reach—powerless against the invisible force that pulled him toward the river. Still, he fought to regain his balance, waving his arms to build momentum in the opposite direction, if possible.

The woman took another step and offered her hand in a desperate attempt to stop his fall. Her reach wasn't enough, and he plunged backward into the murky water of the San Antonio River. At forty-five degrees, the river was cold. Blurred by the water, faces appeared in his line of vision. Holding his breath, he began to right himself to drive his body to the surface, but his feet hit bottom.

Idiot. The river was only three to four feet deep. When he straightened his legs, he stood up and out of the water, which hugged his waist. Gasping for breath as he gathered his bearings, he searched the crowd, ready to unleash his anger. Where was she? Finally, incredulity fueled his lunge back to the sidewalk's edge.

How could a woman have the strength to knock him into the river? Or had it been *his* clumsiness? Whatever the cause, his humiliation grew with the crowd on both sides of the river.

There. Short blond hair wreathed her beautiful face, and striking eyes stared back. Water lapping around him, Joshua gripped the sidewalk's edge, expecting her to extend a hand again, this time helping him from the water. Although, he wouldn't need her assistance, of course. As he stared at her angelic face, all the frustration seemed to wash away with the cold river's current.

Suddenly, the desire to know this woman flooded him. He wanted to learn everything about her.

"Oh, sir. I'm so sorry! Please, accept my apology," she said as she backed away, the crowd parting for her.

An odd sense that she was the woman of his dreams gripped him. *I might never see her again.* But already he was losing her. "What? Where are you going? Wait!"

"Please, I'm late," she said, her eyes compelling him to understand. "I'll find a way to pay for any damage. I promise."

Then, as if she'd been an apparition, she disappeared. "Wait. . ." His words were wasted. She melted into the crowd.

Shivering, Joshua began climbing from the water. Two men assisted him, and an older woman wearing festive-colored waitress attire offered him a large warm towel as he stood. "Thanks." He wrapped it around his shoulders.

"You're welcome. Now, why don't you come inside?" She gestured toward La Cocina del Rio, a popular Mexican restaurant. "Would you like hot apple cider or coffee?"

With both hands, he shoved the wet hair from his face. Feeling numb after the dunking he'd taken, Joshua nodded. "Do you have hot chocolate?"

A twinkle in her eye, the woman smiled. "*Sí.*"

The throng around him began to disperse, and Joshua followed the waitress. It wouldn't hurt to give himself a moment to collect his thoughts about what had just happened. And what *had* just happened?

Before he went inside the restaurant, someone nudged Joshua's shoulder from behind.

He turned to see an elderly man, wanting his attention.

"Can I help you?" Joshua asked.

"The woman left this for you." He winked and held out a business card. "I wouldn't let that one get away."

Still struggling to wrap his mind around the incident, Joshua accepted the card and stared at it. "Thank you," he said and looked up. But it was too late. The man had vanished.

The name Eliza Connors was printed in the center, and underneath, a phone number. That was it? Who was this Eliza Connors who'd knocked him into the river?

As Joshua pondered the questions, little birds busied themselves on the sidewalk, collecting remnants of food left behind by people rushing to and fro.

A slight tug on his arm pulled his attention back to the

waitress and the kindness in her eyes. "Do you still want something warm to drink?"

Joshua shrugged the towel from his shoulders and smiled. "Thanks for your generosity, but no. I'm feeling much better."

Taking the towel from him, she nodded and entered the restaurant, leaving Joshua standing in the cold. He stood on the Riverwalk soaked to the bone. Shivering, he'd never noticed how cold it could get in San Antonio until that moment. A drop of water slid down his forehead and into his eye.

Joshua wiped his eyes and face with his sleeve then headed in the opposite direction of the Paloma restaurant, toward his truck near the Rivercenter Mall. Once inside, he started the vehicle, and since it was still warm from his drive over, he turned up the heat.

He pictured the young woman with silver-gray eyes and short blond hair, staring at him.

One look into those eyes and he knew—*I must find out more about you, Eliza Connors.*

He drove away from the curve where he had parallel parked and into traffic. Facing off with Tom was no longer in his plans today. No, the mysterious woman had seen to that. Still, he couldn't help but be thankful for the collision.

When his eyes had locked with Eliza's, it seemed as if she'd stirred life into his soul—that she'd shined light into the loneliness he held inside, chasing it away.

Could his mother be right? Was there such a thing as love at first sight?

✳

Sitting at a table in the restaurant, Ecko sipped on her water, thankful that her prospective employer was the one who wasn't on time. After the mishap on the Riverwalk, Ecko was fortunate to be only five minutes late.

This day was turning out to be the worst she'd experienced in a long time. The flight delays, missing her interview, and then there was Daddy's news.

"Oh, Daddy, what are you thinking?" She murmured under her breath.

And that poor man she'd sent tumbling into the river. She hated leaving him like that, but she had no time to help him. Likely, she couldn't have assisted him anyway. Still, she hoped someone else had helped him out.

Ecko forced her thoughts back to the interview. A glance at her watch set her nerves on edge even more. If she weren't already panicked from the volatile day, now she was beginning to worry that her interview wasn't going to happen. But with so many things vying for her thoughts, could she even make a good impression today?

One thing would go a long way to help her focus on her job interview. She dialed Daddy. He answered on the first ring. "Ecko, how did your lunch appointment go?"

"I'm still waiting for the woman to show. Listen, how about dinner tonight?" Ecko held her breath, hoping Daddy didn't have plans with—*that* woman. She winced at her sour thoughts of the woman Daddy thought he loved, a woman who could soon be his wife, Ecko's stepmother.

"I have plans with Laura. But I suppose asking you to join us at this juncture would be too much."

Ecko closed her eyes, hating to hear the pain in her father's voice. "I'm sorry, Daddy," she whispered.

"No, it's all right. You're still the most important woman in my life. I want to make you understand."

"Thank you, Daddy." Ecko smiled at the man who began taking his seat across the table from her. "My appointment is here. I'll call you later."

She snapped the phone shut and offered her hand. "I'm Eliza Connors."

The man smiled and shook her hand. "Chris Barnett." He adjusted his silver-rimmed glasses and tugged his tie.

Wearing a blue suit, he had black hair gone silver at the temples. Ecko guessed him to be in his early forties.

"I confess I was expecting someone else," she said.

Mr. Barnett took the menu the waiter offered. "We've had a slight change in our direction, Miss Connors. Or should I call you Miss Lewis?"

❄

That evening, Ecko spotted her father waiting for her. La Canarias was a four-star restaurant on the Riverwalk. If nothing else, she would have experienced the fine cuisine of San Antonio restaurants by the end of her stay. There was nothing like Tex-Mex.

Wearing her nicest dress and a warm velvety jacket, Ecko rushed into his arms. "Daddy!"

When he released her, she stood back and admired his suit. "You're a handsome man. No wonder you're engaged." Ecko attempted to keep the tone light, though she remained greatly troubled with the circumstances, especially considering Mom had only been gone a year.

Once ushered to their seats by the maître d', Ecko smiled across the table at Daddy. "Why the fancy restaurant?"

"Can't a father treat his little girl to a nice dinner at a fine restaurant?" He winked then perused the menu.

"You know you don't need to impress me." She giggled. Why hadn't she noticed before what a handsome man he was? Glad to spend time with him this evening, she dreaded the inevitable discussion regarding his upcoming nuptials.

"How did your day go? Did your lunch appointment finally show?" He peered at her over his menu.

"Yes, finally." She focused on her own, hoping to discourage further questions on the topic.

The interview had been disturbing. Mr. Barnett had assured her that, if hired, she would be working on serious human interest stories, though it sounded more like the publication had changed direction and now resembled a tabloid. She suppressed the sigh that arose at the disappointing thoughts. For the moment, it was her only prospect. She couldn't live more than two months without an income.

"I missed reading your column this week. Are you writing for another segment now?"

Ecko froze. She'd hoped to share good news with Daddy before he noticed her column was no longer in print in the *Kansas City Star*. Though he was her biggest fan, she knew that Daddy would sometimes go days without reading it because he was busy with work.

"Yes." She dipped her head to focus on the menu again, pretending she cared about her choices. "I'm looking into a human interest piece."

The waiter came to take their orders.

Ecko sent him an apologetic look. "I still haven't decided. I'm accustomed to tacos and burritos. But this is seriously upscale Mexican. What do you suggest, Daddy?"

"How about I order for us?" He winked.

"Okay." She handed the menu to the waiter. "Surprise me."

For her, Daddy ordered the seared sea scallops with jalapeño cream and for himself, turkey chipotle–cranberry tortas.

The waiter smiled his approval and left them.

"Now, where were we?" Daddy asked. "Oh, I remember. Will you write this new piece under your pen name, Eliza Connors? Or can the world know my daughter is a famous writer?"

"I'm not famous." Guilt mingled with the heat in Ecko's cheeks. "Oh, Daddy—"

Her cell rang. Maybe this was the call telling her she had the job so she could be up front with Daddy. Her heart raced.

To Daddy, she said, "Excuse me. I need to take this." Into the cell, she answered, "Eliza Connors."

"Miss Connors, I hope I'm not disturbing you."

"No, not at all." Who was this? It didn't sound like Chris Barnett.

"My name is Joshua Sheppard. We met earlier today when you knocked me into the river."

Ecko gasped and looked at her father, hoping he didn't see the disappointment and embarrassment infusing her at that moment. She covered the mouthpiece, "Daddy, I'll be right back." Rising from the table, she hurried to the restaurant foyer and found a private corner. "Sir, I apologized for that. I'm so sorry. Is there something else?"

Ecko cringed, wishing she hadn't left her card. But at the time it seemed like the right thing to do. At least it had been her business card with her pen name—that way the man couldn't track her down or stalk her, if he were crazy. These days, one never knew. She'd covered enough of those stories in her gossip column.

"Yes, there's something else." He was silent for a moment, then, "Would you allow me to buy you lunch sometime?"

Oh no. Ecko pressed her head against the wall, forcing herself to remain calm.

He cleared his throat. "I understand your hesitation. How about a cup of coffee?"

To his credit, he hadn't exactly used her guilt for landing him in the river to force her into lunch. He mentioned it only as a way to identify himself. And, after all, didn't she owe him at least a cup of coffee? In a safe public place, what could be the harm? And, it would be a simple way to ease her conscience in the matter.

"All right. And I'm buying. I owe you. But after coffee, we're good. Is that a deal?"

"Fair enough. Are you familiar with La Cocina del Rio?"

"I'm sure I can find it."

"It's near the place where we met. Ten thirty, tomorrow?"

"I think I can fit that into my schedule." Ecko started to ask how she would recognize him then caught herself. She recalled the surprise in his dark eyes and how his black wavy hair had looked so different when wet. Unfortunately, a small laughed escaped.

"Is something funny?"

Other than the comical way you fell into the river? "No, not at all. I'll see you there." After ending the call, she had the strange sense that he knew exactly why she'd been laughing.

Standing tall, she straightened her dress and headed back to Daddy. Now, to find out why he was in such a hurry to get married. . .

Chapter 3

The waitress who'd offered Joshua a towel yesterday also served him today as he sat at a lone table in La Cocina del Rio. Her name tag read Marcy.

She approached his table again and held out the coffee-pot. "Another cup?"

"Yes, please." This was his fourth, and he was beginning to think that Eliza Connors wasn't going to show.

"Don't worry." Pouring his coffee, Marcy's smile was sympathetic. "She'll be here."

Joshua narrowed an eye and looked up at her. "How do you know it's a she?"

"You were nervous when you got here, like a schoolboy on a first date. Now, your jaw is twitching because she's late." She gave a soft laugh and squeezed his shoulder. "You remind me of my son."

Joshua ripped into a sugar packet and poured it into his cup, stirring, then took a swig of the coffee, feeling it burn his empty stomach. "I'll give her five more minutes."

Fifteen minutes later, he was shaking his head at Marcy when she offered more coffee, this time her eyes telling him she'd lost hope, as well.

I'm a fool. Bad enough, Eliza Connors made him look like an idiot yesterday when he'd fallen into the river, but she'd done the same today. Thankfully, Marcy was his only witness. He wondered if she had an inkling about who he'd been waiting for.

As he stood from the table and tugged his jacket from the chair back, he realized that he wasn't much different than his mother when it came to the opposite sex, or at least with this one woman. He'd allowed her to toy with him.

It would not happen again.

Leaving a big tip for Marcy, Joshua tugged on his cap and nodded at her across the room, forcing a smile to hide his annoyance.

Recalling she mentioned his jaw, he tried to relax that as well. A woman stumbled through the door of the small restaurant. Joshua cringed as Eliza Connors barreled toward a waitress who lifted a breakfast tray just in time for her to walk underneath.

Frowning, Eliza searched the restaurant until her eyes found him then. . .she smiled. When she looked at him with her light gray eyes, he remembered that moment yesterday when he'd felt his irritation wash away with the river current. Now, her smile caused his frustrations to fade in the same way.

Joshua nodded and held out the chair for her where he'd

been sitting as she strolled his way.

"Mr. Sheppard, I don't think we've met formally." Eliza held out her hand, setting the tone like a businesswoman. "I'm Eliza Connors."

Joshua took her soft hand in his and gently shook it. "Joshua Sheppard. Please, call me Joshua."

"All right, Joshua. Call me Eliza." Eliza sat in the chair he held for her. "I'm sorry I'm late. I hope you didn't wait too long."

Joshua took the seat opposite her at the table, wondering if he could down yet another cup of coffee. "I arrived only a few minutes ago myself." He avoided looking at the empty sugar packets surrounding the lone cup—evidence to the contrary. To think, she was supposed to be the one to pay.

Unfortunately, the sugar packets snagged her attention. A small grin slipped into her lips.

Nailed. The woman was observant.

"Thank you for warming the seat for me. Can I buy you an early lunch?"

Joshua owned and operated his own business and could arrange his schedule. Though agreeing would mean he'd have to work late, he needed to spend time with the woman who lit his heart.

"Lunch is good." He wanted to add that he would buy, but feared he would scare her off with the way his heart and thoughts raced out of control.

Slow down, man. He was crazy, no doubt there. If his mother found out, he'd never hear the end of this. But her situation was different. Completely.

Eliza smiled when Marcy approached the table. "I'll have

a cup of coffee and we'd like to see lunch menus."

Marcy poured coffee for Joshua, too, but he had no intention of drinking it. Joshua was aware of her particularly big smile, but she said nothing to him and handed them both a menu.

When Marcy left, Eliza relaxed into the chair, appearing uninterested in the menu. "Tell me, Joshua, what do you do for a living?"

He leaned against the seat back and smiled, surprised at her question. A good conversationalist knew how to draw others out, rather than talking about themselves. "I own and operate Sheppard Christmas Lighting. We install both residential and commercial Christmas lights."

"Ah, so this is your busy season. I'm flattered that you allowed me time to repay you."

He searched her unusual eyes, thinking he could look into them forever. The same words of caution he'd given his mother warned him to slow down. He couldn't be in love—he'd told his mother it was impossible for her to love someone in such a short time.

Yet, here he was, hoping that Eliza would agree to see him for some reason other than to repay a debt. "Your apology is payment enough," he said.

Her gentle laugh and the look in her gaze told Joshua that she felt it, too—there was chemistry between them.

❄

"I hope you know I truly am sorry for dunking you." An image of him plunging backward into the river flitted across her vision. She felt the smile slip into her lips and covered it with her hand as she rested her chin on her palm.

A broad grin spread across Joshua's face. With black hair and eyes to match, a tanned complexion and a strong jaw, he was a handsome one. Despite her earlier hesitation to meet him for coffee, she was glad she'd agreed. And now, coffee had turned to lunch, after all. Marcy returned, and Ecko ordered a chicken fajita salad, Joshua an enchilada dinner.

"So, Eliza, what do you do for a living? Or an even better question, why were you in such a hurry yesterday?" Flashing an easy smile, he tapped a sugar packet against the table.

Though he appeared to pack a lot of nervous energy, Ecko felt comfortable with him. She laughed. "Actually, the two questions are related. I majored in journalism in college, and I'm still searching for the right job. I was running late for an interview—one that I had to reschedule because I missed the first one." She warmed her hands on the steaming mug and watched Joshua's reaction.

"Ah, so that explains it." Elbows on the table, he cradled his cup, as well, then leaned closer. "I hope you made it on time, despite our little mishap."

A mishap that had brought them together. Ecko found she was glad to be sitting across the table from Joshua Sheppard. Feeling heat in her cheeks at the thought, she pulled her gaze from his dark eyes and stared into her cup of coffee.

"Yes, I made it."

He drew back and leaned against the chair. "Then I'm glad you didn't stop to help me from the river."

Before Ecko could respond, Marcy appeared with their lunch and placed a salad before Ecko, dressing on the side, and set Joshua's hot plate in front of him. Ecko noticed the woman wink at Joshua. In return, he gave the waitress a slight nod. What was that about?

Marcy left, and Joshua returned his attention to Ecko. "Others gave assistance. Someone even brought me a towel and offered me something warm to drink."

Ecko realized she'd become tense. She relaxed as understanding dawned. The incident had happened just outside this restaurant. "I have a hunch that our waitress today was there to help you. Am I wrong?"

"You're correct. I was a stranger to her, yet she offered me warmth when I was cold and something to drink when I was thirsty." He took a swig of coffee, watching Ecko over the rim.

He's a Christian. Ecko's breath almost caught in her throat. "The parable of the sheep and the goats in Matthew chapter twenty-five. 'For I was hungry and you gave me something to eat, I was thirsty and you gave me something to drink, I was a stranger and you invited me in, I needed clothes and you clothed me, I was sick and you looked after me, I was in prison and you came to visit me.'"

His expression softened into something Ecko couldn't read. "I'm—impressed."

Suddenly feeling uncomfortable, Ecko looked down at her salad. "Would you say the blessing, then?"

Ecko shut her eyes and listened to the soft words of thanks as they rolled with feeling from Joshua's lips. She slowly opened them to see him staring at her. His lips stretched into a small grin.

Lifting his fork, he said, "Tell me about the interview. It went well, I hope."

Ecko jabbed at her salad, too nervous to eat. What was

happening? Could she really like a guy she'd only just met?

"I feel confident that they want me. I'm waiting to hear back from them." For the first time since hearing Daddy's news she felt at peace. Things might just work out, after all. And though Daddy's engagement could be the right thing for him, she almost let her concerns dampen her mood. One look at Joshua lifted her spirits again.

Before she realized it, she'd divulged her hopes and dreams, leaving out that she'd written for a gossip column. It had only been a stepping-stone, after all. Leaving out, too, that she was beginning to think the serious job she wanted in San Antonio could amount to nothing more than a tabloid. But again, she needed a job, and it would land her near her father.

She set her fork down, realizing she'd only toyed with her salad, the dressing on the side unused. When was the last time a man had made her so giddy? And to think, he'd actually listened to her, seeming to care about her life. Grim regrets of her brief engagement to Brennan flitted through her thoughts.

A new waitress came to remove their plates and offer dessert.

Joshua wiped his mouth then placed his napkin on his empty dish. "Where's Marcy?"

The young woman smiled sadly. "She had a family emergency. I'm taking her place for now. Can I get you anything else?"

Lost in thought, he frowned. Finally, he realized the waitress still waited for his answer, and he looked at Ecko. "Would you like dessert?"

Ecko wanted to know more about Joshua. She didn't want their time to end. Did he feel the same way? "I'll have some if you are."

He studied her, appearing more serious than she'd seen him since she'd watched him fall into the river. "I'm afraid I have to get back to work."

"Oh." The one word revealed her disappointment. Oddly, instead of wishing she'd hidden her true feelings, she wanted him to know.

"I think I'll pass on dessert then, too," she said to the waitress.

Slipping his hand across the table, he took hers. His gentle touch sent a current up her arm—something she'd never felt with Brennan.

"Eliza Connors, thank you for meeting me today. I enjoyed it." He searched her eyes.

What was he looking for? The answer to his next question? *Can I see you again?*

"I did, too," she said.

For an instant, Ecko thought he might lift her hand to his lips. The romantic current was definitely flowing. Instead, he released her hand and stood. He smiled down at her as he tugged on his cap and jacket.

Pulling a large bill from his wallet, he left it on the table and winked. "Take care," he said then headed toward the exit.

Stunned, Ecko watched him leave. Was that it? One minute she was practically basking in his company, and the next he stood and walked away without so much as asking if he could see her again?

As if emptying the coffee cup could somehow douse her disappointment, Ecko drained the last drop for good measure. What had she expected anyway?

Wait. Wasn't she supposed to pay?

Chapter 4

Joshua spent the remainder of the afternoon attempting to answer complaints as well as meet the demands of new customers. Though he had several crews to oversee, there never seemed to be enough hard-workers to meet the needs during the holiday season. Despite the hectic afternoon, a sense of pride and achievement swelled inside. He could easily have lived off his mother's wealth like a spoiled son, but he refused her generosity, wanting instead to build something successful and meaningful with his own hands.

Though swamped with work, Joshua had not stopped thinking about lunch with Eliza. It had taken every ounce of his strength to keep from asking her to meet with him again. To ask her on a real date. But, he reasoned, his emotions were getting away from him. He was moving far too fast and feared he would scare her off. She'd simply agreed to meet him for coffee and, because she'd arrived late, offered to pay for lunch.

He chuckled, remembering that he'd been the one to pay in the end. Joshua searched the radio station for Christmas music while he drove.

There. A popular contemporary Christian artist sang "Angels We Have Heard on High." That was more to his liking. Another angel came to mind. In two days, he would call Eliza Connors again. This time he would invite her to go shopping with him to find a Christmas gift for a special little girl.

Today, he'd learned that Marcy had been pulled away from her job as a waitress to care for her six-year-old granddaughter, who'd fallen ill. Marcy's son, the child's father, had left his daughter with Marcy while he was out of town. Marcy didn't go into detail, but Joshua figured she had her hands full. Staying home from her job to care for the child would hit her already-limited finances hard. He would do what he could to help without making Marcy feel as though she was accepting charity. Somehow he knew she would flatly refuse his assistance otherwise.

Darkness had settled over San Antonio a couple of hours ago. He drove through one of his favorite neighborhoods on his way home to admire the Christmas lights. Depictions of the Christmas story decorating yards and business establishments never failed to inspire him and ease his tension. In a way, he believed he was part of a ministry to spread the Gospel by telling the story of Christ through Christmas lights.

Leaving the neighborhood behind, exhaustion began to lay hold of Joshua. Joining his mother and Tom for dinner was the last thing he wanted to do right now and, as it was, he would be late for dessert. He rushed home, showered, and called her to let her know he was on his way. Then he spent the remainder of the drive attempting to order his thoughts regarding Tom. His mother knew how he felt about the man, but she insisted that Joshua was wrong. Insisted that Joshua spend time getting to know Tom.

The most important thing to Joshua was his mother, and he would bend over backward if that's what it took to keep Tom from hurting her. He would be there tonight, smile and be cordial to Tom, and at the same time, hope Tom would slip in some way, revealing the truth about his unfaithfulness. Though he dreaded seeing his mother hurt, he preferred that the truth come out before the wedding.

Guilt squeezed his heart. Could he consider his actions and thoughts those of one who claimed to follow Christ?

Create in me a clean heart, oh God.

Parking his car in the circular driveway, he trotted up the steps onto the porch and slipped through the front door. His mother's laughter could be heard in the den. When she saw him standing in the doorway, her face lit up.

"Joshua." She seemed to float across the floor to him and kissed his cheek. "You made it."

Tom stood. "Good to see you."

"And you." Joshua made his way to the settee where he took a seat.

The man smiled, but Joshua noticed his jaw working—tension that could easily be spotted if one knew where to look. Thanks to Marcy, Joshua now knew. And Tom's tension? All the more reason to be suspicious of him. Why couldn't his mother see Tom's obvious aversion to her son? That should be a sign to her.

"I can't stay long," Joshua said.

"It's your busy season; I understand." She sat on the sofa across from Joshua. "Thank you for coming."

Tom joined her. "Your mother hopes that you and I will have the opportunity to get to know each other better."

His mother smiled and looked into Tom's eyes. "*Before* the wedding," she said.

Feeling nauseous, Joshua averted his gaze from their shared look. "That doesn't give us much time, does it?"

His question prompted an idea. In fact, this could be the answer. A way for him to discover what he needed to prove Tom's unfaithfulness. "Maybe you can join me one evening on the job. You don't work during the evening, do you?"

"With the approaching holidays and wedding, I'm trying to tie up loose ends and still have time to spend with your mother."

"And Tom's daughter is in town," she said.

"Yes, I'd love for you to meet her." Tom rose and moved to stand behind the sofa.

At that moment, Joshua noticed the turtle cheesecake set out. He took a slice and poured himself coffee while he considered Tom's suggestion. If Joshua had his way, Tom wouldn't be around long enough to bring other acquaintances into the circumstances. He took a long slurp of coffee, enjoying the warmth to his gut.

Tom's cell phone rang, and he looked at it. "Excuse me, I have to take this." He answered and disappeared from the den.

When Tom left the room, Joshua's mother visibly sagged.

"What's wrong with you? We've been over this already. I'm getting married. Accept it."

"Everything is fine. I'm just tired."

"You act so—cold and guarded."

Joshua sighed, wishing his mother would be more guarded with her heart. He moved to sit next to her, leaving his cheesecake. "All I want is for you to be happy. You know how I feel about your engagement, but I'm here, aren't I?"

She touched his hand. "I wish you would find someone to love."

With the words, an angel named Eliza Connors filled his mind's eye. Silver-gray eyes stared back at him.

His mother's gasp drew him from the momentary vision.

"You have, haven't you?"

"What?"

"You've found someone. Oh Joshua, I couldn't be happier."

"Why would you think that?" Now, Joshua felt his own jaw twitching.

"Haven't you witnessed love in someone's eyes?"

Joshua said nothing, but knew that he had. He'd seen it in his mother's eyes when she looked at Tom or spoke of him.

"I saw that look in your eyes when I mentioned you should find someone to love. Who is she? Please, invite her over. I'd love to meet her."

How could Joshua tell his mother that was the last thing he wanted to do? Fame and fortune had a way of changing the way people looked at someone—he'd seen that enough in his mother's relationships.

No.

He could only trust what Eliza Connors might feel for him if she knew nothing about his mother's fame and wealth.

❄

Two days later, Joshua could hardly believe that he stood next to Eliza in the Rivercenter Mall. She'd agreed to join him to shop for Christmas gifts.

Blond hair catching the light, she held out a Madame Alexander doll. "Oh, Joshua. Don't you think she'd love one of these?"

The doll's face was framed with golden curls, and its eyelids slid closed when Eliza cradled it. She tipped it forward to hear a responding, "ma-ma."

The doll's cry elicited sweet laughter from Eliza. Joshua smiled, appreciating the warmth that stirred all the way to his toes. He wondered if he were going crazy, or if Eliza felt it, too. That first day in the restaurant, he'd been so sure she sensed their chemistry.

Joshua breathed in the scent of the doll store—a blend of new toys and women's perfume—restoring calm to his thoughts. Planted as they were next to the large display that had caught Eliza's eye, customers shopped around them as though they were store mannequins.

Suddenly, Eliza's smile faded, and she slowly looked up into his face. All that surrounded him seemed to fade away as he held her gaze. What were her thoughts at that moment? Her lips appeared soft and expectant.

Without thinking, Joshua gave her a quick, gentle kiss. Watching her reaction, he smiled, unwilling to hide his pleasure from her. Still, he feared he'd overstepped.

Surprise shown in her eyes for an instant then was gone. She gave him a quick squeeze. "Well, regardless of what you think, I'd love to give her one of these. I had one when I was a little girl."

Joshua risked a hug and relished that Eliza was receptive to him. "I think that's fine. In fact, we don't need to stop with the doll. Why don't we spoil her?" He winked then led Eliza, who still held the doll, to the cashier's counter.

He pulled his wallet out to pay for the item.

Eliza stepped in front of him. "Oh no you don't. I'm getting this."

"No, please. I invited you to help me, remember?"

Her eyes sparkled. "I was supposed to pay for lunch the other day. Besides, I really want to do this. Let me?"

How could Joshua deny this woman? He stood back while she went through the payment process. His mother had already mentioned she'd seen "the look" in his eyes. How would he ever hide this from her? He was in love.

Really—in love.

❄

While Ecko walked the crowded mall, she admired the gorgeous Christmas trees covered in lavish ornaments and silver tinsel, and the colorful lights strung everywhere possible. Cheerful seasonal music was piped through the mall, and the aroma of freshly baked cinnamon rolls drifted around her, making her mouth water. The Christmas spirit was definitely in the air.

Joshua carried their purchases, but she wished the doll wasn't packaged in a box. How she'd love to hold it to her gently. It seemed that was the only thing missing, because she was happier than she remembered ever being.

His calloused hand was large and strong as he held hers. Odd. It had all happened so fast, but seemed so natural. She couldn't imagine being anywhere else. Being with anyone else. She'd never felt this way with Brennan, and, except for the quick comparison, Joshua had made her forget about her ex-fiancé. Despite everything that had gone wrong between them, she'd continued to harbor the hurt, as though she owed Brennan something, as though she still carried a remnant of the love they supposedly shared.

She glanced up at Joshua, his good-looking face the picture of contentment as he searched the store windows. The man stirred her heart in a powerful way. No, she'd never loved Brennan.

Ecko shopped in a perfume store while Joshua took their packages, including the doll, to his truck. Rummaging through the large display of scents, both old and new, Ecko stumbled upon a bottle of Giselle.

She drew in a quick breath. "Daddy," she whispered. When he'd shared the news that his fiancée, Laura Kimball, was also the infamous Giselle Honors, Ecko could hardly believe it. She pondered that a woman of such beauty could have influence over Daddy, and perhaps that was the reason he seemed so in love, so eager to marry.

Still wary about Daddy's engagement, Ecko had tried to convince him to wait if only a little. But he would not be persuaded to postpone the wedding. Daddy wanted Ecko to meet Laura soon.

Lifting the perfume bottle from its position among many, Ecko held it gently in her hand. Would they have a tester?

After searching through the displays, she couldn't find one. Regardless of the perfume's scent, Ecko decided to buy a bottle for herself.

After completing her purchase, she stood outside the perfume store waiting for Joshua and gazed at the books in the window display next to the perfume store. Strong hands squeezed her waist from behind.

"Eliza," Joshua said into her ear. A delightful tingle crawled over her body. She turned to face him—his handsome face nearly taking her breath away.

How had she been so blessed to cross paths with this man?

"Eliza," he said again and smiled. "I'm sorry it took me so long."

Eliza. Though she was accustomed to going by Eliza professionally, Ecko considered telling him her real name. As she gazed into his dark eyes, she realized the extent of her growing feelings for him—a man whom she'd only recently met. But if things didn't work out, it would be easier this way. How many times had she wished that Brennan had never known her by her real name?—so messy was their breakup.

Suddenly he frowned. "What's wrong?"

She flashed him a bright smile. "Now that you're back, all is well with the world."

He studied her, appearing unconvinced at first, then the crease in his forehead disappeared. "What did you buy?"

"Perfume, of course, what else?" Ecko pulled the box that held the bottle of Giselle from the sack.

If possible, Joshua's dark eyes grew even darker.

Chapter 5

Something was wrong. Ecko sensed that Joshua had grown distant ever since he'd returned from putting away their packages. Gone was the light in his eyes and the easy conversation, zapping her joy and Christmas spirit. Joshua seemed preoccupied because within half an hour, Ecko found herself sitting in his truck as he drove her home. They'd ended their shopping spree too soon in her opinion.

Back at her apartment, Ecko held the door for him as he helped her lug packages into the living room. She'd offered to wrap the presents for Marcy's granddaughter. Stepping through the door to leave, he stood under the mistletoe she'd hung, his breath coming in white puffs—surprising for San Antonio.

Ecko stood on the porch and closed the door behind her to keep the cold out of her apartment. She clung to the hope that she could restore the magic she'd felt all day. "Any chance I can be with you when you take the gifts?"

Hands tucked in his black leather jacket, he smiled. "I'd like that. I have to find out when it's convenient though, so I'll call you." He stared down at her, the shadows preventing Ecko from reading his expression.

She wished she could read his mind. Because they'd shared a small kiss earlier, she didn't believe he needed the mistletoe for a hint now. But she allowed her gaze to drift up until she saw the greenery above.

Joshua tugged her to him and planted his lips on hers. He lingered this time. She breathed in the scent of him, wishing they could remain like this forever, but too soon the cold nipped, and she allowed herself to ease away.

"Good night, Eliza Connors." Joshua winked then made his way down the steps.

When he disappeared around the corner, Ecko released a content sigh.

Oh, Daddy. If this is anything like what you feel for Laura, how can I blame you for wanting to be with her always?

❄

Later that evening, Ecko sat on the floor writing out Christmas cards at the coffee table while she watched *It's a Wonderful Life*. She'd finished wrapping the gifts. Only eleven more days until Christmas. She was beginning to worry that she didn't get the job she'd interviewed for, after all. In the meantime, she'd sent out quite a few résumés and contacted people she knew in the business to no avail.

The holidays weren't exactly the best time to be job hunting. Oh, she felt confident she could land a position somewhere—but it might not be in San Antonio. And if that happened, she wouldn't be closer to Daddy. Of course, he would soon be a newlywed and wouldn't even miss her. Why should he? She hadn't even told him of her plans.

Then there was Joshua. What had distracted him during their shopping? Ecko sighed and rested her head in her palms, watching the movie. If she had to leave San Antonio, she would never find out what could have been between them.

She groaned inside. Who was she kidding? She was worrying about something that hadn't happened yet.

❉

The next morning, her cell rang at seven thirty.

Lord, please let this be the call I need.

One look at the caller ID and, though it wasn't Chris Barnett with a job offer, her heart leaped. "Joshua?"

"Good morning. I hope I didn't wake you."

"Not at all. I'm researching potential employers, considering I haven't heard back from the other."

"I made arrangements to take the gifts to Marcy this afternoon. It should only take an hour or so and then I have to get back to work. I can't believe that with only ten days left, we have at least twenty new customers wanting lights."

Ecko heard both excitement and distress in his words. "Oh, Joshua. That's wonderful!"

"Can you be ready at twelve thirty?"

"Of course." After he ended the call, Ecko stared at her cell, marveling at the miracle of their whirlwind relationship.

She could hear Daddy now, repeating to her the very same words she'd said to him. *Isn't that fast?*

By early afternoon, Eliza rode next to Joshua as he drove

through a neighborhood of older homes. She held several gifts in her lap, while others were stashed in the backseat of his truck. While he drove, he answered her questions about his business. The tone in his voice told her everything—he loved his work. But it went deeper than that—Joshua Sheppard was for real.

He pulled up to the curb in front of a small frame house in need of another coat of white paint. "This is it," he said, flashing her a grin.

Her heart lurched. That he would go to such great lengths to help a stranger in need!

By now, of course, Marcy and her granddaughter had become more than strangers to Joshua. The way he spoke of them, they sounded like family. As he assisted Ecko from the truck, holding the gifts, she gave him a side glance.

Funny. He never talked about his real family. But then, she hadn't told him about Daddy, either. Ecko frowned. The decision to withhold her real name hadn't been the right one no matter how much difficulty her breakup with Brennan had caused. Keeping the truth from Joshua had been the wrong choice. But how would she tell him?

❄

"You ready?" Joshua held her hand as she climbed from his truck, clinging to two gifts—one the Madame Alexander doll. He would come back for the rest after letting Marcy know they'd arrived.

He smiled, thinking about how much Eliza loved the doll. He could imagine her as a little girl. Instead of short hair, long golden curls would have hugged her face.

Together, they strolled up the sidewalk to the little house.

He'd see to painting once spring arrived. Though the house was small and run-down, Joshua was jealous of the warmth and love he'd felt inside upon his initial visit with Marcy—a far cry from the home he grew up in, though he knew his mother loved him.

Joshua had only lifted his hand to knock when the door swung open. Marcy beamed at him then turned her smile on Eliza. "Come in, come in. I'm so glad you were able to come. A neighbor is willing to watch Maria this evening, and I'm going back to work."

Eliza walked into the home ahead of Joshua.

"That's wonderful news. Please, let me know if there's anything else I can do," he said.

"Mr. Joshua, you've done more than enough." Marcy appeared embarrassed. "I only allow your help"—her eyes teared up—"for my granddaughter's sake."

"I'm so glad you did, Marcy," Eliza said. "I picked something out that I hope she'll love as much as I did when I was a little girl."

Marcy smiled at her behind moisture-rimmed eyes. She took both Eliza's hands in hers and gazed at Joshua as though giving him her approval. He and Marcy hadn't known each other long, but she could read him well. In fact, he thought she might even love him like a son. Maybe one day he would take her to meet his mother.

Suddenly, all eyes turned to Maria—a frail little creature with long black hair—standing in the doorway. "*Abuela*?"

Marcy rushed to her. "You remember Mr. Joshua? He's brought a special friend. They've brought you presents."

"Would it be all right if Maria opened at least the one

present before Christmas? I would so love to see." Eliza's soft, pleading eyes would easily persuade Marcy, Joshua thought.

With a smile, Marcy nodded her agreement and guided the little girl to a chair. Eliza handed the gift to Maria, whose eyes filled with wonder. Appearing to have difficulty opening the package, Eliza gently helped her rip at the tape and folds until the paper finally gave way. She held the box up so that Maria could see the doll inside.

Maria took the box, her face lighting up. "A doll, *Abuela*!"

"I thought you might like it," Eliza said. "Here, let me remove it from the box for you."

After freeing the doll, Eliza handed it to Maria. Tugging the doll gently to her, Maria cradled its head in the crook of her neck. "She's beautiful just like you. I'll keep her forever and ever because she'll remind me of you. I want to name her after you. What is your name again?"

Eliza appeared startled at the question, and her smile melted into a slight frown. She glanced up at Joshua, an unreadable emotion in her eyes.

❄

Before Ecko could think of how to answer the precious little girl, her cell phone rang. A glance at the caller ID sent her heart soaring.

"Yes!" She bolted upright almost too fast. "I'm sorry for the interruption, but this is the call I've been waiting for."

She sent an apologetic look Joshua's way, believing he would understand, and saw warmth in his eyes. Stepping outside, she answered, "Eliza Connors."

"Miss Connors. We've made a decision. The job is yours if you can complete our test assignment satisfactorily."

Chapter 6

Back at her apartment, Ecko stared at the e-mail explaining her test assignment. To think that she'd traveled from Kansas City to San Antonio for an interview with this publication. She'd wanted this job. And now, she needed this job.

But as she read through the assignment, her spirits sagged. Her hopes slowly bled out her feet. They wanted her to write what appeared to be nothing more than a smear campaign. If she didn't take this assignment, she wouldn't get this job. Her dreams of living in San Antonio near Daddy would die, and now she had a new dream—to be near Joshua Sheppard.

"It's just a stepping-stone, after all. I can always work up to something better," she murmured.

Why were things always so complicated? Chocolate was in order. She unwrapped several pieces of candy until she had had her fill. Decision time.

Ecko drew in a breath then replied to the e-mail, agreeing

to the assignment. Once she agreed, Chris would e-mail the final details. Apparently, he wasn't about to share any news or gossip tidbits with her until receiving confirmation from her.

Within a few minutes, she received his answer. He'd heard a rumor that Giselle Honors would soon marry, and, though the ex-model had hoped to keep things quiet, the *San Antonio Sun* would expose everything.

For what seemed like several minutes, Ecko sat in stunned silence. *Oh, Daddy. What have you gotten yourself into?*

Ecko rested her head in her arms on the table and sobbed. Once the tears subsided, she went to the bathroom and tugged several tissues from the box to wipe her nose and eyes.

"Lord, please show me what to do here. I have no direction. Help Daddy, too. I'm scared for him."

Sitting at the table, she faced her laptop again. Ecko had never for an instant considered what marrying a celebrity, even one from days gone by, could do to a person's private life. In fact, her own life could be under scrutiny once Daddy was married. Of course, Ecko would refuse to complete the assignment, given the circumstances, but now that she'd accepted it, she wasn't certain of the repercussions for declining after the fact.

She admitted, too, that she probably couldn't regard herself as much of a human interest journalist since she'd not done any research on Daddy's fiancée. While she considered how best to decline the assignment, she utilized a search engine to find out more about Giselle Honors.

After several pages, she found only one small reference to Laura Kimball, which was surprising. It wouldn't be long before the media dragged out her real name. Another name caught her attention.

This time, Ecko stood from the chair and backed away.

No. . . *This can't be.*

Joshua Sheppard is Giselle Honor's son?

❄

Sitting on the sofa with swollen eyes, Ecko stared numbly at the television game show. She'd lost her job before she had even begun. The time had come for her to be up front with Daddy. But explaining would be difficult because a good part of her story involved his fiancée.

Again, she wondered if his decision was the right one. But then, it wasn't really hers to make.

There was the matter of Joshua, whom she'd fallen in love with. She knew that now beyond a doubt. Otherwise, why did she hurt so much? Joshua hadn't been up front with her about who he really was. He'd seen the bottle of Giselle—could have told her then. She recalled his reaction and knew now that the perfume had put him into the dark mood. Were he and his mother estranged?

She squeezed a pillow to her face and screamed, then slid over until she lay on her side. How could she blame him when she'd been equally dishonest? What a mess.

Ecko prayed silently for answers and drifted to sleep.

The familiar ring of her cell pulled her awake. It was Daddy. Though she wasn't prepared to talk to him, she answered anyway.

"Baby, so glad I caught you. I know this is last-minute, but can you join me? I want to introduce you to Laura. We've just been so busy lately; I'm sorry I couldn't get you two together sooner."

"Oh, Daddy. Something's come up."

Daddy's breath caught. "What is it? What's wrong?"

Ecko thought about how best to share her disappointing news. News that involved Daddy's fiancée and their wedding plans. In a public setting, Ecko could better keep her emotions in check. "Can you meet me somewhere?"

Daddy hesitated. Ecko hadn't ever known him to do that.

"Can you tell me on the phone?"

"Remember when you knew it was best to tell me in person? This is one of those times."

"Okay, I'll have to give Laura an excuse. You're the most important woman in my life. La Paloma at seven?"

"Oh, Daddy, Laura will soon be your wife. I'm not so insecure that you can't admit how important she is to you. I'll see you at seven."

"I love you. You know that will never change," he said.

❄

Joshua's pulse hammered in his neck.

Finally. Standing just outside the den, he'd once again stumbled upon Tom expressing his affections for another woman. The man didn't even have the brains to keep his indiscretions private.

I'll have to give Laura an excuse. You're the most important woman in my life. La Paloma at seven?"—a pause for what Joshua presumed was the woman's response, then—"*I love you. You know that will never change.*"

The words burned in his mind, just as they had before. He squeezed his fists, wanting nothing more than to march into the den and pummel Tom Lewis.

"Joshua, what a pleasant surprise," his mother said as she descended the ornate staircase. "What brings you here today?"

He'd come to speak with her about Marcy, but with his temper raging, now wasn't the time. "I'm sorry. I've just been called away." He pecked her lightly on the cheek. "I'll be in touch."

His mother's brow creased, and she opened her mouth to object, but he was out the door before she could speak. Speeding away toward the Riverwalk, Joshua planned to be there in time to witness Tom with the other woman. Confront him. Despite his fury, the corner of his mouth curved when he remembered the last time he'd tried to catch Tom.

He'd collided with Eliza—journalist extraordinaire. He was so proud of her for landing her dream job. It would mean, too, that she could stay in San Antonio. An answer to his prayers.

For that, he supposed he could thank Tom and his indiscretions—an irony, really. Eliza was the woman of his dreams.

As he parked near the Rivercenter Mall to begin his surveillance, memories of shopping with Eliza flooded his mind. He recalled little Maria's expression when she saw the doll Eliza had chosen for her.

A pang squeezed his chest. In his kindness toward Marcy and her granddaughter, Joshua knew he was merely exhibiting his Christianity, but not in his treatment of Tom. Still. . .

Lord, I must protect my mother.

Once inside La Paloma restaurant, he produced a large bill, allowing him to choose a table in a dark corner. From his perch, he could easily watch Tom Lewis. It was only six thirty, so he ordered a coffee and waited, the smells of Tex-Mex taunting him. He refused to give in, instead focusing on his task.

With less than two weeks until the wedding, this would most likely be his last opportunity. In fact, once he confronted Tom, catching him meeting with the other woman, perhaps Joshua could reason with the man to gently back out of his engagement, sparing Joshua's mother from the hurt and embarrassment of yet another failed engagement.

The media would have a feeding frenzy. Of that, he had no doubt. The crowd began to grow, pleasing Joshua because the throng would better hide him. Still, he tugged his cap lower and sipped his coffee.

Then he saw Tom. Joshua's pulsed raced. Tom strode between the tables, the hostess leading him to one at the opposite end of the large dining room. Good. Joshua remained out of Tom's line of sight, but he would still be able to see Tom.

He watched Tom order. The man left his menu on the table and kept glancing at the restaurant entrance, expecting to see his mistress.

Watching Tom, Joshua clenched his coffee cup.

His waitress approached. "Sir, can I get you something else?"

The look on her face told him she wasn't pleased at having to give up a table for a customer only wanting coffee. She stood in Joshua's view, and when she moved, he spotted

Tom standing to greet someone. She was wearing a hooded coat—pretty, like something Eliza would wear—and had her back to Joshua so he couldn't make out the woman. But it didn't matter.

He bolted from the corner and marched toward Tom, maneuvering between the tables. He'd reached the middle of the room when he saw the woman remove her hood and coat then slide into the booth to face Tom.

Almost mid-stride, Joshua froze. Cold shock slammed his gut.

He might as well have been thrown into the river again. "Eliza?"

But she hadn't heard his heart's cry over the multitude of patrons. Joshua fled the restaurant.

Chapter 7

Ecko wasn't sure when she'd been so relieved to see Daddy. Just being in his presence comforted her, giving her a sense of security. And yet, she still had to share the horrible news.

"Ecko, what's wrong?" He reached over the table and gripped her hands.

Don't, cry. Don't cry. Feeling the tears behind her eyes, she couldn't meet his gaze. "I don't know where to start."

"I can't remember when I've seen you so upset. What could be so bad?"

Ecko knew exactly when Daddy had seen her this upset—when she and Brennan broke off their engagement. She made the decision. Ecko had waited until the day before the wedding, and Brennan was furious. His pride shattered and reputation ruined—at least from his point of view. Ecko wasn't sure she'd recovered from the aftermath.

She released a breath. "All right, Daddy. Here goes. I lost

my job with the *Kansas City Star*."

"Oh, Baby, no." Daddy squeezed her hand again.

"Wait until you hear the rest. That's only the beginning. And really, it's not such a bad thing. I wanted to be a serious journalist, not some gossip columnist. And—I wanted to be near you in San Antonio."

She risked a peek into his eyes and saw his pleasure.

"I would love that. But surely, you're not upset over losing your job, then."

"No, there's more. I had an interview here in San Antonio. That's why I stayed in a friend's apartment. I didn't want to let on that I was unemployed. Daddy, I wanted to surprise you with my new job."

"Oh, Ecko. I'm so sorry you didn't get that job. But you're young and talented. There will be other opportunities."

"That's just it. I *did* get the job."

Daddy appeared confused. "I'm listening."

Ecko's chest rose and fell with a sigh. "I get the job if I complete their test assignment to their satisfaction."

"I have no doubt that you can do this."

He didn't understand. This time, Ecko reached for Daddy's hand. "The assignment is to write what amounts to a smear campaign against Giselle Honors. Against Laura."

Daddy looked as though someone punched his heart. He leaned back, pulling his hand free of Ecko's. "What?"

Ecko could hardly stand to look in his eyes. She felt tears stinging hers. "You know I won't do it."

"How or why would anyone want to hurt Laura like that?"

Here came the difficult part. Ecko tugged a tissue from

her purse. She had hoped meeting him in public would help her remain composed. "You know Laura's past as a famous model. She's a celebrity of sorts. And celebrities are fair game. Daddy, this will mean your life will come under scrutiny once you're married. My life, too."

The waitress approached to take their orders. They hadn't even looked at the menus.

Frowning, Daddy kept his eyes on Ecko as he spoke to the waitress. "Please give us a minute."

Ecko couldn't look at him any longer and stared at the table.

"Ecko, I'm hurt that you would use this to attempt to persuade me not to marry Laura. I love her. I won't change my mind."

She searched Daddy's eyes, hoping he would understand. "I've miscommunicated. I'm only trying to make sure you are informed and understand all that you're getting into. I know that you love her." Despite the gravity of their discussion, Ecko smiled. "In fact, I think I'm in love, too."

The lines around Daddy's eyes eased into a smile. "Now that's the best news I've heard all night. Tell me about him."

Ecko couldn't help herself. She laughed. Daddy gave her a strange look, as though he thought she'd lost her mind.

"That's the last piece of this story. Please don't be upset, but I did some research on Giselle Honors—Daddy, I had to know what you were getting into."

His smile flattened. "And?"

"I'm in love with Laura's son, Joshua Sheppard."

To Ecko's surprise, Daddy's mouth dropped open. He shook his head. "Ecko, you don't know him like I do. And you've been in San Antonio all of what—six days?"

Ecko held up her hand to stop Daddy's tirade. "I doubt you've seen the side of him that I've seen, either."

Daddy laughed. "I suppose you're right. It looks like we're both stepping on each other's toes when it comes to love. But that's just because we love each other, right?"

"Right. And maybe you see Joshua differently, because he, too, is trying to protect his mother. Maybe he shows you a different side."

"I think you might be on to something. He certainly doesn't like me."

The notion saddened Ecko. She wanted the man she loved to adore her father as much as she did. "None of this solves the fact that I don't have a job. And once I find one, I might not end up in San Antonio."

"I have an idea. I had hoped to introduce you to Laura tonight. If you're willing, I think she'd love to hear your tale." Daddy winked. "Including the fact that you're in love with her son."

❊

Joshua walked the Riverwalk that night, not caring as tourists and busy shoppers bumped him coming and going. The bustle of the crowd was far from his mind.

Where did I go wrong, Lord?

He'd honestly believed that Eliza was the woman of his dreams. And once he'd completed his task of exposing Tom's indiscretions to his mother, he hoped for an opportunity to make Eliza a permanent part of his life. In an appropriate time frame, of course. His mother would need time to recover.

Never would he have thought that Eliza Connors and Tom Lewis were seeing each other. But what did he really know about the woman? He'd spent such a short amount of time with her—what had convinced him that she was the one?

Pain had coursed through him for so long now that he'd become numb. Somehow, he found his way home. He sat on the sofa in his lonely apartment, staring at nothing. He had to regain his handle on the situation—there was still a wedding to prevent.

Who was Eliza Connors, after all? A quick Google search told him the worst of it.

Why should he be devastated that he was right and his mother wrong? Love at first sight didn't exist. He'd known that, yet he'd allowed himself to believe in it. He'd wanted to believe in it.

The next morning, Joshua took the day off, disregarding the fact that he was in the middle of his busy season. Considering his mood, interacting with customers or his employees wasn't a good idea. He phoned Eliza and invited himself over. The sound of her voice, seeming to drip honey as though she were pleased to hear from him, made him nauseous.

The ruse was up. But he would save the words.

On the drive over, he recalled her face when she'd given the doll to Maria. She appeared completely sincere. In fact, he didn't doubt that she was sincere when it came to her giving spirit. But the way she'd used him was beyond excuse.

Finally, he stood outside her apartment door and knocked.

When the door swung open, she smiled—so beautiful his heart ached—and stepped aside for him to enter.

"I won't be staying long."

Immediately, he sensed when her guard came up.

"Joshua, what's wrong?"

"The ruse is up."

Her hand went to her throat. "Joshua, I—"

"Save it. I know the job you so desperately wanted is for a tabloid. And I know all about the sorts of stories tabloid reporters write. You used me to get to my mother, so you could further your career. Worse, you're using my mother's fiancé, Tom, as well. How does a person stoop so low?"

Her mouth fell open, leaving her speechless. Good, he didn't want to hear her excuses. He left her standing there. Descending the steps, he heard her cry out from above.

"Joshua, wait. You don't understand."

With no intention of stopping, he climbed into his truck. Now, to take care of Tom. He sped from the parking lot without another look back. But he felt no better for having said the words to Eliza. In fact, he felt worse. Bitterness and resentment seemed to eat away at his insides.

"Lord, help me. I'm trying to set things right, but why doesn't it feel right?"

Joshua mulled over waiting to speak to his mother. But with her wedding just a few days away, he couldn't wait, no matter how much he wanted to put it off until his own pain subsided. With the way he felt, that could be an eternity.

He found his mother in the kitchen, drinking coffee and reading the morning paper. She rose when she saw him and as always gave him a peck on his cheek.

She took a second look at him. "What on earth is the matter?"

"Please, sit down." He wished he could wipe away the grim look he knew was on his face, but it was no use.

"Joshua, you're scaring me. Has someone died?"

"I know you don't want to hear this."

"Oh, please, not your suspicions of Tom's unfaithfulness again. I love you, but you're going too far to stop this wedding."

"Mother, I saw her."

"Oh? Who exactly did you see?" His mother appeared only vaguely interested as she perused the paper.

"Tom's girlfriend. I saw him with her."

That got her attention. She stared up at him. Joshua sat down, too, and took his mother's hand in his. "I'm so very sorry, but I warned you of this."

"Tell me about the other woman, Joshua. Do you know her name?"

"Yes, mother. She's a younger woman, much younger than Tom." Joshua felt an ache all the way to his bones. "She's a reporter for a tabloid. I believe she's using Tom to get information on you. But it doesn't change the fact that he met with her."

"Is that all?" A strange smile spread over her face.

Perplexed, Joshua continued. "Isn't that enough? I overheard Tom making plans with her. His exact words were"— Joshua tugged the paper from his pocket—" 'I'll have to give Laura an excuse. You're the most important woman in my life. La Paloma at seven?' Then, 'I love you. You know that will never change.'"

"Does this person have a name?"

"Eliza Connors." He flinched. Saying her name aloud, hearing it, tore through his gut.

To his surprise, she smiled softly and slid her hand down his cheek as though he were a child. "Oh, Joshua, I appreciate you trying to save me. A mother couldn't ask for more. I'll take what you've learned under consideration. In the meantime, the engagement party will not be canceled, and I expect you to attend. I promise to have a big surprise for you."

Chapter 8

Baby, I have an idea." Daddy sounded excited over the cell.

"What's that?" She stared at the e-mail she composed to let Chris Barnett know that she had decided against taking the test assignment. She hadn't hit SEND yet.

"First, let me tell you how impressed Laura was with you last night."

"I can see why you love her so much." Ecko had been impressed as well. Beautiful and refined, Laura was also warm and loving. "I'm glad I finally got to meet her."

Ecko struggled to keep disappointment from seeping into her words, but she hadn't told Daddy about Joshua's accusations.

"I know your job situation has been disconcerting for you. Laura has offered to give you an exclusive interview. Her exact words were 'an elegant interview.' I'm not sure that's something your tabloid will appreciate, but it's worth a try, don't you think?"

Ecko stared at the e-mail. "You know, I like that idea." She would make sure they understood the article belonged to her before she sent it. If Mr. Barnett didn't like it because it didn't fit in with their gossip guidelines, then Ecko could attempt to sell the interview elsewhere.

Feeling more encouraged than she had in two days, Ecko sat up straight. She could freelance. Plenty of writers did.

"Good. Now, about the engagement party. It's only three days away."

Ecko's heavy sigh gave Daddy pause. She wished she was better at hiding things from him.

"What's the matter now?"

"I'm not sure I can go, Daddy." She regretted having to say the words. "I've had a falling-out with Joshua."

Daddy didn't respond. Ecko gave him time to think.

"I'm sorry about that. Can you tell me what happened?"

"If it's all the same to you, I'd rather not. At least not yet."

"All right." Daddy's breathing sounded heavier now. "But I need you at the engagement party. I know that Laura expects you there. I talked to her earlier this morning, and she made a special request, asking that I pass it on."

"A special request?" Ecko couldn't imagine what.

"At the time I thought it odd. But now I think she knew something that I didn't. She asked that you avoid speaking to her son, if possible, until the party."

Incredulous, Ecko laughed. "I don't think that will be a problem."

A thick knot grew in her throat, despite her attempt to

sound cheerful. They said their good-byes, and Ecko grabbed a few pieces of candy. Joshua resented her for writing an article about his mother. Resented Ecko because he thought she'd simply used him to get to her. No wonder he hadn't shared her identity with Ecko.

Joshua's words had stung, giving Ecko a piercing ache in her heart, and a throbbing head. But his accusations about Daddy—well, that was something different, entirely. Nobody accused her father. At the moment, her fury over that kept Ecko from crumpling into bed.

Joshua believed that Ecko's father was unfaithful because he hadn't known that Ecko was Tom's daughter. What made a person that crazy with suspicion? If Ecko fell back on her minor in psychology—courses that helped her toward her journalistic goals—she'd think that Joshua had had a few bad experiences in his life. A cheating father came to mind.

Sighing, Ecko admitted that she was as much to blame as anyone.

She could have prevented the misunderstanding if she'd been up front with Joshua. Now, he had the wrong idea about her. She didn't blame him, though. After wiping away the tears for the hundredth time in the last two days, Ecko decided she wouldn't call him to explain.

After everything she'd been through with Brennan, she'd had enough of men who would rather accuse her than give her the benefit of the doubt. Or at least ask for an explanation.

❄

Ecko parked her car in the hotel parking garage, wondering if this was such a good idea, after all. She stepped out of the vehicle and into the cold night. The private engagement party was to take place in an elite hotel along the Riverwalk. Ecko shook her head. They were having a party to officially announce the engagement and would marry less than a week later.

She straightened the teal satin dress she'd purchased just for the occasion—compliments of Daddy—and tugged her black velvet wrap around tight and snug. Though she hated heels, the dress wouldn't work without them. Clicking her way through the parking garage, she entered the hotel, found the elevator, and pressed the button for the twelfth floor. The invitation said seven thirty, but Laura had asked Ecko to arrive at least half an hour early.

Alone on the elevator, she marveled that she should be nervous, and yet her heart drummed in her throat, and her palms grew more moist by the second. This was Daddy's night, his event. What was wrong with her?

Joshua.

Joshua was what was wrong with her. Had he learned the truth yet? It had been three days since he'd accused her. She hadn't heard a word from him since. And if he did know the truth, would he continue to think negatively of her because she'd not been up front with him? Because she worked as a gossip columnist and had interviewed with a tabloid?

Living with a celebrity mother more than likely had given Joshua his fill of media attention. Still, Laura had done an excellent job of keeping family matters private.

The elevator doors slid open. Ecko took a deep breath and stepped into the hall, wondering if Joshua would be there early, too. She couldn't decide if she wanted to see him or not.

She knocked on room 1233. The door quickly opened to reveal Daddy beaming at her.

"Ecko, you look stunning." If possible, his smile grew brighter as he gestured for her to enter.

The chic suite was dimly lit. A large Christmas tree stood in the corner, stylishly decorated in shades of violet. Tables were adorned for Christmas, as well, along with hors d'oeuvres of every kind. Tuxedoed waiters stood nearby, waiting to serve guests.

"Am I the first to arrive?" Ecko asked.

"Yes, but not for long. Come with me," Daddy said, and led her to another room off the suite.

Once inside the room, Ecko saw Laura standing before a long mirror, completing the final details of her appearance. She smiled at Ecko through the mirror as she applied soft pink lipstick.

"You wanted me to be here early," Ecko offered.

"Thank you for coming." Laura seemed to float across the room. She took Ecko's hands in hers. "You're a lovely woman. I know that my son loves you." Her smile faded but only slightly.

Ecko felt the burn of tears behind her eyes. *Please, Lord, don't let me cry.* Unsure of her voice, she said nothing in response.

"But he's confused right now. I would like for you to wait in this room until I introduce you as Tom's daughter. If you will accommodate me in this one thing, I'm sure we'll both get what we want."

Though Ecko nodded her agreement—she wouldn't do anything to hurt Daddy or ruin his night—she was uneasy with Laura's request. She doubted anything Laura could do or say could make things right for Ecko or give her what she wanted.

※

"Lord, let me see things through Your eyes," Joshua prayed, pouring out his heart on his drive to the party.

Without God's help, he wouldn't make it through this evening. The way things looked right now, the situation was beyond tolerable. Yet, there wasn't any way he could avoid attending his mother's engagement party.

If only he could stop thinking about Eliza. He'd been a fool to fall for her so quickly, to believe, like his mother, that he could be in love with someone he barely knew. Yet, despite all he'd learned about her, his heart ached to be with her again. He missed her glowing smile. The way her hair caught the sunlight. The look in her eyes when she'd found the doll, and when she'd given it to Maria. Before he discovered the truth, she'd been the light of his life, if only briefly.

And—he loved her, still.

Images of the conversation he'd had with his mother came to mind. Joshua released a weighty breath. He'd done all he could to convince his mother about Tom.

But she was a grown woman. Her choices, her own. And likewise, her mistakes.

Joshua parked his truck and rushed through the parking lot. Already late, he hoped to avoid much of the celebration and leave early, too, diminishing his time spent in an uncomfortable situation.

Standing outside room 1233, he heard soft music and light chatter. He hoped to avoid the customary toast, but chances were his mother would wait until he arrived, expecting him to give words. Before entering, Joshua tugged at his collar and adjusted his tie. Without knocking, he simply entered the gathering, noting his mother's friends and a few of her important business contacts mingling in several small groups around the room.

He wished he could melt into the wall behind him, become invisible. Then he spotted his mother standing next to Tom near the table. She looked radiant as she stuffed hors d'oeuvres into his mouth. Her laughter reached Joshua across the room. Shoving down his frustrations, he collected his thoughts and forced a smile.

His mother raised her stemware and tapped the glass with a spoon. Joshua didn't move as all eyes turned to her. What was she up to? He hadn't even spoken with her yet.

"Ladies and gentleman, we have a special guest tonight. Someone I'm delighted for all of you to meet." A connecting door to the suite eased open. His mother spoke softly to whomever stood in the doorway. "Come, dear."

Eliza stepped into Joshua's line of sight. It was clear she was uncomfortable with the attention.

Pressure buzzed in Joshua's ears. What did his mother think she was doing? Didn't she know? Eliza was the woman that. . .

The room swayed. His mind scrambled.

Chapter 9

I'd like to introduce you to the lovely Ecko Lewis, Tom's daughter," his mother said, and smiled for the crowd. Though she'd forbidden pictures and media of any kind—this was a small private party—she appeared to be performing for the camera.

Joshua didn't miss that the act was for him as she flashed him a knowing grin and a small wave.

Ecko Lewis? The name reverberated through his mind. Ecko Lewis was Eliza Connors? His head spinning, Joshua pressed his hand to his forehead, the gathering around him seeming to fade. Tom wasn't unfaithful to his mother? Eliza wasn't the other woman?

For an instant, his heart leaped, and hoped surged. He'd been wrong about Tom. Equally close to his heart—he'd been wrong about Eliza, or Ecko, her real name.

He understood about using another name. Life with his mother had taught him that. But why had Eliza—er—Ecko kept that from him?

Ears still humming, he risked a glance at her. She did not look his way, but rather smiled softly in conversation with his mother and her fiancé. Joshua stood frozen, feeling the fool. But—he supposed—he deserved this.

His mother had warned him that she had a big surprise for him. He wished he could laugh, join her in the joke. And he would, except he'd said those terrible words to Ecko. It was difficult thinking of her as Ecko rather than Eliza.

Had he also misread Ecko's intention to use him to get to his mother? Probably. It was too much to absorb. Joshua wanted to flee the celebration. He needed time to grasp what he'd just heard, to understand all the ramifications.

Lord, help me to comprehend it all, and—thank You for letting me see things through Your eyes, for letting me see the truth.

With the simple prayer, he knew that he should immediately seek forgiveness. Joshua tugged the hem of his suit jacket and strode toward the long food-laden table, toward Ecko. If God saw fit to answer the rest of his heart's prayer, Ecko wouldn't have already tossed aside her feelings for him. She'd forgive him for being an idiot.

Upon seeing Joshua's approach, Tom stiffened, though subtly. Now, it was Tom's turn to be the protective one. Certain that Tom was well informed of the situation, Joshua didn't blame him.

"Tom." Joshua nodded.

"Joshua, good to see you." Tom thrust out his hand.

Joshua gripped and shook it with a smile. He'd grossly misjudged Tom. "I owe you an apology."

Tom stared back. "Apology accepted." He glanced at his daughter.

Ecko smiled, but it resembled the performance Joshua's mother gave. Behind her eyes, he could see all the pain he'd caused. If only they were alone, he could tell her all that she meant to him.

"And—Eliza." Wincing, Joshua cleared his throat. He hadn't said her pseudonym intentionally.

Her faced paled. He admired her ability to remain composed, despite the impossible state of affairs.

"I'm sorry. It will take me time to learn your real name. Ecko, please accept my apology."

She said nothing and smiled at one of his mother's friends who had approached and now drew Ecko into conversation, oblivious to the fact that she was already in one. The gathering had grown hungry, and the table was surrounded. Joshua wished they could leave. He needed to speak to her privately, to convey the depth of his regret.

People pressed against him, and the room grew stifling hot. He leaned near Ecko, to speak in her ear, noting she wore the soft scent of Chanel No. 5.

He closed his eyes, breathing in the essence of her and whispered, "I need to speak with you alone. Can we go somewhere?"

Ecko stiffened and continued to choose her hors d'oeuvres. She'd managed to comb her short hair in a fashion that covered her face when she leaned forward. He could not see her expression. Was she angry, happy, or sad?

"Eliza," he whispered again. "I'm so sorry."

A man across the table began chatting with her.

Impossible. The situation was impossible. He could do nothing more without drawing too much attention.

Again, the clinking of the glass. His mother's voice rose above the chatter.

"Can I have your attention again, please? I'd like for my son, Joshua, to share a toast."

Joshua had not grown up without training in performing for the camera and backed from the table, a smile firmly planted on his face. Despite his own debacle, his mother had found the man of her dreams. Finally, he should be happy for her.

And he was.

He buttoned his suit jacket as he strode to where she and Tom stood, holding hands. Joshua lifted a flute of sparkling apple cider. He knew this was expected of him and had vaguely considered his words throughout the evening's struggles.

Lifting the glass, he began. "Here's to my mother, the bride-to-be. You've finally found him, Mother; you found the man of your dreams. And to Tom—the groom-to-be, you found something rare when you found my mother. May your lives together be long and filled with love deeper than the ocean and happiness that takes you higher than the mountains."

The crowd sounded their approval. But Joshua wasn't finished yet. This could be his opportunity.

"And to Tom's daughter, Ecko. . ." Joshua's heart hammered as he searched the room. "Where are you, Ecko?"

There. All eyes turned to her. Ecko stood halfway out the door, looking like a small animal caught in the headlights of a car.

Ecko looked straight at Joshua, into his dark eyes. As she stared at him, she shook her head so subtly, she hoped only he could read her answer, then slipped the rest of the way through the door. She could not hear what he wanted to say. Remaining one second longer would end in embarrassment, as Ecko could hold back the tears no longer.

As she rushed down the hallway and onto the elevator, Ecko relived the moment when Joshua had stepped into the room. She'd ignored Laura's requests to remain hidden, but had lingered near her father. Ecko alone appeared to notice when something changed in the room, almost as if she could feel his presence. She'd instantly glanced around the suite, searching.

Once she'd spotted him across the room—though the partygoers blocked much of her view—she noticed how handsome he looked in his dark suit and tie. Her knees had gone weak. Yet, how could she continue to feel the same about a man who had treated her that way?

Ecko stepped into the lobby, intending to dash to her car. But something stopped her. Better to get fresh air amid the Christmas madness on the Riverwalk. She rushed outside into the cold air and onto the sidewalk that rimmed the San Antonio River, tugging her wrap even tighter. Walking fast would keep her warm, though her heels would be a hindrance.

Seeing Joshua had sent all the hurt rushing back to her. It hadn't even occurred to the man to trust her or to ask her for an explanation. Not so long ago, she'd gone through the same realization but with Brennan—his lack of trust had also led to his lack of respect for her. She wouldn't allow that to happen again.

The activity surrounding her drew her from the gloomy thoughts. Ecko could never have imagined the Riverwalk bustling as it was on a cold night. People were everywhere. Christmas lights hung from every venue, including trees and arbors. Tourist-filled riverboats floated down the river. Restaurants were busy catering to customers, plenty of whom sat at the tables outside, even on a cool night.

The scene warmed Ecko's heart, if only a little. Festive music assailed her from every direction as she walked. An elaborate display of lights caught her attention, and she stopped. The presentation depicted the manger scene, including the heavenly hosts of angels hanging from high above.

Overcome with awe, Ecko stood for several moments, looking at the lights. Was this display a product of Joshua's company, of Sheppard Christmas Lighting?

Beautiful beyond words, it was a simple reminder of the birth of Christ, the Savior of the world. Farther down, the lights continued and were fashioned into a crucifix with the words "While we were still sinners, Christ died for us."

Ecko's breath caught in her throat. A single tear slipped down her cheek, and she knew many more could easily come.

Hadn't Joshua apologized to her? And even if he hadn't, as a Christian, she was supposed to forgive. Christ had forgiven her.

She should forgive Joshua, even if she didn't. . .

Ecko sucked in a breath. She still loved him.

❄

Joshua had almost made it to the door, his every intention to follow Ecko. Chase her if he must. Win her back. No one was going to stop him, but Tom grabbed his arm, doing exactly that.

Though frustrated, Joshua would not disrespect the man. He sighed as he turned to face Ecko's father.

His mother appeared next to her fiancé. "Maybe you should let her alone for now, Joshua."

"I agree. Give her some time," Tom said.

Though he wasn't baring his teeth like an angry dog, Joshua could easily have imagined Tom as such, protecting his daughter.

"I made the biggest mistake of my life by accusing the woman I love. I have no intention of simply letting her go until she knows how sorry I am. Until she knows how much I love her."

Joshua had no idea how—if he loved her—he could have accused her without hearing her explanation. On the inside, he felt like dying.

Tom slowly released his grip. Joshua was thankful that his mother's guests appeared to have lost interest and were busy with discussions of their own lives again.

He released a pained breath and looked at his mother. Even thirty years past her modeling prime, she was still so beautiful. "I see now that I've done the same thing to all the men in your life. Always accusing them. I'm sorry for that, Mother. And we can thank God that I didn't run Tom off, too."

His mother's eyes filled with tears. "Oh. . .Joshua," she said, her voice trembling.

He couldn't remember the last time he'd seen her cry,

especially in a public gathering. Maybe never.

"You had reasons for your distrust. We both know that," she added.

Not wanting to delay further, Joshua simply dipped his head, gesturing he understood exactly whom his mother referred to. He left them standing there to pursue Ecko. But where had she gone?

Lord Jesus, lead me to her. When the elevator opened on the lobby floor, Joshua stepped off and searched the area. At the concierge desk overlooking the lobby, he asked a young woman if she'd seen Ecko, describing her dress and hair.

The woman's eyes grew bright and she nodded. "Yes. She was so beautiful in that dress she stood out from the crowd, especially with the pained expression she wore. I saw her rush through the doors to the Riverwalk."

"Thank you." Joshua hurried after her.

"Merry Christmas, and I hope you find her," the young woman called to Joshua from behind.

Stepping out into the shock of cold, he was greeted by the joyous mood on the Riverwalk, and it warmed his spirits, even in the face of possibly losing Ecko for the second time.

He looked left then right. Which way should he go? *Where are you, Ecko?* Recalling their first encounter, he headed in the direction of La Cocina del Rio.

With his hands jammed into his leather jacket, he made his way through the crowd, all the while searching for the beautiful blond woman in a teal dress and black wrap. Surely, as the woman at the concierge's counter had said, Ecko would stand out.

His throat thickened with regret as he considered the

consequences of his actions. It was wrong for him to think every man was like his father. Wrong for him to continually harbor suspicion of others.

Lord, help me to forgive my father for cheating, for his unfaithfulness, for all the pain he caused us. Help me to forgive him for leaving us. Though his father had died years before, Joshua still carried the anger and resentment toward him. Forgiving his father would begin the healing process for Joshua. He knew that. And with the words of his heart, he felt it, too.

Hadn't his heart been pricked with every Christmas light installation? He always tried to include the message of Christ's forgiveness along with the story of His birth. But now he realized—*Thank You, Lord*—that the message had been meant for him.

God had been speaking to him through his lighted displays all along. Even as he had the thought, one of his company's displays came into view.

The baby Jesus with Mary and Joseph tucked warmly in a manger scene and surrounded with shepherds, animals, and a host of angels. Then. . .Christ on a cross.

Slowly, he read the words. "While we were still sinners, Christ died for us."

Joshua felt the release in his heart. "Thank You, Lord," he said, not caring who heard.

Many potential customers had complained at first about his insistence that the Cross be included in his displays, but soon enough, Sheppard Christmas Lighting was recognized everywhere to include the full Gospel message.

Now, if he could just find Ecko. With difficulty, Joshua

pulled his eyes and thoughts from the display, knowing that he shouldn't forget the pain he'd caused her. He turned his back to the lights and faced the river, allowing his gaze to travel over the Riverwalk.

Then, he saw her.

Chapter 10

Joshua was too far behind for Ecko to hear him if he called out to her. He hurried through the bodies, seemingly bouncing off them as if he were in a pinball game. Fearing he would lose her again, he called her name.

"Ecko!" He continued moving in the direction he'd last seen her.

He stood on his toes to see above the crowd. No! He'd lost her. But surely, she couldn't be too far from him.

Ahead of him a large gathering congregated around a mariachi ensemble that featured violins, trumpets, guitars, the works. "Feliz Navidad" seemed to be the song of the evening, echoing from all corners of the Riverwalk.

Joshua slid his hand down his face. How would he get through the crowd? Excusing himself as he went, he pushed gently between the men, women, and children, their faces filled with the wonder of Christmas joy. The images brought to mind Maria's face when she first saw the doll Ecko had chosen for her.

Lord, please, if it's Your will, let me find her. Give me a chance to make this up to her.

Pushing further through the crowd, the music grew even louder. Joshua pushed up on his toes to see above heads.

There! Ecko neared a bridge in the distance.

"Ecko! Ecko, wait."

In return for his shout, he received a few glares—but he continued pushing through.

"Ecko, I love you!"

A strange event began to unfold before his eyes. The music subsided, slowly, and the crowd around him began to part. Joshua knew his eyes were wide in disbelief.

What was happening? Were they stopping for him?

"Go get her, son." An older man was the first to speak.

"Yeah, don't let her get away," a little boy said and tugged Joshua's hand, pulling his gaze down to see warm eyes staring back.

Feeling as if God had done this, God had opened a way for Joshua, tears of joy almost overcame him. The noise subsiding, the crowd opening up for him—it was nothing less than a Christmas miracle.

"Thank you," he said, the words barely audible. "Thank you, all."

Confidence returned to his voice, and he shouted at the top of his lungs, this time with permission and encouragement from the people around him.

Let the world hear it, let them know. "Ecko, if you can hear me—I love you!"

❄

The chill of the night began to eat at Ecko. She'd finally walked off the ache in her heart, emptied her emotional angst. Her prayers asking the Lord to help her forgive Joshua were working.

She was responsible for his knee-jerk reaction—she'd kept the truth from him. Even though she'd felt justified in playing things safe by using her pen name, it was wrong to withhold her real name.

Still, even if she hadn't played a role in the misunderstanding, even if he had no reason to react the way he had, she had to forgive him.

Oh, Joshua. . .

Standing near a bridge, she drew in a deep breath of the night air, feeling spent. She now wished she had stayed to hear what he planned to say to her during his toast. Oh, how she loved him.

If only she hadn't run out.

"Ecko! I love you!"

The words filtered to her from somewhere on the Riverwalk. Was she dreaming? Simply wishing too hard that he was here? Was there someone else named Ecko?

She made a full circle. A distance away, she spotted Joshua with a crowd behind him as though they were his followers. The band on the stage near them also watched.

What was going on? Had he arranged this just for her? Her pulse increased at the sight of him. Tears streamed down her face.

With his actions, he melted her heart as though it were a candle, the flame his love.

Thank You, Lord. She couldn't have asked for a better Christmas gift than to see Joshua announcing that he loved her to the world.

The mariachi band started their music back up, this time playing softly. Soon enough she recognized the tune, "*Si Nos Dejan,*" "If They Allow Us."

"If they allow us, we will love each other a lifetime," she sang under her breath in English, though the band sang it in Spanish.

Ecko was more than familiar with tune. She recalled an article she'd written—the song was used as a proposal.

She took a step toward Joshua. Was he proposing to her? Each step came faster, and as she drew near, she could see the love in his eyes and hear the words of his voice—a beautiful singing voice. She hadn't known him long enough to hear it.

Joshua placed his hand over his heart, and Ecko stopped short, so stunned was she. He was proposing—he was really going to do this. Swaying back and forth, his melodrama would almost have been comical if she didn't adore him so much. To give him room, people eased away from him on all sides. Ecko could see the river mere inches behind him.

Would he go down on one knee now?

She closed the distance between them, wanting to be there to answer, though she hadn't given much thought to what that might be yet. But, with the way she loved him, she doubted it required much thought.

Finally, she stood face-to-face with the man she loved. "Joshua," she said, feeling breathless. "I love you, too."

Joshua grinned. She thought he would lean in to kiss her.

Instead, he took a step back.

❄

Cold water engulfed him, taking his breath away. He drew in an untimely gulp of water and felt the pain in his nose. Coughing and sputtering, he stood, almost instantly going numb with the bite of the San Antonio winter. What had just happened?

Idiot! He had planned to go down on one knee and propose to the woman of his dreams. Wanting to make things right with Ecko, he knew in his heart that a romantic Christmas proposal would heal them both. But Ecko had stood so close to him—oh, so close—he could have kissed her. Instead of going down on his knee, he took a step back.

As he caught his breath and shook the water from his hair, smiling faces hovered over him as hands reached into the river and pulled him out. Ignoring his protests, Ecko hugged him to her.

Against his ear, she whispered, "Yes, my love, yes."

Shivering, he could barely respond. In his peripheral vision, he spotted Marcy, throwing towels around each of them.

"Hurry inside, you two," she said.

Before he took a step, he gained control over his chilled body. "Did you hear that?" he announced. "She said yes!"

The crowd cheered and applauded. The mariachi band began again, this time playing *"Gloria in Excelsis Deo"*— "Glory to God in the Highest."

Joshua couldn't agree more as he tugged his bride-to-be close, and together, they escaped the night into the restaurant and Marcy's nurturing.

He would never regret having a second chance to fall into the San Antonio River.

Epilogue

Mmm. Ecko drew in the aroma of the cinnamon rolls she'd placed in the oven to bake. By the smell of them, they were close to being ready. Joshua always loved the smell of cinnamon when he came home. Since this was his busy season, he wouldn't be home until late and hadn't wanted her to cook dinner. Instead, he assured her he would bring takeout with him. Still, she loved to think how it made him feel to come home to something freshly baked.

And to come home to his new wife.

"Italian, Mexican, or Chinese?" he'd asked.

"Surprise me," she'd said. Oh, but her mind was drifting from the task at hand.

Knitting her eyebrows, she stared at the page and finished typing the last line of the human interest article she'd been working on regarding Tommy Hernandez, of the Hernandez-owned La Cocina del Rio.

Tommy has reached his goal of walking again and looks forward to finishing his Associate degree in Computer Information Systems. He's a testimony to the fact that someone's past doesn't dictate their future.

Pressing her hand into the small of her back, she waddled into the kitchen to check on the cinnamon rolls. She tipped the oven door open to peek at the rolls. "Hurry up, will you?" Her mouth was watering already. Plus, she wanted them ready and waiting for him.

He was working to complete a huge light display for a downtown bank. She was so proud of her husband.

Her husband.

She released a contented sigh, marveling at the way things had turned out. A photograph of her and Joshua on their wedding day was stuck to the refrigerator door. Ecko ran her finger over it.

A year ago she'd come to San Antonio, hoping to land a job to keep her near Daddy. But the Lord had so much more in mind for her. Though she'd not taken the job offer, she'd found that she loved freelancing, writing what she wanted and when she wanted. There were plenty of heart-wrenching and life-changing stories out there to draw an editor's attention.

Ecko tugged the photo from the refrigerator door and held it to her heart. Much more important than her career, she'd fallen in love, and what a whirlwind romance it had been.

"That man is still sweeping me off my feet." She spoke softly to the child inside.

From behind, arms wrapped around her bulging waist.

"I hope so. I have plans to do just that tonight," Joshua said, whispering into her ear.

Tingles crawled over her, and she rested her head against his shoulder. "Mr. Sheppard, how did you get in without me hearing you?"

"I have a key, and you were talking to yourself, Mrs. Sheppard."

She giggled, enjoying his loving embrace. Turning to face him, she wrapped her arms around his neck, but she couldn't get nearly as close as she wanted with her middle protruding as it was.

"And what do you have planned?"

"It's our anniversary, don't you remember?"

Ecko frowned. "But we were married in February, not December. What are you talking about?" Her father and Joshua's mother had wed the day after Christmas as planned, and Ecko wanted to give Daddy and his new bride their special day. She and Joshua waited a whole two months—an eternity!

"It's the anniversary of the day I proposed to you." He drew near, close enough to kiss her, and spoke softly. "And if we don't get out of here now, we may not leave."

"Ah, you mean the second time you fell into the river because of me." She snuggled her head against his chest, smiling at the memory.

"The third time I fell, actually."

Ecko drew back to search his dark eyes. "What are you talking about?"

"I fell the first time I met you, and then again when I fell in love with you. So, my proposal is the third time that I fell because of you." Releasing her completely, he winked, then grabbed the pot holders and tugged the rolls from the oven.

Ecko almost cried. "Oh, honey, I'm so sorry."

"They're only a little burnt. But they can wait. I thought it would be nice to have dinner at La Cocina del Rio."

"You're so sweet," Ecko said and nuzzled his neck. His thoughtfulness flooded her heart with joy. Again, she thought she might cry. Joshua was probably tired of seeing her tears. It was only the hormones, she was sure. "But, I certainly don't want to see a repeat of you falling into that river."

He pressed his lips against hers. "Not a chance of that tonight."

A sudden tightness, then a deep ache rippled through Ecko's abdomen. She backed from Joshua and bent forward. Wrapping her arms around her belly, she moaned. "No, not a chance of that tonight. Not if Little Josh has anything to say about it."

ELIZABETH GODDARD is a seventh-generation Texan who recently spent five years in beautiful Southern Oregon, which serves as a setting for some of her novels. She is now back in East Texas, living near her family. When she's not writing, she's busy homeschooling her four children. Beth is the author of several novels and novellas. She's actively involved in several writing organizations including American Christian Fiction Writers (ACFW) and loves to mentor new writers.

Find out more about Beth at www.elizabethgoddard.com.

KEY TO HER HEART

by Martha Rogers

Dedication

To my ACFW encouragers and mentors DiAnn Mills,
Kim Sawyer, Lena Nelson Dooley, Deborah Raney, Brandilyn
Collins, and Connie Stevens because you believed in me
and prayed with me to bring me to this point.

To my crit partners Janice Thompson, Linda Kozar,
and Kathleen Y'Barbo.

And as always, to my husband, Rex, for
his patience, understanding, and support.

Chapter 1

The ledger book closed with a *thud*. What a mess. Valerie Murray needed more than four years of business classes at the university to fix this hodgepodge of numbers. Half of Aunt Cora's notations and entries were like a foreign language. Apparently, her aunt knew nothing about computers and spreadsheets. Ever since Uncle Will's death, Cora had tried to take care of the books, but she sorely lacked her husband's business knowledge. No wonder she wanted to get rid of the shop and had handed over the lease to Val.

Val closed her eyes and massaged her temples. She needed help and needed it soon or Cora's Cards and Gifts would be closed by Thanksgiving if not sooner. The numbers she could work out on her laptop, but the inventory, invoices, and sales figures would take weeks to translate.

Aunt Cora had warned that she had trouble keeping up with the accounting, but Val had no idea of the quagmire produced by poor records, missing receipts, and cryptic remarks. How her aunt managed to keep the store going for the past few years posed a big mystery at the moment and one Val would have to solve in a hurry if she wanted to stay open.

She pushed back from the desk in the cramped office and wandered out into the store itself. This had been one of her favorite places as a young girl. The gifts on display now reminded her of those wonderful afternoons she'd spent helping out when in high school.

It'd been only three days since Aunt Cora handed her the keys and smiled. "I know how much you loved this place when you were a child, and if anyone can take care of it, it's you."

There had been no time for her to look over the merchandise in those three days with anything more than a cursory glance, but now she bent closer to scrutinize the items more closely. They looked exactly like the figurines from those days. Val gasped. Surely her aunt hadn't kept inventory around that long. As much as she loved all the angels in the special display, some of them had to be nearly ten years old, if not fifteen. No wonder the store was sinking. This place needed a thorough inventory check. She should have thought of that sooner, but the garbled books took so much time to decode.

She wished Uncle Will were still around to help her, but then Aunt Cora would not have given up the store. Her aunt and uncle had managed the store quite well until his death four years ago. He'd taken his nights and some weekends to oversee the business out of love for his wife, and she been the one to work with customers and merchandise.

With a nod to the lone salesclerk on duty, Val scurried back to the office and began rummaging through the piles of papers there. After an hour of sorting and stacking, some semblance of order began to take shape. Not to her surprise, some of the invoices did date back ten years ago, around the time she had left to attend college, and a few further back than that. She tapped her chin with her pen. Surely Uncle Will had seen to it that new merchandise was ordered.

She delved back into the stack, but the more papers and receipts she found, the more dismay filled her. The first thing in order was to evaluate the inventory, check it against the invoices, and determine when Aunt Cora last ordered new merchandise. The only current bills to be found were those for the cards. At least those were kept up-to-date, but Val had to decide what to do with the old cards she'd found in the storeroom.

Susie poked her head around the door. "Miss Murray, there's someone here to see you. Actually he asked for Mrs. Bennett, but I told him she wasn't here at the moment, so he asked to see the manager. I guess that's you."

Val shook her head and blew out her breath. "Please call me Val. Miss Murray makes me sound as old as my aunt." Then she bit her lip. Surely one of Aunt Cora's creditors hadn't come to demand payment for a delinquent bill. "Tell him I'll be right out."

One glance back at the ledger affirmed she had no money to pay a large bill at the moment. *Aunt Cora, how could you have made such a mess?*

She squared her shoulders to meet whatever faced her in the shop. When she stepped through the door, she spotted a tall man in a tan knit shirt. Her shoulders relaxed. Probably just a customer. She pasted on a smile and headed toward him. The man turned around...and Val's world turned upside down. Colt Jamison was back in Texas and standing in her store.

When he had left with no explanation five years ago, her heart had broken, but she had managed to glue the pieces back together. Seeing him now, smiling as though the five years didn't exist, caused a rumble of anger to begin deep inside. Val clenched her fists and pressed them to her sides in order to control her emotions. She had loved him so much, but with no letters or attempts to contact her the first year, she'd locked her heart against ever being hurt like that again.

❅

Colt's heart jumped and his nerves tingled as he locked gazes with Val Murray. She was the last person he expected to see in Cora Bennett's shop. He had expected to run into her before he left town, but he wasn't prepared for it to be so soon. He searched her face for any of the feelings he had once seen there, but now only a mixture of surprise, wariness, and distrust filled her features. He could hardly expect more since she hadn't answered any of his letters.

"Hi, Val, I had no idea you worked here. I thought you were still in Dallas." He glanced beyond her shoulder. "Where's your aunt?" He had a thousand other questions for her, but that was the only one to make it out of his mouth.

"I don't just work here. I own the place now. Aunt Cora retired and handed it over to me." Her gaze narrowed. "What are you doing in San Antonio? Did New

York lose its glamour?"

Now that Cora Bennett didn't own the store, he wasn't sure how to answer her questions. He pulled a folded letter from his pocket but then decided not to reveal its contents to Val. "Just wanted to check up on an old friend." No need for her to know he'd quit his job to come back because of her aunt.

"Aunt Cora has retired, and I imagine she's with some of her friends playing bridge, or she's volunteering for some project at church."

Her words carried no welcome, only disinterest, and he shook his head. "That's Aunt Cora, always busy."

Val glanced at her watch. "I have a lot to do, so if you'll excuse me." She turned to leave.

"Val, wait. How's the store doing?" It couldn't be doing well according to Cora's letter, and the place looked just the same as it had five years ago when he left. But he wasn't ready to let Val go yet.

She hesitated a moment and tilted her head as though contemplating an answer. Finally she shrugged. "I'm not sure. The books are a mess, and I'm trying to decipher all of her codes and notations."

The contents of Cora's letter burned in his memory. She had asked for his help, but at the moment he didn't think Val would be very accepting of that fact. Still he had to offer. "Would you like me to take a look at them?"

She stared at him for a moment, indecision in her eyes. "I don't know what you'll find that I haven't, but a fresh look may help." She turned on her heel and beckoned him to follow her. "Everything's in the office."

The stacks of papers and piles of folders that greeted him brought forth a long, low whistle. "Wow. You do have a mess on your hands."

Val handed him a stack of files. "See if you can put these in any kind of order, and I'll work on the ones here." She picked up another stack and sat down at her desk.

Colt moved papers from another chair and settled himself for the task ahead. They worked in silence for a few minutes before he sensed a movement beside him. He glanced up and caught her looking at him. For one brief moment, pain glittered in her eyes and burned through to his very soul. Then a veil dropped over her eyes and covered any emotion he may have seen.

He blinked then returned to his task. If he kept looking at those amber-flecked brown eyes, his mouth might speak before his brain could think, and he wasn't ready to open those old wounds yet.

"How's your job in New York?"

Colt's heart jumped in his chest, and his throat closed so that he couldn't speak. After a moment he said, "I've been with an advertising agency there." That much was true, but now was not the time to reveal the rest.

"Then you've been using your creative juices to sell stuff."

He nodded and shuffled a few papers. "I guess you could look at it that way. I take a product and build a campaign around it with slogans and ads for television or magazines, but all my artwork is done on the computer."

"You should have been a salesman with your ability to talk people into doing whatever you wanted them to do."

The acid in that remark cut through Colt like etching on glass. Her hurt went deeper than he'd imagined. Perhaps that was the reason she hadn't answered his letters, but he couldn't ask about that now. He didn't want a second rejection. "Is that what I did? I thought y'all just wanted to have a good time." The words hung in the air, and he wanted to snatch them back and stuff them where they'd never be heard again.

Her brown eyes flashed in anger for a moment then filled with something he couldn't quite determine. She slapped a folder on her desk. "I think we're done here."

The urge to explain the truth of his departure rained down on his soul, but the words he needed wouldn't come. He'd done it once, and she'd ignored him. Telling her again would only add fuel to the anger filling her now.

"I'm sorry, Val." He placed the folders on her desk. "Maybe this wasn't such a good idea." He turned to leave.

"Thanks for nothing. Have a good life."

Those parting words sent more slivers of pain through his heart. He could never explain to her now.

✳

Val fought back the tears that threatened to fall. Colt Jamison was not going to ruin her life again. For years she'd hoped he would come home for a visit, but that hope never materialized. Now when she'd finally put him to rest in the past, here he showed up to create havoc in her present.

Tears blurred her vision and finally caused her to push aside the work. If she didn't stop this now, she'd never get anything done with the shop. Her vow to Aunt Cora to keep the place open and running looked even more hopeless.

Her remarks to Colt had been rude, but the lock she

had on her heart had been threatened, and she had taken the only route she knew to keep it locked. If he thought he could waltz in here after five years of absence and silence and sweep her off her feet again with his charm and good looks, he was sadly mistaken.

She grabbed a tissue to dry the moisture, and a knock on the door sounded behind her. If that was Colt, she just might hit him.

"Val, do you need me right now? I thought I'd go ahead and take my lunch break."

Susie's voice sent relief through Val's bones. She nodded, but didn't turn around. "Sure that's fine."

"Hmm, who was that good-looking guy who left a few minutes ago? He looks familiar."

Val swallowed hard. "That was Colt Jamison, a friend of Aunt Cora's."

"Colt Jamison? I didn't know he was back. He and my brother were best friends in high school, but I haven't seen him since he was in college. He's even more of a hunk now than he was then."

Ryan Morrill and Colt Jamison had not only been friends but also teammates on the state championship basketball team. Val remembered some good times with Ryan and Amber, the girl he'd married after college, and Colt during those hectic days of high school. She slammed the door on those memories and grabbed for her purse in the bottom drawer.

"I guess he's back for the holidays." Val fumbled for her billfold then took out a ten-dollar bill. "Will you bring me back something? I'm going to keep sorting out this jumble of papers."

"Be glad to. Want your usual ham on rye with swiss cheese, honey mustard, and bread and butter pickles?"

"Yes, and a diet soda." She handed Susie the money. "Let me know if it's more than that."

"Will do. See you later." With that she was gone, and Val turned back to her task. She rummaged through the desk looking for another pen. Her hand grasped a pad of sticky notes. They would be useful in sorting out the different vendors and receipts. Her aunt's handwriting on the top note caught her eye. Then shockwaves of disbelief rolled through her. She read the words a second time.

Write to Colt. I need his help. I can't do this alone anymore.

Chapter 2

Aunt Cora must have written to Colt, and that's why he'd come back to San Antonio. After struggling with the mess in the office, Val understood why her aunt thought she needed him. With his creative genius, he was her hope for saving the shop.

Val tapped her pencil on the desk and considered Colt's relationship to her aunt. After his father's death, his mother had shut herself away from the world, and that included her sons. Childless since the death of their two babies, Uncle Will and Aunt Cora had taken teenaged Colt and his younger brother under their wings, and were responsible for the two boys going to church and becoming Christians.

Now Colt had returned in response to Aunt Cora's plea for help, but he had taken his time getting here. Surely her aunt had written before giving the lease over to Val. More questions than answers filled her mind. She had to confront Aunt Cora, but then she'd only insist that Val let Colt help.

That wasn't possible. He'd already created havoc in her heart, and she wasn't about to let it continue. She sighed. No time to worry about that now. With Susie gone, someone needed to man the floor.

The store appeared as empty as it had earlier in the day. Not many people noticed the card and gift shop situated between the candy store and the jewelry boutique. She sauntered to the front windows, which still bore the original name, Cora's Cards and Gifts, in red and gold painted letters. She'd already picked out a new name, Unique Boutique, but needed someone to scrape off the old painted letters and apply the new.

The bell over the door jingled when an elderly woman stepped inside. Sweet little Myrtle Bronson had been a customer as long as Val could remember. "Good afternoon, Mrs. Bronson. How can I help you today?"

"Oh, hello, Valerie, I forgot you would be here." She headed for the card section. "I've just come in to buy a few thank-you and get-well cards."

"Take your time, Mrs. B." Val retreated behind the cashier stand to check on bags and tissue for purchases.

A few minutes later, the gray-haired woman laid her cards on the counter. "I saw Colt Jamison a little while ago down at La Cocina del Rio. I didn't know he was back in town."

Val's breath caught in her throat. Good thing she had decided to eat in today because La Cocina was her favorite restaurant, and she'd have been there for lunch. San Antonio may be a city, but sometimes it was more like a small town when so many of her or her family's friends were around. "He came by the store earlier."

"I see." She tilted her head and peered at Val. "Seems to me I remember you and he had a thing going before he left."

Right now Val wished she'd stayed in Dallas. There she was lost among the millions of people, and no one knew her past history. "We dated in high school and some while we were in college, but it was nothing serious." At least not to him, or he wouldn't have left so abruptly.

She finished ringing up the transaction and returned the woman's change. "Here you go, Mrs. B."

"Thank you, dear. I'm glad to see you back and taking over for Cora, although I do miss seeing her behind that register." Mrs. Bronson gripped her bag and turned to leave, but she stopped. She glanced over her shoulder at Val. "If I were you, I wouldn't let Colt Jamison get away again. Don't let him run from his troubles this time."

Before Val could react, the woman disappeared through the door and into the crowd outside. Her parting remark hung in the air like a spiderweb, and if she took a step or two toward it, Val would be entangled in her past all over again. Not this time.

The bell jingled again, and Susie strode through carrying a white paper bag. "Here's lunch and you get some change back." She set the sack and the money on the counter. "Just saw Mrs. B. Did she come in for her usual supply of cards?"

"Yes, she did. Does she ever buy anything else? She didn't even look at the shelves."

Susie laughed. "One time I asked her if she wanted anything else, like a gift or something, but she just laughed. She said she'd bought one of just about everything Cora had in the store, and it was time for some new merchandise. When it came in, she'd buy."

Val started to laugh then recognized the truth in the statement. Everything on the shelves was old and some even out-of-date. She needed to buy new inventory, but until some money came in, that couldn't be done.

She picked up her lunch. "I'll be in the office if anyone needs me." Back at her desk, Val unwrapped her sandwich and contemplated the note once more. If Aunt Cora really thought she needed Colt's help, maybe it was time to talk with her and see what her aunt wanted before contacting him.

A new thought leaped into her mind. If that had been the reason Colt was here in the first place, then he should've mentioned it. Not that it would have made a difference, but it might have lessened the shock to know that Aunt Cora had summoned him for help. On the other hand, if she'd known he was coming, Val would have made arrangements to be somewhere else and let Aunt Cora settle the situation.

Now she found herself in a no-win situation. If she called him for help, she'd risk opening up old wounds and unsettling her settled-on routine. But if she didn't, the store might have to close, and that would break Aunt Cora's heart.

She opened a drawer and pulled out her Bible. Only place to go when she needed solutions to a problem. God had given her peace through the years, especially after Colt left, and she needed the Lord's guidance now more than she'd ever dreamed.

❄

Colt left the restaurant and headed for his car. It had been good to see Gabriela, an old friend from high school. So many good friends he'd left behind five years ago, and it reminded him he needed to call Ryan and Amber. He prayed they would greet him as Gabriela had and not as Val had. Of course he hadn't hurt the others as he had her. He'd been a real coward in those days, but who was to say he was any better today? Coming back was the first step, but whether or not it would lead to reconciliation with his mother or with Val, only God could know.

He pulled his cell phone from his pocket and called Cora's number. When she answered, he said, "Hi, Aunt Cora, it's Colt Jamison."

"So you did come. I suppose you found out I don't run the store anymore."

He chuckled. "Yes, I did. Quite a shock to see Val there."

Her laugh resounded. "I imagine it was."

Colt cleared his throat. "Do you mind if I come out to see you?"

"Not at all, dear boy. I have some fresh-baked snick-erdoodles and a pot of fresh coffee. You know how to get here."

"Indeed I do, and the cookies sound great. See you in a few." Not that he had room for them, but those cinnamon-sugar cookies had always been a favorite. Besides her retire-ment, no telling what other surprises Aunt Cora would have waiting for him.

Fifteen minutes later he drove up to her house and parked on the street. She must have seen him because the door opened wide before he was halfway up the walk.

"I can't believe it's really you." She peered at him as he drew closer. "And you haven't changed a bit. Just as handsome as ever."

Heat rose in his cheeks, and she welcomed him with open arms. At the moment a hug from her was just what he needed. He followed her into the living room. Everything looked the same as it had five years ago when he'd last been in the room.

"Have a seat and I'll get the cookies and your coffee. Still like it black, I suppose."

"Yes, ma'am, black it is." He gazed around the living room with its comfy upholstered chairs and sofa. Despite it being mid-afternoon, the lamps were on and lent a cozy feel to the room. He'd spent more time in this room the last year before he left than anywhere else. Here, the love he missed at home could always be found.

Aunt Cora returned with a tray laden with mugs and cookies. She set the tray on the coffee table in front of the sofa. "How long have you been in town?"

"Got in last night. I'm staying with Chase and Julie, but with their baby due in a few weeks, I should find somewhere else." They had the space, but new parents didn't need an extra mouth to feed or entertain.

"You can always stay with me while you're here." She handed him the plate of cookies.

He slipped three of them onto a napkin beside his mug. "I know, but I want a permanent place." Her eyebrows raised in question. "I quit my job in New York and came back to San Antonio to try reconciliation with Mother and to help you."

Aunt Cora set her mug on the table with a *thud*. She

moved to sit beside him on the sofa and wrapped an arm around his shoulder. "Good. It's time you came home and set things right. Have you been to see your mother yet?"

Guilt seeped into his heart, but just as quickly, he pushed it aside. "No. I've called three times and left messages, but she won't return them."

"I'm so sorry, but don't give up on her, Colt. She can't shut the door on you and your brother forever, especially since Chase and Julie are going to have her first grandchild very soon."

"I'm not sure even that will make a difference. When Dad died, something inside of Mother did, too. You know she hasn't accepted anyone or anything in her heart since then." If it had not been for Aunt Cora, Colt and Chase would have been more like orphans than children of the wealthy socialite turned recluse, Sylvia Cantrell Jamison.

Cora reached over and grasped his hand. "I know. I tried to talk to her when Chase married, but it was like no one else existed but her, and she can't accept the idea that you boys are Christians."

"When she cut us out of her life, she said she never wanted to see us again. She didn't understand how we could believe in a God who was so cruel as to take away the one person she loved more than anything."

"Your mother and I were best friends at one time, but bitterness and depression have taken their toll. She's not the same Sylvia I once knew. I could see how hurt Chase was that she didn't come to the wedding."

"I wish I could have been here longer for that, but I had work facing me in New York. Maybe Chase and I could have done a better job of reaching out to her if I had stayed around." Although she had refused to see them when they went by her house, they had both hoped she'd at least try to contact them or say something about the wedding.

"I don't think there was anything you could do. All my attempts meet with failure just as yours have. It's as though we had never met or been friends."

Colt sucked in his breath then expelled it in a puff of air. His mother had been a matter of prayer for a number of years, but lately he'd given up on prayers. God would take care of her in His own time, but Colt didn't have the patience to wait. Of course, with things the way they were now, all he could do was wait. He nibbled on the cookies and became the boy he'd been when Aunt Cora came to his rescue.

She tilted her head. "So what did you think when you saw Val and the store?"

He choked on a crumb and grabbed his coffee to take a deep swallow. "You left a little bit of a mess for her."

"Like I said in my letter, I needed help. I learned I had no business sense whatsoever. As long as Will was alive, he kept the books. When he died, the store was the only thing to keep me going. When things got into such a mess, I knew I couldn't do it alone anymore."

"So that's when you wrote to me."

"Yes, and when I didn't hear from you right away, I decided to give it over to Val. She always loved the place, so I figured she could straighten it out. After all, she was a business major at UT, and that should give her what she needs to figure out my papers."

It'd take more than a business degree to make sense of the

hodgepodge of invoices and orders and inventory he'd seen. "When was the last time you ordered new inventory?"

"Why, just last month when I ordered cards for the holiday season."

"No, I mean real merchandise."

Cora twisted her mouth and wrinkled her nose. "I really don't remember. I hate to buy new things until I've sold the old."

"But you need new merchandise to get customers to come into the store." Even with his experience, Colt doubted he'd be much help, but he'd have to see Val again and go over the invoices. With an inventory of what was on those shelves, he might be able to devise a plan for getting rid of it and getting new, but without Val's cooperation, he couldn't do anything.

Cora poured more coffee into his mug. "Do you think you'll be able to help Val?"

"I don't know. Besides, even if I came up with an idea, she may not even speak to me or want me anywhere around. And even if she did, we would need money for new merchandise."

"I may not have any sense of business where the shop is concerned, but Will took care of us quite well, so don't worry about the money. I can supply what she needs." She leaned forward in a conspiratorial manner. "So, will you help?"

He sat for a few minutes to sort through the meaning behind the letter and the words she had just spoken. If she had the money to take care of the store, she didn't need him to help her with it. She could have easily hired a new bookkeeper. Then his suspicions grew, and his eyes narrowed as he peered at Aunt Cora. "Just exactly why did you give Val the store and want me to come home?"

Chapter 3

Colt stood outside the gift shop and took a deep breath to bolster his courage. Aunt Cora's heart was in the right place, but her manipulations could backfire and cause more hurt.

With renewed determination, he opened the door and entered the all-but-empty store. One customer occupied the attention of the lone clerk, and Val was nowhere around. He headed back to the office, waving at the clerk as he passed her, and received a huge smile of welcome. At least one person was glad to see him. She looked vaguely familiar, but he couldn't place her at the moment. He'd have to ask about her later.

The office door stood open, and Val sat at her desk with her chin on her palm and her bottom lip between her teeth, a sure sign of her puzzlement over some matter. He knocked on the frame and cleared his throat.

She whirled around and dropped her pen. "Colt, what are

you doing back here?"

He pulled the letter from his pocket and unfolded it. "Aunt Cora sent for me."

The expressions on her face changed faster than a blinking sign, but he caught fear, distrust, and anguish before resignation finally settled in. She reached into the desk drawer. "I found this sticky note yesterday after you left." She thrust it toward him. "Why didn't you say something when you were here?"

He hesitated in order to choose his words carefully and to keep from further antagonizing her. "When I found she was no longer running the place, I figured she'd found help from someone else, and—"

"And things didn't go well between us." She massaged her temples with her index fingers. He recognized the sign of her distress and waited until she was ready to speak again.

Finally she peered up at him. "Up until Uncle Will's death, the records are clear and concise on the computer. Since then, I can't figure out what she's done except not buy any new inventory."

"Will you let me help you?" Colt's breath caught in his throat. If her answer was no, he'd have no choice but to back off despite Aunt Cora's best intentions.

Val lowered her gaze and clasped her hands in her lap. "I don't know, Colt. Can we work together and make sense of all this, or. . ." Her voice trailed off.

"Let me give it a go. If you don't like my suggestions or ideas, just say so."

She delayed her answer for what seemed an eternity but in essence was only a moment or two while she stacked papers and folders. He sensed the debate raging in her mind and probably her heart. Remorse for the years he'd lost with her ate at his soul, but he'd taken the coward's way out of what he viewed as an impossible situation.

Aunt Cora's words yesterday came back to him. *"It was time for you to come home and mend the bridges you burned behind you five years ago."* His only hope now was that those bridges hadn't been completely destroyed.

Val let her breath out in a puff. "This is against my better judgment, but if Aunt Cora thinks you can help me, I have no choice but to accept." She shoved a folder into his hands. "Take this and see what you think."

His throat constricted with joy, and he could only nod and secure the folder under his arm. He swallowed hard, but his voice still squeaked. "The first thing I want to do is a complete inventory of all merchandise on your shelves and in the storeroom."

"Whatever you want." She turned to a cabinet beside the desk and opened it. "Here's a clipboard and some blank inventory sheets. Aunt Cora didn't know anything about computers and did it all by hand. Once we get it counted, you can work up a spreadsheet and we can see where we stand."

"Okay. You're the boss." He turned to leave.

"Colt, wait a minute." She stared at him a moment, swallowed a few times, then said, "Never mind. Go ahead with the inventory." She picked up a folder and swiveled around in her chair.

The anguish seen in her eyes in that moment sent pangs of guilt to his soul. It contradicted everything he'd believed the past five years. He had hurt her, but if she had cared that much, she would have answered his letters and known he still loved her. He tapped the clipboard on his fingertips then pivoted on his heel and headed for the display shelves.

❄

Colt's footsteps faded away, and Val dropped her pen to the desk. Her stomach churned, and her heart pounded in her ears. She breathed deeply then exhaled. He couldn't affect her this way after all she'd done to forget him. He was here only to help Aunt Cora, and the sooner they finished, the sooner he'd leave, and she could get on with her life.

The CD player on her desk filled the room with the words of a Christmas carol. "Joy to the world, the Lord is come." Her shoulders slumped. With the holiday only weeks away, she should be singing along, but no joy filled her world at the moment.

She tried to work, but the songs only added to her distress. Tears stung her eyes with the memories of past holidays. Christmas had always been her favorite time of year. Mom and Aunt Cora decorated everywhere they could find a space in the store and at home. Val jerked and pushed back her chair. That was what was missing. Not a single Christmas decoration could be seen anwhere.

"Susie." Val rushed to the store area.

Her clerk turned from helping a customer. "What do you need, Val?"

"Where does Aunt Cora keep her Christmas decorations?"

"In the storeroom. The boxes are marked."

"Thanks." Val hurried to the back room and began shoving boxes. Sure enough, she found the labeled plastic bins. The first one contained tinsel and strands of lights in a jumble and tangle of wires and gold foil. They must have been stuffed back in the bin last year with no concern about getting them out later. She worked several minutes on the lights but gave up and searched through another bin. Garlands of greenery and bows appeared to be in good enough shape to use again. She glanced overhead to see a box with a Christmas tree pictured on the side. These would be a good start to a holiday feeling in the store.

Susie poked her head through the door. "Need any help?"

"Yes, you can help me get these boxes out where I can see what's in them." She lifted the lid of a second box and found several nutcrackers, an artificial greenery wreath with a large red bow at the top, and boxes of red ornaments. "I hope I can remember where all this stuff goes."

"Why not decorate it the way you want?" A deep voice sounded from the door.

Val peered up at him. "Tradition. Aunt Cora always did it a certain way." Her memory pictured the tree in the window, the wreath on the door, and the lights on the tree.

Colt picked up a large container. "Let's get these things out in the open where we can see what all you have. I may have an idea for a promotion, but I need to know what's available."

Val shrugged and carried out one of the smaller bins and nodded to Colt. "After you set that big one down, climb up and get the box with the tree."

He grinned and headed back to the storeroom. A few minutes later, the three of them sat surrounded by decorations. Val sighed with a bit of disappointment in the assortment, but at least it was a start. Some were tattered and faded, but the nutcrackers and the tree looked to be in good shape.

Colt assembled the tree and stood back to inspect it. "I'd say this has seen better days."

Val nodded in agreement. "It has, but with the ornaments and tinsel, it'll look fine."

He shrugged and set it in the corner. "Whatever you say." He swiped his hands together and knelt beside her. "What else do we have?"

For the next ten minutes, they continued to pull out decorations. Val designated two piles for discards and keepers, and it didn't take long for the discard pile to outgrow the keeper stack. She sat back on her heels. "Looks like I'll have to raid Mom's attic or buy a bunch of new stuff."

Colt laid aside a nutcracker. "I have an idea, and it includes all these decorations, or what there is that we can use now."

Susie smoothed out a red velvet bow. "I'm so glad we're doing this. All the other stores around are all ready for Christmas, but I hated to say anything."

Colt snapped his fingers. "Now I know you. You're Ryan Morrill's sister." A grin covered his face. "You've certainly grown up."

Susie's face turned a bright pink. "I'm a senior at Trinity this year."

"Good for you. I need to give Ryan and Amber a call."

"They'll be glad to hear from you." Susie held up a wreath. "This just needs a little cleaning up and a new bow."

"With all the other stuff going on and trying to get the

records straight, I completely forgot about decorations." Val peered at Colt. "So, what's your idea?"

He rubbed his chin a moment. "Let me work on some things tonight, and I'll have a complete plan for you tomorrow."

Whatever he could come up with now would be better than anything they had at the moment. Although disappointed at what she'd found, Val wanted to decorate like old times. She loved Christmas, and she didn't intend to let any more slips like the decorations keep it from happening here in the store. "Okay, but in the meantime, I'll check with Mom. I know she has some things we can borrow, and Aunt Cora might have some."

Susie stood and dusted her hands against each other. "I bet my mom has some leftovers we can use, too. She never gets all her decorations put out."

Colt shrugged into his jacket. "I'll leave this with you ladies and get to work on some ideas." He headed for the door then stopped. "Do you have someone scheduled to repaint your sign in the next few days?"

Val frowned. "No, I haven't had time to get anyone yet."

"Good, because I have a few ideas about that, too." This time he strode through the door and out to the street.

Val gathered up the lights that all seemed to be working. "Well, let's see what we can do with what we have." From the corner of her eye, she spotted the clipboard Colt had laid aside. She shifted the lights to one arm then reached to pick up the clipboard.

The columns were nearly all filled. Val gasped at the

amount of work he'd accomplished in such a short time. If he worked as fast at coming up with a plan to put the shop in the black, then she might be able to survive after all.

Chapter 4

Val opened the door to her parents' home, and wonderful smells wafted down the hallway from the kitchen to greet her. She breathed deeply and let the spicy scent fill her nose. Gingerbread, her favorite and one of Mom's most delectable homemade treats, led her to the kitchen.

One advantage of living at home had to be the cooking, and her mom's was the best. Still, she longed for the privacy afforded in her own apartment. As soon as the store was in the black, finding her own apartment headed the list of things she needed to do. But for the time being, she'd enjoy Christmas at home.

She entered the kitchen to find her mother preparing greens for salad. Two pans of gingerbread sat cooling on the counter. Val reached for a carrot stick. "Nothing like gingerbread to make the house smell like Christmas."

Mom smiled and sliced a red pepper. "It'll get even better

119

the next few weeks as I get started on my Christmas baking."

Val grabbed a bottle of water from the fridge. "Still baking your banana and cranberry breads for all your friends, I suppose."

"Of course, and I'll make candy later to have ready for visitors." Mom washed her hands then dried them on a towel. "How did it go at the store today?"

"Pretty good, I guess. We got out the Christmas decorations, but they're in sad shape. Colt has some ideas on how to help us get more business during the holidays, and I'm hoping I can find some of the things you're not using to take to the shop."

Her mother's eyebrows shot up, and her eyes opened wide. "Colt was there?" She turned her back to get potatoes from the bin in the pantry. "Do you think it's wise to let him have that much say in your business? I hate to see you open old wounds."

Val downed a swig of water. Doubts clouded her mind, but if Colt could turn things around, then any pain she suffered would be worth it. "I'll be okay, Mom. After all, he's only going to be here for the holidays. If Aunt Cora didn't think he could help, she wouldn't have asked him to come."

Her mother attacked the potatoes with the peeler. "I just wish Cora had consulted with your father and me before going off and seeking help like that. Especially from Colt. He left town without a word to any of us. I just don't want to see you go through anything like that again."

A sigh escaped Val's throat. Mom would never forget those days and nights after Colt left when Val spent most of her time in her room crying. Then the job offer came from Dallas, and it gave her the perfect opportunity to start over in a new place. Now here she was back where it all started. This was not the time to dredge up those memories. Val tossed her water bottle into the recycle bin. "If Colt can help put the store in the black, I can endure his presence for a while. I'm going up to my room, but I'll be back down in time for dinner."

She raced up the stairs to the room she'd shared with her sister so many years ago. All the mementos and decorations from those high school years had been packed away to make this into a guest room. A few of Val's personal pictures and other items brought from her place in Dallas adorned the room. The rest was in storage waiting until she found a place of her own once again.

Mom meant well, but Val couldn't let her mother's ill feelings color her own actions for the next few weeks. Aunt Cora had put her trust in Val to turn the store around and had even managed to provide the one person with the creative ability to help. As much as being close to him did dredge up the old memories, the desire to prove Aunt Cora had made the right decision in giving Val the store was more important.

Val's heart didn't always want to cooperate and still flipped and flopped when Colt was around. Sheer determination to keep it locked up tight would get her through the holidays. She pulled her laptop from its case and sat cross-legged on her bed. One way to keep Colt off her mind was to keep busy. A list of what she needed to do the first week she had taken over the store appeared on the screen, and she added the task of acquiring newer decorations. Maybe after supper, Mom would get out the boxes of extra items for Val to sort through. The area by the display windows needed the most help, so customers would be attracted and come into the store.

Colt's inventory sheets lay in a folder in her computer bag. She extracted them now and glanced over what he'd written. A quick scan revealed no new items for Christmas. How in the world did she think she'd be able to entice buyers to come inside if she didn't have appropriate merchandise to offer them? Maybe Colt would come up with a few suggestions for making the old look new and attractive.

She sighed and opened the calendar on her computer. No matter what she did, Colt managed to invade her thoughts. Today's date stared back at her. December 2 meant a little more than three weeks until Christmas. Most folks would have their shopping done by now as well as have all their cards ready to sign and mail. She let her breath out in a puff. The whole thing looked hopeless.

Tears misted her eyes. *Aunt Cora, why did you wait until things were in such a mess before calling me or Colt?*

❄

Colt stared at the gate that protected his mother's property. He punched in the numbers that would let him gain entrance and prayed they still worked. A moment later the wrought-iron gates, with the circled letter J decorating the center of each, swung back and cleared the way to the house.

The long curved drive led to the massive portico that protected the brick access to the front door. He sat in the car a few moments, drawing in deep breaths to bolster his courage. His mother hadn't spoken to him since the day he left San Antonio, and then it was only to tell him that she had transferred his trust to his name. As soon as he graduated from college, she'd fulfilled his father's instructions in his will then had dismissed him from her life.

The many times he'd tried to contact his mother had each been met with a rejection. The biggest mistake of his life had been to run away to New York to pursue his career and leave behind all that he loved and held dear. With his courage a little stronger, he rang the bell and heard the chimes from within the house.

When the housekeeper, Mrs. Barnes, opened the door, she gasped in surprise. "Mr. Colt, is it really you?" She stretched out her arms and wrapped them around his shoulders. "It's been too long, my boy." When she stepped back, her eyes glistened with tears. "Come in, son, it's good to have you home."

Colt's heart lurched with emotion on seeing the gray-haired woman who'd cared for him and Chase as young boys. "And it's good to see you again. I'm sorry it's been so long, but it was time to try to see Mother again. How is she?" He stepped into the massive entryway and glanced up the curved stairway leading to the rooms where his mother would be.

Mrs. Barnes's eyes clouded, and sorrow filled her face. "Not good, Mr. Colt. It's not a disease that's making her ill. It's her own sadness and how she's cut herself off from all her friends."

Colt shook his head. "It's been over ten years since Dad's death."

"I know, but her heart still grieves for him. She's a

shadow of her former self." She hugged him again. "I'm just so thankful you and Chase had someone like Cora Bennett to take care of you when she went into seclusion." She stepped back and a smile lit up her face. "I must say you've become a fine-looking young man, and you look just like your father when he was younger. What brought you back to San Antonio?"

"Cora needed my help with her store, so I came to see what I could do." He paused then plunged ahead. "I want to be with family again, so I've come back to stay, especially with Chase and Julie's baby due soon."

"Oh, yes, I heard. It's wonderful to know another little Jamison will make his or her entrance into the world." She glanced up the staircase. "I'll go up and see if your mother will see you." She hesitated then said, "But don't get your hopes up."

A few minutes later he heard loud voices, and then his mother's distinct, shrill tones carried to his ears. "Tell him to leave. As long as he believes in that God of his, I don't want him in this house. God doesn't exist, and he's a fool for believing it."

Colt didn't wait for Mrs. Barnes to return. Instead, he strode through the door and back to his car. As much as his heart hurt from her words, he would try again later. God brought him back for a purpose, and he was determined to find that purpose. He headed home to work on the plans he had developed for the card shop. Somehow, with God's help, he'd get through to his mother and bring her back to the beliefs she'd held dear before his father had died.

At his brother's house, he holed up in the guest room. If

he didn't find a place of his own before Christmas, he might end up in a hotel. Chase and Julie needed this room for her mother when the baby came, and from the looks of his sister-in-law, that would be soon.

His thoughts returned to his mother. Her first grandchild would be born, and he wasn't even sure if she knew the baby was coming. Even if she did know, it probably wouldn't make any difference to her. He bowed his head to pray for her as he had done so many times before.

Lord, here I am again. Mother hasn't changed her feelings at all. It's Christmas, and her first grandchild is on its way. Thousands of years ago, one tiny baby You sent made a difference in our world. Please let this little one coming soon make a difference in Mother's world. Even if she doesn't want to believe in You anymore, You can still change her heart. In Jesus' name, amen.

He blinked back the mist in his eyes and turned to his computer. Time to work on those ideas he had for the shop. Soon he had a plan in shape, and the wonderful aromas from downstairs reminded him that with helping Val at the shop and going by to see his mother, he hadn't taken time to eat. His stomach rumbled in protest as he sniffed the herb-filled air.

Time to work on these ideas later—now Julie's homemade lasagna called to him.

Chapter 5

Her arms laden with boxes and bags, Val managed to unlock the shop doors and go inside. Susie rushed from across the street to help her. Val grinned and relinquished the bags. "Thanks, I was about to drop the blue box. It's some of Mom's stuff she didn't use."

"I brought a few things, too. We should have fun with our decorating today."

Val set her load on the counter. "We will. Colt suggested we do what we want, so let's get to it."

For the next half hour, the two decorated the tree for the window display. When she plugged in the lights, tiny sparkles lit up the branches and gave it a festive look. "Lights do make a difference." She placed the tree between the door and window, where it could be seen from the outside as well as first thing upon entering the store.

Susie fluffed the bows on two wreaths and hung one in each window on either side of the doors. She began humming the tune "It's Beginning to Look a Lot Like Christmas."

Val laughed then began singing the song as Susie hummed. Val hung a jingle-bell cluster on the door then stepped back to admire their work. "I must say, the place looks much more like Christmas now. Aunt Cora told me about a Christmas delivery made just before Uncle Will died. She never got it out and then forgot about it until I called her last night."

At that moment the bells jingled as Colt opened the door. "Hey, I see you two have been busy since I left yesterday."

Val's heart skipped in a happy dance. Not trusting her voice, she simply smiled, but Susie's laugh tinkled as merrily as the bells on the door. "Thanks to our moms, we have all we need to give us a festive air around here."

"And you've done a great job." He nodded to Val. "Can we go back to the office? I have some ideas to run by you."

"Sure." Her hand trembled as she handed Susie a strand of tinsel. Susie tilted her head and raised her eyebrows in a way that meant she'd have questions later. Val breathed deeply to calm her emotions before turning to follow Colt to the back.

He had his laptop open and tapped on the keys when she entered. "Thanks for doing so much with the inventory list yesterday. Aunt Cora told me about some merchandise she'd ordered but never unpacked, and it's Christmas stuff."

"That's good. It'll fit right into what I have in mind." He plopped into the chair by her desk. "The first thing I want to do is change your sign. I talked to a buddy of mine, and he'll come over today and take off some of the old. The new name could be Cora's Collectibles in big gold letters with smaller letters that say Gifts for All Occasions.

Val furrowed her brow. It did convey more of what the store was than the name she'd chosen, and it would honor her aunt. "That sounds nice. I like it, but what about all the outdated stuff we have?"

"That's what will make it 'collectible.' We can advertise a big clearance sale of everything in the store. Since all of it has already been paid for, whatever price you charge will be yours." Colt opened a file on the computer.

A diagram of a floor plan filled the screen. On closer inspection, Val realized it was the store. He had divided the space into sections, and she bent closer to read the print. As she scanned the wording, she began to see the plan emerging.

Colt pointed out the different areas. "Since we're saying 'all occasions' in the advertising, we'll have a special place here for wedding, shower, and other bridal merchandise. Then we'll have a section for babies and young children. Another space will be for special holidays; another for cards, paper, and other wrapping supplies; and another for special-event decorations and supplies."

She noticed right off his use of the word "we" in everything he described. He must be planning to stay and help her see it through. Her body stiffened. No, that was just advertising talk for clients. He'd help her get started, and then he'd be off again and out of her life. That's what she wanted, wasn't it? But her heart raced at the thought he might stay.

"Well, what do you think?"

Val started. He'd been waiting for her reaction, and she'd

been thinking about his staying or leaving. She cleared her throat. "I think it might work. I'm willing to give it a try."

"Good. Now let's put a sign in the window that tells people a sale is going on. Then we can start rearranging the shelves and move things around."

Val nodded and followed him back into the showroom. The day passed in a blur of moving things to new locations and grouping items together for quick sale. During the lunch hour, Val perused the catalogs Aunt Cora left and ordered merchandise for each new area of the store.

Susie found the boxes of Christmas items Aunt Cora had ordered and opened them. Val gasped at the quality of the merchandise she found. One box contained nothing but Precious Moments figurines and decorations, while another one contained items from Willow Tree and Dayspring.

At least her aunt had good taste. She and Susie unwrapped each item with care and checked it against the invoice, so she could put it on the computer later. Val glanced up to where Colt supervised the man repainting the sign. Through the windows she spotted a number of people looking in with curiosity. A few even made their way into the store.

Watching Colt talk with the customers and explain what they were doing to the store warmed her insides like her favorite latte. She shook her head. This would never do. Each time she stood, sat, or even walked near him, her blood tap-danced through her veins. If she didn't get things under control immediately, her life would tumble back to those days of heartache.

All afternoon customers strolled in and out of the store as merchandise sold at an amazing rate. At four o'clock, Susie handed a customer two bags of cards and gift items. When the jingle bells signaled the lady had left, Susie punched keys on the register then whooped. "Val, Colt, come look at this."

Val hurried to the counter and gasped at the numbers on the tally. "I can't believe it. We've made more in this one day than in the past month."

Colt joined them. "Hey, that looks great."

Val's arms went around his neck. "Thank you, thank you. Just a few little changes and it made such a difference." His arms encircled her back, and the spicy scent of his after-shave hit her nose. The memory of the last time he held her close flooded her mind, and she jerked away.

Heat crept up her neck. "I'm sorry. Got a little carried away there." She headed for her office. "I need to call Mom and tell her that we're staying open late and I won't be home for dinner."

When the door closed behind her, a sob escaped her throat. "I can't do this. He's out of my life." Her words hung in the air, mocking her vow to not let him have any effect on her feelings.

With her heart pounding, she sat down at her desk. He'd be gone after Christmas, and she could get her life back on the track she'd laid out for it. Until then, she'd just have to make sure her heart remained locked tight and out of his reach. She reached over and picked up the phone to call her mother.

❄

Colt stared at the closed door. For one brief moment, time had reverted to five years ago. The warmth of Val's body against his still permeated his being. If only he could really go back to that time and do things differently.

Susie cleared her throat. "You still care about her, don't you?"

Heat filled his face. "Is it that obvious?"

"Oh, yeah, just like it was when you were in college. I thought for sure you two would marry just like Ryan and Amber."

"So did I." He shook himself. "That's water under the bridge. She's moved on with her life."

The bells jingled to signal the entrance of another customer, and Susie turned away, but not before a last remark. "Why don't you just tell her how you feel? You might be surprised at her response."

He wouldn't go there again and set himself up for another rejection. Val had made it clear when she didn't respond to his proposal in his last letter to her. A call would have been better perhaps, but he could always express his feelings better on paper. Apparently the words meant nothing to her, or she would have at least written to turn him down.

Another customer walked in, and he busied himself with helping Susie. Val returned but avoided him for the next hour. Business slowed then, and he took the opportunity to grab his jacket and computer and leave. "Bye, you two. Congratulations on your sales today. I'll drop by tomorrow to check out a few more things."

Without waiting for a reply, he hurried outside. A cold blast of wind greeted him, and he pulled his leather jacket around him and zipped it. The cold front the weatherman predicted had come in, and now it really began to feel like Christmas. The feelings didn't quite reach his heart. He shoved his hands into his pockets and walked along the river where the reflections of decorations and lights sparkled in the water. He'd forgotten how beautiful the Riverwalk could be at Christmas.

Rockefeller Center in New York City was well known for its Christmas tree and ice skating, but as far as Colt was concerned, the Riverwalk outshone the Big Apple. Boats filled with carolers meandered along the curving river and added to the festivities. Any other time it would have filled his heart with joy, but tonight it only brought back memories of the holidays with Val.

He headed for his car. It was time for another visit with Aunt Cora, and to seek her wisdom as to what he should do now. Before heading in that direction, Colt drove through the posh neighborhood where he had grown up. He paused near the gate to the mansion where his mother lived like a hermit.

God, I just don't understand why mother turned away from You, Chase and me, and all her friends. The woman I saw before I left looked nothing like the fun-loving beautiful woman she was when Dad was alive. Please, God, for the sake of Chase and Julie's baby, I pray You will turn her heart around. What a wonderful Christmas gift that would be.

With a sigh, he stepped on the gas and turned his car toward the Bennett home.

Chapter 6

Val sat cross-legged on her bed reviewing the day. The sales had been so much more than she expected. If it kept up, she'd have enough for the rent and overhead to keep her shop open a while longer. Colt's ideas were right on the money, and when the new merchandise arrived, she and Susie would be able to set up the areas as he had suggested.

She hugged her knees to her chest. The scene with Colt replayed itself over and over in her mind. Her spontaneous hug and the scent of his aftershave had unnerved her more than she could ever have imagined. Her mother was right. Being near him would only bring more heartache.

The rest of December loomed ahead with Colt coming into the store to oversee the changes as she implemented them. *Lord, I need every bit of strength You can give me to get through these next weeks. Help me to keep my mind clear and alert to business and not romance.*

Her thoughts then returned to the number of customers who had come in that day. She and Susie would never have made it without Colt's help. His charm and wit had sold more than a few items. If this increased traffic continued, she may have to hire another clerk.

Then an idea popped into her mind. Aunt Cora could come back and work during the holidays. She had loved that aspect of owning the store, and would probably get a kick out of doing it again. Tomorrow would give an indication if that would be necessary.

Satisfied with that decision, Val picked up the invoices for the items she and Susie had unpacked that day. At least those bills had been paid, so any money made from the merchandise would be all profit and available to be put right back into the shop.

The more she worked, the more excited she became about actually owning the business and running it herself. The only cloud to mar the bright sunshine of optimism was the matter of seeing Colt so much in the next few weeks, but for the moment, she refused to let that cloud rain on her parade of good feelings.

❄

Colt pushed back from the table and picked up his plate. "Cora, you're still one of the best cooks around. Nobody makes stew and corn bread to beat yours."

"That's because you haven't eaten anyone else's but mine." Cora grinned and placed her dishes on the counter. "Remember the first time you ate it here?"

A grin split Colt's face. "I certainly do. You had picked up Chase and me and brought us here to stay a few weeks after Dad's funeral. We'd never had such good home-cooked food." Not that the cook his mother hired was not good, but her menus were more like restaurant fare than the plain, good food Cora dished up.

He leaned against the counter edge. "You know, you fed us more than good food to nourish our bodies. The food you gave us from the Bible nourished our hearts, and for that I'll be forever thankful."

Cora turned from the sink and hugged him. "I just wish I could take care of your heart now. I know it can't be happy because your eyes tell me otherwise."

He hugged her tightly as he would his mother in times past. Cora could always see straight into his soul and know when he was unhappy.

She stepped back from him. "Is it Valerie, or is your mother causing the pain I see?"

"I really don't know. Both of them send my heart spiraling. Val's closeness sends it into a nosedive toward memories of what I walked out on, and Mother's sends it into the depths of despair trying to figure out what I can do to bring her out of her depression."

Cora placed her hands on his shoulders. "I see your love for Valerie and know it's as deep now as it was five years ago. Chase told me about your mother the day after you left. I'm glad you wrote me and let me know how and where you were. Have you talked with Val about what happened between you and your mother that caused you to run to New York?"

"I wrote to her several times and even asked her to marry me and join me in New York, but I never had an answer." Remembering that rejection now sent more pain into his soul. "She didn't bother to write back, so I figure she doesn't want to know about it."

"Why didn't you call or come back to get her?"

"Good question, but you know I always express myself better on paper than I do with the spoken word." If he'd had the courage, he would have returned to San Antonio and asked in person, but when she didn't respond to his first letter, he'd taken the coward's way out. Better a rejection on paper than in person.

"That may be so, but a phone call might have made a difference." She knit her brow and peered at him. "You say you wrote to her. How many times?"

"I sent four letters the first two weeks I was gone, but never heard a word back from her." The fourth letter asked her to marry him, but he had said he'd leave her alone if she didn't answer, and so he had—until now.

Cora shook her head. "I don't recall Valerie ever saying anything about a letter from you. She did ask me once if I knew why you had left, but I told her you could explain it better than I could."

"I guess she was so angry because I left so suddenly that she didn't want to discuss the matter with anyone." That wasn't like Valerie, since she had always gone straight to her aunt whenever she had a problem.

"Well, I think you need to tell her now what happened. You still love her." She wagged a finger at him. "And don't tell me you don't because I can see it every time her name is mentioned."

He held up his hands in surrender. "Guilty as charged."

She led him into the living room. "Then let's do

something about it. I say you tell her everything about that time and see what her reaction is. Maybe you can start all over again with trying to win her heart."

That may be well and good, but the Valerie he'd seen at work was not the same one he'd left. Her attitude and actions when around him spoke of a woman who had dismissed him from her life. "I'm not sure if that will work. What if she rejects me again?"

"Son, nothing worth having comes without some risk. I think you'd be surprised by her response. Pray about it and go where God leads you."

Prayer was the one thing he'd neglected these past few weeks. Once a regular part of each day, his time talking with the Lord had become sporadic. "I'll do that. Working with her each day for the next few weeks should give me some hints, and then I'll do whatever I feel the Lord is telling me to do."

Cora's smile lit up her face. "That's my boy." Then her face turned serious again. "I've been praying for your mother every day for over ten years. I don't know what's taking God so long to fix things because I'm sure He wants them to be fixed."

"I've prayed for her, too, but nothing I say seems to have any success. Just a few nights ago I went by the house. Mrs. Barnes was glad to see me, but when she told Mother I was there, I heard ranting and shouting telling me to get out and never come back."

Cora sank onto the sofa beside him, and her arms wrapped around him in the comforting hug he remembered from years ago. "Colt, your mother doesn't know what she wants. We'll have to keep praying for a miracle to help her see that her life isn't over. In fact, I'm going to go by to see her again, and this time I won't let her turn me away."

"Thanks, but I wonder what good it will do, if any." If she hadn't come around by now, he didn't see how one more visit from Cora could make a difference.

"It may not, but I have to try. It's time for Sylvia to realize she has a family, and it's about to get bigger when that grandchild comes along."

"I pray you are successful." As much as he loved Valerie, if he could only have one wish granted for Christmas, it would be for his mother to wake up and realize she would have a precious grandchild to love. If a baby made such a difference in the world over 2,000 years ago, perhaps a baby could make a difference in their world today.

Chapter 7

After a week of more business than usual and new merchandise on the shelves, Val called Aunt Cora to come in and help with the Christmas rush. She gladly accepted and came to work with Susie while Colt finished the redecorating and arranging of sections. That left Val time to take care of the business end without spending late hours at the store. As far as she was concerned, the arrangement worked to perfection.

Val rolled her shoulders and closed the spreadsheet on her computer. The numbers showed the shop to be in the black for the first time in months, and that sent warm pleasure through her system. She could do this.

Laughter from the front drew her out of the office. Mrs. Bronson stood at the cash register with Aunt Cora. She waved at Val. "I was just telling your aunt what a wonderful job you were doing here. Why, I hardly recognized the place when I came in."

"Thank you, Mrs. Bronson. Colt Jamison deserves most of the credit. He had some great ideas for redecorating." Val glanced around to find him.

Aunt Cora leaned on the counter. "He left a few minutes ago. Said he'd be back later."

Disappointment filled Val, but she smiled. "Oh, well then, you'll have to come back and thank him later."

Mrs. Bronson raised an eyebrow. "I'm surprised he's still in town. Of course, with his brother and sister-in-law expecting that baby, I suppose he wanted to stick around for Christmas. I imagine that made you happy."

Heat rushed to Val's face. "It doesn't matter to me one way or the other. He can stay here or go back to New York."

Mrs. Bronson gathered up her packages. "Well now, if you ask me, it should matter. I was just telling Cora that you two belong together."

Val shot a glare toward Aunt Cora, but she just shrugged her shoulders and turned to talk to another customer.

"And I think she's right on with that." Susie stepped up behind the counter to ring up another sale.

Val grimaced. "You all need to think again. Colt didn't want me five years ago, and he doesn't want me now. When this week is up, I won't need him anymore, and he can go on back to New York and his job there." Before any one of them could retort, she turned on her heel and headed back to her office.

She slumped into the chair at her desk. Why couldn't they see that things would never work out with Colt? He was water under the bridge, and she couldn't let her heart live in the past. Val blinked to ward off tears that threatened to form. He'd be gone as soon as Christmas was over or when Chase and Julie had their baby.

The store had been so busy the past few weeks that there was no time to talk about anything but business during store hours, and Val had made sure she wasn't anywhere around to discuss anything else afterward. Susie had told her that he'd been over to see Ryan and Amber, and they'd gone out to dinner. Val almost wished she'd been there. They'd had so much fun together years ago. A shudder passed through her body. She couldn't go there.

A few minutes later, she grabbed her jacket and went back to the floor. "Aunt Cora, I have to run some errands. I'll be back in an hour."

Her aunt called out, "Wait a minute, I have a question."

Val stopped and stood by the counter until Aunt Cora finished her sale. "Okay, what's the big question?"

"You said something that bothers me. What makes you think Colt didn't want you five years ago?"

"What makes me think—Aunt Cora, he didn't write to me, call me, or anything. He just disappeared and that was that. Pretty clear, don't you think?"

"You sure about that? You and he need to sit down and talk this through. Find out why he left and what he did. I believe you'll be surprised."

Val's mouth gaped open before she snapped it shut. She hitched her purse over her shoulder. "It doesn't really matter now. We've gone our separate ways, and he doesn't need me in his life right now." She fled through the door before her aunt could make another comment.

He may not need her, but she needed him. If he hadn't come when he did, her store might now be dark and closed instead of brimming with life.

She didn't actually have any errands, but getting out of the store and into the cool air would help rid her mind of Colt. By habit and without realizing it, she headed home. When she pulled up into the driveway of her parents' house, once again she wished for a place of her own. If the store continued to show a profit after Christmas, she may be able to have just that.

Since she was here, she could pick up a few snacks and goodies to take back to the shop. Mom always had plenty on hand this time of year. When Val opened the front door, the aroma of cinnamon and sugar filled the air. She headed straight for the kitchen where her mother was putting the finishing touches on her Christmas cookies.

"Mmm, it does smell and look like Christmas in here." She reached for a cookie and bit into it before her mother could stop her.

Her mom laughed. "I never could keep you from eating them before they were completely ready." She wiped her hands on a dish towel. "What brings you home this early? Did you close up?"

With her mouth full of cookie, Val shook her head and held up a finger. In a moment she said, "No, I thought I'd see what you had on hand to take back as a surprise for the gang. They're working so hard, and I want to give them a little something to celebrate."

"Now that's a fine idea. Let me see what I can put together." She opened the cabinets and reached for the decorated tins she had stored away. "These will be nice and festive. I have cookies, nut bread, and candy, and I can put some wassail into a thermos for you."

"Sounds great. I'll help." Mom had come through as usual. Aunt Cora and Susie would really be surprised, and Colt, too, if he'd returned by the time she got back.

Val covered the pralines with waxed paper and snapped the lid on the tin. "Susie will love these, and your banana bread is Aunt Cora's favorite."

"Yes, and that's why I put in an extra mini loaf for you to give to her. Remember to ask her to dinner on Sunday." She turned the heat off under the wassail. "Is Colt still around helping you?"

"Yes, but I don't know for how much longer." Val bit her lip and tore off another sheet of waxed paper. "You know, he's been a tremendous help, and I've really been pleased with what he's done."

Her mother narrowed her eyes. "You're not letting him soften your resolve are you?"

"No, Mom. Besides, he'll be gone as soon as the holidays are over." But she'd miss him more than she'd ever admit to her mother.

"That's right. Just remember he hurt you once, and there's no sense in letting it happen again."

Val let her breath out in a long sigh. "You know, I still don't understand why he never wrote to me or explained why he left. I really thought he loved me."

An expression almost like guilt crossed her mother's face, but she turned toward the sink before Val could be sure and said, "Don't think about it. It's best to leave the past in the past." She picked up a two quart–size thermos. "I'll pour this and then you can get back to the shop." Her hands shook as she poured the hot liquid into the container.

"That's fine, Mom, they'll appreciate it." Val furrowed her brow and frowned. Her mother's words and abrupt actions were not like her at all. Mom had never been that fond of Colt because of his wealthy background, and she'd always said he'd someday break Val's heart. She'd been right, but that didn't explain her strange behavior at the moment. Val sensed her mother hiding something, but had no clue as to what it was. Maybe Aunt Cora would know.

Loaded with good things to eat, Val headed to her car. She secured the tins and thermos so they wouldn't shift and fall during the ride back to the shop. Between her mother's strange behavior and Aunt Cora's statement earlier, Val sensed something wasn't right, but if it involved Colt, it never would be.

❄

Colt sat on a bench near the river. How he loved it all decked out for Christmas. The lights gave it a magical look, but his heart felt anything but magical. So far he'd had no success in trying to speak with Val about what happened five years ago. He'd been so hurt by his own mother that he couldn't see how his running away would hurt Val, the one person who could have made him truly happy.

His mother's words came back to haunt him even now. "Take the money I put in your account and get out of my life. God doesn't love us, and your saying you have become a Christian hurts me. If God did love us, your father would still be here. God is cruel and doesn't care what happens to any of us. Right now I don't even believe He exists, and I don't see how you can, either. I hate you, I hate God, I hate Chase, and I hate everything you say you believe."

The words poured over him now like cold wind and chilled his soul. He squeezed his eyes shut. *God, how can I get through to her? Help me somehow, someway make her see and understand what Chase and I know to be true. You do love us and want what is best for us.*

What was best for him? At the moment he doubted he could truly be happy back in San Antonio. It had been a mistake to return. If he left, he'd just be running away again, but this time he'd make sure Val understood why. He had to tell her one more time that he loved her and always would, even if she turned away from him.

Surely there was a way to open her heart and unlock those feelings from five years ago. Christmas was a time of wonder and great love and had always been her favorite time of year. He began making plans for things to do with her that would remind her of all the good times they'd had. But would she agree to do things with him?

He glanced at his watch. He should be getting back to the store. His stomach rumbled in protest at not getting the meal he'd planned on having while out. No time for that now. It'd just have to wait another few hours.

The bright lights and colorful displays of the store beckoned him as it did the customers. The window glittered with the bright red and gold lettering that matched the new overhead sign proclaiming this to be CORA'S COLLECTIBLES. If sales kept up like they were going, Val wouldn't have a lot of merchandise left over for clearance after Christmas.

The closer Christmas came, the more he realized he had to ask Val why she'd never answered his letters. He stared through the window to the scene inside. Several tins sat open on the counter as the three women shared cookies and what looked like pralines, one of his favorite candies. Val laughed at something Susie said. She swept her fingers through her hair in a gesture so familiar that his fingers itched to grab hers as he'd done so many times in the past. He swallowed the lump in his throat. Let them have their fun tonight. He wouldn't spoil it by walking in now.

He turned to head back to his car. Somehow he had to come up with a plan to win Val's trust. A box in the jewelry store caught his attention. A seed of an idea planted itself in his mind and took root.

Chapter 8

Colt hadn't been back to the store since the night she'd brought back the treats from home. That ought to show Aunt Cora he didn't have any interest in taking up where they left off. The numbers on the screen blurred. She clenched her fists and her shoulders tensed. In just the few weeks he'd been back, Colt had managed to stir up all the old feelings of rejection and disappointment.

She should never have let him start working on the store or thought that she could work with him without it affecting her. Christmas, once her favorite time of the year, brought heartache as she once again remembered all the good times she and Colt had had with Christmas on the Riverwalk.

The boats filled with carolers each evening no longer thrilled her heart with their songs, and the lights everywhere did nothing for her spirits. The happy couples and families strolling along the walkways only served to remind her that she was alone.

Susie's boyfriend had started picking her up each evening when the store closed, and Val watched them with envy in her heart. Her prayers for God to squelch the envy and bring peace to her soul had not been answered.

At least the shop was doing good business. Colt's plan was working well, and each section had brisk sales with the holiday section having the highest number, as they'd hoped. Upgrading the merchandise and changing the types of items sold had made a big difference, and for that she would be grateful in the months ahead. Now the day before Christmas Eve, customers filled the aisles and bought rather than browsed.

Her stomach rumbled, reminding her that she had eaten only half a sandwich for lunch. After one glance at the now-stale bread and limp fries, she grabbed for her jacket. She waved to Aunt Cora and Susie. "I'm going to get something to eat. Do you need anything?"

Her aunt shook her head, but a big grin split her face. Val smiled in return then turned to bump headlong into a broad chest in a black leather jacket. She slipped backward, but strong hands reached to catch her. She gazed up into Colt's blue eyes. Her heart flipped, and if not for his hold on her, she would have collapsed.

"Hi, I was just coming to find you."

His dimpled smile sent her heart racing. "Oh?" She cringed at the squeak that emerged from her mouth.

"Yes, it's dinnertime, and I stopped by to ask you to have it with me."

Objections rose to her lips, but she swallowed them. One more time with him, and then she could get on with her life.

"I think I'd like that."

With Aunt Cora and Susie both telling them to have a good time, they left with Colt holding Val's arm. The spot where his hand grasped her elbow burned even through her jacket. This was not a good idea. She should have said no, but she wanted to be with him. Besides, maybe she would take Aunt Cora's advice and ask him about why he left. Better to know the truth than to second-guess herself the rest of her life. If he didn't want her around, he sure had a funny way of showing it.

When they entered La Cocina del Rio, memories of all the other times they'd been there skipped through Val's mind. This evening could be more difficult than she thought, but she'd get through it.

Gabriela, an old friend, greeted them. "Welcome, you two. It's good to see you together again." She led them to a table by a window that looked out over the patio area and the river. Only a few patrons braved the cold to sit outdoors, and Val was glad for the warmth of the dining room. She picked up the menu and barely glanced at it, as did Colt. They both had their favorites, the quesadilla and enchilada dinners.

Val munched on a few chips and some salsa. "I want to thank you again for the wonderful job you did with rearranging the shop, and all the ideas you gave us for it. Sales are going great, and Aunt Cora loves helping out."

"It's nice seeing my ideas put to work and how much they helped bring in customers. You know how much I love your aunt."

"Yes, I do." Aunt Cora and Uncle Will had been life-savers for Chase and Colt, and had led the boys to become

Christians. That's when things began to spark between Val and Colt. He couldn't have forgotten all the good times they'd had with the youth group in high school and then in college, but apparently they hadn't meant anything to him after all.

All through the meal, Val searched her mind for a way to approach the question foremost in her heart, but a crowded, noisy restaurant was not the place to ask anyway. Colt looked as though he had something to say, too, but held back. He probably wanted to tell her when he planned to leave. At least this time she could say good-bye.

After the meal, they walked along the river. Val shoved her hands into her gloves and wrapped her scarf about her neck. Colt grasped her hand and tucked it under his elbow. How good and comfortable it felt to be walking like this. The years fell away, and Val was back to the good times. No questions tonight. She planned to enjoy every minute of this time together as long as it lasted.

❄

Walking with Val's hand under his elbow felt as natural as breathing. All the love he'd harbored for so long filled him with hope and confidence. The first part of his plan had worked, but he still had many pieces to put in place before it would be complete.

He'd held his breath back in the shop, afraid she would turn down his invitation to dinner. When she agreed, his heart sang, and he'd wanted to shout. He led her toward a bench where they could sit and watch the boats and carolers pass by. Val had always loved doing that and usually sang along with them.

Tonight was no different. Her clear soprano voice lifted in the night air as the group floating by sang "Oh Come, All Ye Faithful." She waved at them, and the people on the boat waved back as they completed the song and then shouted, "Merry Christmas."

A sigh of contentment came from Valerie, and he wanted to hug and kiss her right then, but that would be too much too soon. First he had to regain her trust.

"Val, I have some things I need to tell you." His throat tightened at the worried expression on her face. He had to choose his words carefully so as not to hurt her and make her angry.

"I thought you understood why I left home the way I did, but it seems I must have been mistaken." She didn't respond, so he took a deep breath and plunged ahead.

"Mother called me in right after I graduated from the university. She lashed out at me and told me that since I was now an adult and out of college, I could stand on my own two feet. She would no longer offer any financial or moral support. She said she never wanted to see me again unless I could come back and tell her I was no longer a Christian because God was cruel and only hurt people."

Val's eyes clouded over and she blinked. "Colt, I'm so sorry. Why didn't you tell me then?"

"I was so hurt and defeated that all I could think about was getting as far away from her as possible. I took all the money left in my account and went to New York where I'd had a job offer."

"You never said anything about a job in New York."

"Because I didn't plan to take it until that night. You were in Dallas at your cousin's wedding, so I just got on a plane and left. I wrote to you and explained it all but never heard back from you."

Val's mouth dropped open. "You wrote to me? I never got any letter or phone call, not even an e-mail message."

A cold chill raced through Colt. "How could that be? I wrote and even e-mailed once. I don't understand."

"Neither do I. I believed you ran away from me and all that we'd had together. I was furious with the way you waltzed back into my life as though nothing had happened. If I hadn't seen that note from Aunt Cora saying she needed your help, you'd never have been asked."

"And I would never have intruded into your life if you hadn't accepted my help." He grasped her hands in his.

"Where do we go from here? I'm sorry for hurting you."

She narrowed her eyes. "How can I believe you really tried to reach me all those years ago?"

"You have my word. I know I should have called, but putting words on paper or e-mail is so much easier for me. I never dreamed you didn't get them."

Val pulled her hands from his. "I want to believe you, but I'll have to think about this and see if I can find out why I didn't get those letters you say you wrote." She stood. "I need to get back to the shop now. Thank you for dinner." She strode away from him.

He wanted to go after her, but his good sense told him she needed time to think about what he'd told her. At least she hadn't completely closed the door, and that left it open for step two of his plan to unlock her heart and be let in once again.

❄

Tears blinded Val's eyes as she raced the few blocks back to the store. Her mind couldn't wrap itself around the idea that Colt had written her. How could she believe what he said when she had nothing to show for it? Something wasn't right, and she had to find out what that something was.

Two hours until closing and several customers still browsed the aisles. Val waved to Aunt Cora and Susie but headed straight for her office without stopping. She grabbed a handful of tissues from the box on her desk and pressed them against her eyes. Nothing made sense. If Colt wrote to her and e-mailed her, why didn't she receive any of his letters?

A knock on the door frame was followed by a voice. "Want to tell me about what happened with you and Colt?"

Val lifted a misty gaze to her aunt and nodded her head. Aunt Cora closed the door and pulled a chair to sit beside Val. "Talk to me, child."

"We were having such a good time. We ate at La Cocina del Rio and visited with Gabriela then went for a walk like we used to do. We were watching the carolers and even singing with them, and afterward Colt told me about why he left." She paused then peered at her aunt. "You do know what went on with his mother. I remember asking you, and you said Colt should tell me."

"Yes, Chase told me all about it."

"But why didn't you tell me then or when I asked you? I was heartbroken because he left, yet you let me believe he didn't care."

"I told you I didn't think it was my place to tell you his business. I really thought he'd write and explain, and he said he did. You never mentioned it, so I just thought you'd decided to let him go."

Tears threatened again, and this time Val let them fall. "I don't know what to do. He told me he wrote, but why don't I have the letters or the e-mail?" Her whole being ached with the realization that perhaps five good years had been lost because of a letter she never received.

"I say give him the benefit of the doubt, and work things out with him. Go slow and make sure you both understand what the other is saying and feeling."

Val sniffed and wiped her nose with another tissue. "You're right, but I need to know what happened to those letters."

"Don't worry about them, and concentrate on making things right with Colt." She glanced at her watch and stood. "It's near closing time. I'll help Susie, and you decide what you have to do next." She paused at the door. "I have a little something else that needs to be made right. Pray that it works."

Whatever it was must concern Colt and Chase. Her aunt loved them like her own, and the fact that both their names started with C, like the names she'd chosen for the two baby boys she'd lost, made Colt and his brother even more special.

Val swept her hair back from her face with her fingers. She loved Colt and wanted to believe him. She leaned back in her chair and closed her eyes. *Dear Lord, help me trust Colt. Don't let us make the same mistakes. I love him and want him in my life. Show me the way, Lord, and help him to reach out to his mother. Soften her heart and show her Your love. In Jesus' name I pray. Amen.*

She'd taken the first step toward her future, but whether or not that future would include Colt lay entirely in God's hands.

Chapter 9

Colt waited for Cora outside his mother's home. His curiosity as to the reason for the visit grew as he remembered the last rejection. Whatever Cora had in mind must have to do with Chase and Julie's baby, due any day.

Cora arrived a few minutes later, and Mrs. Barnes buzzed them through on the intercom. At the front portico, she met Colt on the steps. "I've already talked to Mrs. Barnes. She's agreed to let us go up to your mother's room. I'll go in, but you stay in the hall until I call for you."

"If you say so, but I don't see how this is going to do any good at all. What's going to change her mind after all these years?" As futile as it may sound, he would still try anything in hopes of getting his mother to once again accept her sons.

Mrs. Barnes greeted them and led them to the second-floor bedroom. Cora hugged the elderly housekeeper. "Thank you, Mrs. Barnes. Send up a prayer that this will work. I may have to say a few harsh words, but if those words hurt her and open her eyes to what she's done, then it will be worth the effort."

Mrs. Barnes nodded and went back downstairs. Cora pulled her shoulders back and lifted her head. "Say a prayer, too, Colt. This is for you and Chase." With that she walked through the door.

She left the door ajar, and Colt leaned close to listen. Cora's voice greeted his mother who shouted back. "What are you doing here, Cora Bennett? Who let you in? Mrs. Barnes, where are you?"

Colt cringed but heard Cora's soothing tones trying to calm his mother. He couldn't hear her words, but they must have had some effect because his mother lowered her voice and the conversation resumed.

"Sylvia, I've been your friend for more years than either of us would like to count, and it hurts me to be turned away every time I try to see you. I begged Mrs. Barnes to let me come up, and she finally agreed."

"I'll talk to her about that. She knows better. I don't want to see anyone, especially you or any of my family."

The bitterness in her voice sent a chill through Colt. Cora would never get through to her.

"I know you had a tremendous loss. You loved Trent with all your heart, just as I loved my Will, but you have two wonderful sons to help you carry on. I lost the only two boys I had. Charles and Christopher would have been a blessing for me when Will died."

"But you had Will for a lot longer than I had Trent. He died too young. God was cruel to let that happen. God has given me nothing but grief."

"Don't you think I had plenty of grief with the death of my babies? Remember how we both promised to give our boys names that started with C because it was our favorite letter? Your boys lived, but mine didn't."

Colt's heart ached for the woman who had given him so much. She would have been a wonderful mother, and the fact that she didn't let death defeat her was a testimony to her faith in a loving God. He couldn't understand why his mother's reaction had been so completely opposite.

"I'm sorry for your loss, Cora, but I don't want to talk about this anymore. I don't want to see Colt or Chase, and I don't want to hear any more about God or any of that religion stuff. I'd appreciate it if you'd leave right now." She raised her voice. "Mrs. Barnes, I need you."

Colt didn't wait to hear any more. His mother would never change. Satan had such a hold on her heart, no one could get through. He raced down the stairs and out to his car. The only person he wanted to see at the moment was Val, but he wasn't even sure about how she'd greet him.

After the walk last night, he'd wanted to call her, but she needed space to think through everything. She would be at home now, as the store was closed early for Christmas Eve. He planned to attend the late candlelight service at church as he'd done so often in years past. Perhaps Val would go with him since she always went, too.

His fingers caressed the two velvet boxes in his jacket pocket. If she went with him, and things worked out like he prayed they would, step two of his plan to win her back would be in place, and he'd be ready for step three.

With renewed courage, he headed to Val's house.

❄

Christmas Eve, a time of joy and celebration—but at the moment, Val felt no joy and was in no mood to celebrate. Colt hadn't made an appearance today at the shop, so she'd had no chance to talk with him about the letters.

A cup of hot cocoa would be good since a cold front had come in and the temperatures had dropped considerably. That was Texas for you. Nice and warm one day, and the next could be bone-chilling cold.

When Val stepped into the hallway, her mother came up the stairs. "Where's Dad? I need to talk to you about something."

"He had an emergency at the clinic. He hopes to be back in time to go to church with us. Come on into our room. We can talk there while I decide what to wear since it's turned so cold."

Val followed her into the room and sat on the bed. How many times she'd done this when she wanted to talk with her mother about different things in life? The memory of one of those times filled her now. Her mother's words came back in a rush. "I say good riddance to that boy. He's too wealthy for his own good. Never had a sense of responsibility, and this proves he never will."

Realization dawned and Val gasped. "Mom, do you know anything about any letters Colt wrote to me five years ago?"

Her mother's back stiffened, and she didn't turn around. Her hands clenched the coat hanger she held. "Letters? Why would you ask that?"

"Because Colt said he wrote me and even e-mailed, but I

never received any of them."

"Then there must be some mistake. Are you sure he's telling the truth?"

"Why would he lie to both me and Aunt Cora?"

Her mother still stood with her tensed body facing the closet wall. "Well, you know, he wasn't trustworthy then, so it stands to reason he isn't now."

Val jumped from the bed and grabbed her mother's shoulder. "Look at me, Mom. What are you hiding?"

"I'm not hiding anything." She turned to face her daughter, anguish written across her face. "Oh, Val, why can't you leave well enough alone?"

Val's insides churned with the possibility of the truth staring at her. "What happened to those letters?"

"I—I did what I thought was best for you at the time. You were getting ready to—"

"You took them?" Val clenched her fists and fought back anger. "What did you do with them?" Colt had been telling the truth. Her heart cried for the time they'd lost and her belief that the man she loved deserted her.

Her mother turned and reached up for a box on the closet shelf. "I don't know why, but I saved them." She handed the box to Val.

Val clutched the letters, her heart soaring with the proof that Colt had tried to reach her. At that moment her cell phone rang. She reached for it, and when Colt's number appeared, she flipped it open. "Colt, I'm so glad you called. I have so much to tell you." She had to see him. This was something she didn't want to explain over the phone.

"Then come to the door. I'm right outside."

She raced down the stairs, the phone still in her hand, and flung open the door. Colt stood there with his phone to his ear, and a grin spread across his face. "I take this to mean you're coming?"

Her first impulse was to throw her arms around his neck, but she held back and slipped her phone into her pocket.

He reached for her hand. "Get your coat and let's go for a ride."

Val simply nodded and headed back for her coat. Now that he was here, all the things she wanted to say scrambled in her brain to incoherent thoughts. She folded the letters and tucked them into her pocket.

Now bundled up against the cold, she met him at the door and they headed for his car.

He started up the motor. "Let's go to the river. I know it's cold, but it's Christmas Eve, and the lights are so pretty."

Glad that she'd wrapped a wool scarf about her neck and pulled on both gloves and her hat, she nodded. "I think that's a great idea."

Fifteen minutes later he parked, and they walked toward the lights. As they crossed one of the bridges, he stopped and leaned on the side. "It's almost like magic, a fairyland of light and beauty."

She tucked her arm under his and leaned against his shoulder. "Yes, it is." She searched for a way to tell him about the letters and her mom, but she didn't want to spoil the moment.

His hand covered hers. "Cora and I went to visit Mother again tonight. Cora got in to see her, but it didn't help. Mother still doesn't want to see or have anything to do with me or Chase."

"Oh, Colt, I'm so sorry." That must have been the other thing Aunt Cora had wanted her to pray about. Now was the time to tell him her news.

"I'm also sorry to have doubted you. When I hadn't heard from you, I believed you no longer loved me and went to New York to get away from me."

He grasped both her hands in his. "I never wanted to get away from you. I wanted you to come with me. That's what was in those letters I sent you."

She pulled one hand from his and extracted the letters from her pocket. "You mean these letters?"

He gasped. "But I thought you didn't get them."

"I didn't. Mom intercepted them and hid them from me. She had just given them to me when you called. I should have known something was wrong and that you would never have just left me dangling with no word at all."

"Of course I wouldn't." He leaned forward as though to kiss her but stopped.

Fear clutched her heart. He had second thoughts and didn't want to kiss her.

Then he grinned and held out a black velvet box. He flipped it open to reveal a gold key.

"This is a key that I hope and pray will unlock your heart and release all those feelings of anger, doubt, and resentment you held against me and fill it with my love for you."

Tears filled Val's eyes, and she didn't trust her voice. The key gleamed in the light and beckoned to her. She grabbed it and held the key close to her heart. "It's unlocked and empty, just waiting for you to fill it again."

This time he did kiss her, and when his lips touched hers, all the good memories of the times they'd kissed before swirled in a kaleidoscope of color.

His lips lingered, and then he stepped back. "Let's go to church. It's Christmas Eve, and I have so much to be thankful for tonight."

Val couldn't argue with that. This was a perfect ending to a perfect day with her heart so full of love at the turn of events that right now she held no anger at all against her mother. They had a few things to get straight, but love and forgiveness were the main themes for tonight, nothing else.

Chapter 10

Val's heart filled with peace as she walked out of the church with Colt. Mini lights twinkled on the trees lining the walk from the sanctuary to the parking lot, adding to the magic already in the air. A few minutes past midnight on Christmas morning gave her renewed hope for her future with Colt. He still loved her—after five years of thinking she'd rejected him. But then her love for him had remained, too.

The only blemish on the entire evening had been Colt telling of yet another rejection from his mother. A chill that didn't come from the cold air caused her to shiver. Colt would be gone in a few days. The time she had left with him became even more precious.

She hugged Colt's arm. "I'm not ready to go home just yet."

"I'm not either. After that wonderful message and the beautiful music, it seems wrong just to end it."

His cell phone rang out, and he fumbled to retrieve it from his pocket. "It's Chase. Hi, bro, what's going on?" Colt's eyebrows shot up, and he grabbed Val around the shoulders. "We'll be right there."

He snapped the phone closed. "Come on. This night is far from being over. Chase and Julie are at the hospital. Looks like we'll have a Christmas baby."

What a perfect ending for an incredible day. Val ran with Colt to his car and jumped in. As they drove from the parking lot, she asked, "How long has she been in labor?"

"I'm not sure. He said they'd been there since just after seven. This is the first chance he's had to call. Guess it's been a few hours."

"Then we should have plenty of time to get there for the birth. First babies usually take awhile to make their appearance." A lot she knew about babies and birth, but that's what she'd heard. But being a Jamison, this baby wouldn't do the ordinary. "Do they know if it's a boy or girl?"

"Yeah, it's a girl. Name will be Chelsea. Chase wanted to keep the C thing going."

"Oh, I like that name. But what made your mother and Aunt Cora want all C's for their children's names?"

"I overheard her talking with Mother about it. Something about it being their favorite letter. We can ask Cora. I'm sure she'll be there tonight."

With the way her aunt felt about Chase and Colt, Val had no doubts about Cora being at the hospital for the birth of this little girl. Her mind envisioned a time when she and Colt might be having the same experience as Julie and Chase. She blinked her eyes. Too early for those thoughts. He said he loved her, but that was all. No talk of marriage yet. Still she could hope.

They both jumped from the car and ran into the hospital. Colt slid to a stop at the front desk. "Mrs. Chase Jamison, Julie."

The woman there smiled and peered at the screen before her. "Oh, yes, she's on the second floor."

"Thanks." He made a beeline for the elevators with Val on his heels. When they reached the floor, they didn't have to ask for a room number. Chase greeted them with a smile as wide as the Mississippi River across his face.

"She's here. Chelsea Dawn Jamison has arrived." He glanced at his watch. But on the phone, he just said she was in labor. No baby yet. He led them into the room where Julie held a bundle wrapped in a pink blanket. A pink cap covered the baby's head.

Val's heart raced at the beautiful sight before her. So much for first babies taking a long time to arrive. "She's beautiful, Julie." Val bent closer to observe the tiny girl who yawned and blinked her eyes before settling back to sleep.

Colt pumped his brother's hand. "I can't believe it. I'm an uncle. I'm so glad I'll be around to watch her grow up."

Val's eyebrows shot up. He'd be around? "What did you just say?"

Colt moved to her side. "I said I'd be around to watch her grow up. I'm not going back to New York."

A squeal escaped her lips, and she grabbed him in a hug. "For real? You're staying here?"

He laughed and hugged her in return. "Yes, how could I

leave the most beautiful women in the world?"

How good his arms felt, and his words sent her heart soaring. Then she remembered the baby and turned to the bed. "Oh, I'm sorry. I didn't mean to make so much noise. I didn't wake her up, did I?"

Julie giggled. "I don't think anything will wake this little girl. She's worn out from all the kicking she did before she was born."

Julie's parents burst into the room, and her mother rushed to the bedside. "We're too late. I wanted to be here with you." She hugged her daughter then gazed down at the baby. "She's so beautiful. I can't believe I'm a grandma." She turned to her husband. "Come here and see this precious little girl."

Mrs. Burns shook her head and teased Julie. "You never were one to waste time. When you started something, you got it done in a hurry. I see it was no different with giving birth. I'm sorry we're late, but the traffic from Houston was terrible, even on the interstate."

Val stepped back to the door to let the family enjoy this time together. Her mind still reeled with the idea that Colt was not going back to New York. She didn't know what he was going to do here, but she didn't care. All her hopes had risen to a new peak with his announcement.

Colt gestured for her to come to his side. When she did, he wrapped his arm around her shoulder. "Isn't she the most beautiful little girl you've ever seen?"

At the moment she was. Julie had turned back the blanket for her mother to see more of Chelsea. Her tiny hands curled around her grandmother's fingers. Chelsea's bud of a mouth made sucking sounds, and she blinked again.

Val's breath caught in her throat. To her, birth was a miracle, and for the first time in many years, she had the hope that such a miracle would occur for her. Tears filled her eyes, and she sent up a prayer of thanks for what had happened this evening.

A voice from the door said, "I've come to see the latest addition to the Jamison family."

Colt's arm tightened around Val, and a choking sound came from his throat. "Mother?"

Mrs. Jamison stood in the doorway with Aunt Cora right behind her. Colt hurried to her and wrapped his arms around her, as did Chase. Val swallowed the lump in her throat and wiped tears from her cheeks. Aunt Cora smiled and nodded at Val. Her aunt's prayers had been answered, and another miracle had happened right in this room. God sure had a lot of surprises for them tonight, and this was one of the best.

Chase and Colt stepped back, and Chase led his mother to the bedside. "Mom, meet your granddaughter, Chelsea Dawn Jamison. She's going to be a real beauty, just like you."

Julie lifted the baby up to Mrs. Jamison, who took her and cuddled her to her chest.

Colt turned to Aunt Cora. "How did you do this? When I left, she was ordering you out of her house."

"I wouldn't leave. I made her listen to me, and she finally realized what she'd be missing if she didn't come. When I called Chase's house, and they didn't answer, I tried the hospital. That's how we knew you were here."

Mrs. Jamison swayed back and forth with the baby. "She's so precious." Then she nodded toward Cora. "My friend here hammered me until I gave in. I was so mad at her then, but now I'm glad she didn't give up."

Val hadn't seen Colt's mother for ten years, but her beauty was still evident in the perfectly coiffed hair and smooth-as-silk skin. Her smile now lit up her face and warmed Val's heart toward the woman even though she'd been the cause of Val's heartache. Two mothers, one doing what she thought best, and the other refusing to do what was best, had sent Val's life into a tailspin. Tonight, neither could take away the joy of learning Colt would be here to stay.

Colt wrapped his arm around Aunt Cora. "This is the most wonderful Christmas present you could ever have given us."

She blinked back tears and nodded. "She's not ready to admit all her mistakes yet, but she's on her way back to us, and with patience and love, I think she'll come back completely."

"One thing Val and I are curious about. What's with the tradition of all the names beginning with C?"

Cora laughed and hugged Colt. "Sylvia and I both were in love with a boy named Charles. We decided, at age fourteen mind you, that all our children would have C names. We even made a list of them. Seemed like a good idea at the time."

Colt grabbed Val's hand and pulled her to the center of the room at the foot of Julie's bed. "This isn't the place I planned to do this, but I think it's the best place and better than my original idea."

Everyone in the room stopped, as did Val's breath. Colt reached into his pocket and took out another black velvet box. He opened it and held it out to her. "Valerie Jean Murray, I love you. Will you do me the honor of becoming my wife?"

Every fiber of Val's being sang with joy. The words she'd wanted to hear five years ago were just as sweet tonight. "I thought you'd never ask." She held out her hand for him to slip the ring on her finger.

She threw her arms around his neck, but he turned her face to his and bent his mouth to hers. A cheer went up in the room, and Aunt Cora clapped.

Val heard, but the only thing that interested her at the moment was the man who held her and the promise for the future in his kiss.

Martha Rogers is a fourth generation Texan who has made Texas her home all her life. She is a retired teacher of both the secondary and college levels and now lives in Houston with her husband Rex, also retired. Martha and her husband are both active members at church where he is a deacon and she sings in the choir as well as co-leads a First Place 4 Health group. They enjoy spending time with nine grandchildren, a grandson-in-law, and a great-grandson. She is the author of several novellas as well as a series of historical novels. She is a member of American Christian Fiction Writers (ACFW) and writes a weekly devotional for the group. She is also a member and treasurer of Inspirational Writers Alive! and Writers On the Storm, the Woodlands Chapter of ACFW. For more information, visit Martha at www.marthawrogers.com.

LIGHTS OF LOVE

by Lynette Sowell

Dedication

To Beth, Martha, and Kathleen: We've been friends for years, and I'm so glad we had the chance to work on this book together. I'm the only non-native Texan in our bunch, even though I did get here as soon as I could. Thank you for your big hearts and your friendship. You all inspire me in many ways, as writers and as women. May God continue to bless you, your families, and your writing as you use your gifts for Him.

To my own Mr. Christmas: here's another Christmas story.
I love you!

Chapter 1

The people walking in darkness have seen a great light;
on those living in the land of the shadow of
death a light has dawned.

ISAIAH 9:2 NIV

Order up, chicken molé, enchilada plate!" Gabriela Hernandez slid the chicken molé plate across the stainless-steel counter. She dabbed her forehead with the back of her sleeve. "Lookin' good, Hector."

The newest sous-chef at La Cocina del Rio grinned. "*Gracias*, Señorita Hernandez." He bobbed his head, his teeth white on his tan face. "Next week, molé *verde*?"

She shrugged and glanced toward the doorway to La Cocina's office. "If the boss says it's okay, but I doubt he will. Please, it's Gabriela."

"You're boss's daughter. Not right for me to call your name."

"Okay then. Call me chef."

"*Sí*, chef." Hector continued plating. "Maybe one day Señor Hernandez will let you make the green molé."

"Maybe. Until then, we stick to the menu." Gabriela was proud of their newest sous-chef. He held promise. She liked his adventuresome way of plating food. Pop didn't care much for it sometimes, but as long as a customer didn't complain, he only raised his eyebrows and let them cook.

Another tray of Wednesday specials went out to the lunch customers who not only craved a mouthwatering Mexican meal but also wanted to eat that meal on San Antonio's Riverwalk.

Gabriela smiled at the packed dining room lined with tables covering the terra-cotta-tile floor. La Cocina had been her second home since she was barely eye-level with the wooden dining room tables. The restaurant had plenty of little corners that made good hiding places.

One of the latest diners slid onto one of the chairs at a table for two. His back to Gabriela, he leaned on the table and glanced out at the narrow, winding river. He looked familiar, especially his tousled hair.

"Is he here yet?" Pop plucked her elbow.

"Is who here yet?" Gabriela switched to Spanish.

Hector slid another trio of finished plates in Gabriela's direction. She nodded. "Order up, Maria!"

"The contractor, *m'ija*. I invited him here for lunch. I'm showing him the plans for our kitchen."

"I don't know. Did you ask Maria to watch for him?"

"*Sí*, I asked her to let you know. I want his order to be perfect because I want perfection from him when he starts our kitchen remodel."

Gabriela froze, her hand poised over an enchilada plate. "You and Mom are redoing the kitchen *now*? When did you decide that?"

"Last night, after church. We had some ideas and found the contractor." Pop beamed. "So it'll be done by Christmas."

"Christmas? That's one of our busiest seasons here." Gabriela didn't know what Pop was thinking of. The restaurant demanded many hours of their time. No, it didn't demand. Something you love didn't demand. It lured them, day after day, and Gabriela was happy to give in.

She garnished one of the plates with her latest creation, deep-fried, thin strips of tortilla. "Here you go, Maria."

Their hostess, wearing a simple white blouse and festive embroidered skirt, grabbed the tray. "Gracias. Oh, Señor H, your contractor's here. Table Eight."

Gabriela glanced in that direction. The dark-headed stranger, seated solo at a table for two. "Who is it?"

"He has high recommendations and does good work; plus he's trying to expand his business." Pop patted Gabriela's arm. "Show him our best."

The ringing phone in the office clamored for someone's attention, but Pop headed for the dining room. Aunt Celi would answer it, efficient as always.

Gabriela went back to the blur of the lunch rush. Hector didn't miss a beat, even when they ran low on fresh tortillas and another of the prep cooks had to roll out some fresh dough.

Aunt Celi emerged from the office. "Gaby, your

mama's on the phone."

Was it something about Tommy? Her brother had been complaining of back pain again last night at supper, after he returned from physical therapy. She took the phone from Celi.

"Mama? Is everything okay? How's Tommy?"

"Tomás is fine, he's fine. Did your papa tell you about the kitchen? Oh, I've always dreamed of a new kitchen."

"But now? I mean, Thanksgiving is next week, and we're having dinner at Aunt Celi's—" At this, Aunt Celi grinned, the same grin that Pop had. She'd followed him from Mexico forty years ago and never looked back.

"Yes, now."

"But our Christmas dinner. . .plus Mark and Hayley want Christmas at their *abuelo* and *abuela's*." Her nephew and niece always brought a ton of laughter to the family.

"We'll be done by the twenty-third."

"Are you sure? I mean, contractors always take twice as long, and people end up always blowing their budgets."

"My worrywart. Don't worry. Your papa has everything planned, and if anyone can squeeze a penny and make it squeal, he can." Her musical voice had chased away many a nightmare when Gabriela was a child.

"I hope so, Mama."

"But you'll be moving out soon yourself anyway."

Gabriela bit her lip. "I'm pretty sure I will."

"What does that mean? Aren't you going to buy a house? I don't see why one woman needs a whole house for herself, especially if—"

"I know, especially if I'm not seeing anyone, or married,

178

or. . ." She hadn't meant her reluctance to move out to show through, especially since she'd talked about her plans for the last couple of years after culinary school. Finish her business degree then buy her house. She'd finished the degree, but found herself in the restaurant kitchen yet again.

"*Mi corazón*, all in good time."

Something crashed behind Gabriela. "I know."

"And you must go. My cell phone's ringing, and I think it's your sister. So we'll talk more tonight."

Gabriela placed the phone on the counter's edge, closest to the office, and hurried back to the worktable. Something smelled burnt. She followed the scent to the chile roaster and found a cluster of blackened poblanos.

She dashed to the prep sink with the chili peppers. Time to quit thinking about the kitchen at home and focus on the business here. One bad plate of food, one dissatisfied customer, and Pop's reputation was at stake. La Cocina del Rio was their livelihood.

Gabriela turned on the faucet and stuck the burnt chili peppers under the running water. Being here wasn't a bad thing. She'd ended up at La Cocina after culinary school, and Pop paid her well. The money in her savings amounted to a tidy sum, and instead of a house, Gabriela envisioned something far greater.

La Cocina del Mercado. She'd already scouted for a possible restaurant location close to El Mercado, blocks away from the Riverwalk yet close to another San Antonio attraction. The Mexican marketplace drew plenty of visitors.

But she kept wondering about the diner, the contractor Pop had just sat down across from, even as she peeled the charred skin from the poblanos.

❄

Miguel Rivera took a long sip of sweet *horchata* water. He never tired of the taste of milk, sweetened rice, and cinnamon blended together with ice. His mama used to make it the same way, and he'd hover around the kitchen while she mixed up the beverage.

He tried to contain his excitement, feeling almost like a kid again. Getting the contract for the Hernandez's kitchen remodel would help Rivera Remodeling end the year in the black, if barely. For his first year in business, not bad. Not at all. He was surprised when Tommy's father approached him the other night at church.

"Señor Rivera," Juan Hernandez had spoken as if to a business equal, "I understand you do kitchens."

And so after a few minutes of conversation, they agreed to meet for lunch today to talk more about the project, or so he hoped. He needed one more project for the year. Pablo, his friend and fellow contractor, told him business usually screeched to a halt from November through January.

Miguel perused the menu and ordered the special, beef fajitas, knowing whatever he ate at La Cocina would be delicious.

Gaby was working today back in the kitchen. He'd glimpsed her once at the pass-through window, her serious face focused completely on the food going out on trays to customers. A strict planner like her father, but with a warm side like her mama. Maybe she still had that warm side, but he hadn't seen it in a long time, and since his return to the fold, she seemed to steer clear of this formerly lost sheep as much as possible. Not that he blamed her.

"You've ordered?" Señor Hernandez took the seat across from him. He placed a manila folder on the table between them.

"Yes, the special."

"It's on the house, as they say."

"You don't have to do that."

"I insist."

"Okay. Well, what do you have in mind for your kitchen? Give me your ideas, and I'll give you an estimate. Of course, it depends on the materials you want for cabinets, countertops, sink, and floor, and if you want to use the appliances you have now or buy new ones. And your budget."

"Ah, I see. And my Rita isn't here. She knows what she wants. But I can tell you the floor plan, where our appliances are." Mr. Hernandez scratched his chin and frowned.

Miguel opened the portfolio on the table and showed him the graph paper with small cutout pieces to arrange and form kitchen layouts. "Show me the layout. I'll need to go by your house and take measurements."

"Sí, sí, of course you will." Mr. Hernandez looked intently at him for a moment, and Miguel fought the urge to swallow the lump in his throat. Maybe he was changing his mind about the whole idea.

His waitress, a blond, glided past, steam rising from her tray, and the scent of peppers and tomatoes and melted cheese drifted in their direction. Miguel's mouth watered. The donut he'd inhaled at six that morning had disappeared long ago.

Mr. Hernandez slapped the table with both palms and made the silverware jump. Miguel almost jumped, too. "I have it, I have it. You come for supper tonight. Rita has cooked something. There's always enough. Like the old days."

Miguel tried not to exhale his pent-up breath. Only a few diners glanced in their direction. The piped-in mariachi music featured a great drum solo at the moment. At first he sensed Gaby's father was going to change his mind about hiring him. But he wasn't expecting an invitation to supper at the Hernandez's home. "Like the old days, the good ones."

Mr. Hernandez nodded. "The good ones. Miguel, a man can make mistakes, bad ones that he does not think he can untangle himself from. But when the day comes and he travels a new path, he will look for the old path and see only weeds growing over what once was his favorite walkway. Do you understand?" Again, he gave the intent look, his dark brown eyes nearly black.

"Sí, Señor Hernandez. I understand that very well now. My old path is definitely overgrown." *And thorns might emerge from the weeds and try to track him down.* But he didn't say this to Gaby's father.

"Come at six. Gaby won't be home until seven at least." Mr. Hernandez glanced up at an approaching waitress. "Ah, here it is now."

"Here you are, Sir," the waitress said as she slid the plate in front of Miguel. The beef, peppers, and onions sizzled on the hot plate. "Señor H, will you be having anything?"

"No, no." He waved the waitress away. "Gracias, Katie."

"I'll be there, then." Miguel didn't reach for his fork. So, Mr. Hernandez wasn't blind to the tension between him and Gaby. Who was he kidding? There was no tension. Just a yawning chasm and he had no idea what to do to close the space between them.

Chapter 2

Miguel couldn't remember the last time he'd laughed so hard. Maybe it was the day he'd been baptized at the New Life Center. Sure, he'd made his peace with God and was forgiven, but something happened that day almost two years ago, when he'd come up out of the water hanging on to Brother Pete's hand. He felt like he'd left something behind down in the tank of water, something that wasn't a part of him anymore. Pure joy surged through him, and he'd had no choice but to release the laughter.

It also reminded him of the day he'd first played with Tommy Hernandez, when the fire department opened the fire hydrant on their San Antonio street. The rushing water drew the children like a magnet that hot June day. Everyone stayed out of trouble, for once. If only an open hydrant could have kept them that way.

Tonight's meal with Tommy and his parents showed him a glimpse of that joy. Miguel grinned at his old friend across the table. "Tommy, I don't know how you eat like this every day. If I did, I'd have to live at the gym. Your mama's the best cook in San Antonio."

"Nah, I don't think so. My sister is." Two years younger than Miguel, Tommy shot a glance toward the kitchen sink, where his mother stood.

"I heard that, Tomás." Mrs. Hernandez turned and faced the two men, one hand propped on her hip. "Keep it up, and you'll be doing these dishes."

"But, Mami, Gaby learned it from you, of course."

Mr. Hernandez paged through the newspaper. "She should be home soon. That girl works too hard."

"That, mi corazón," Mrs. Hernandez said as she wrapped the last of the tortillas, "is what she learned from you."

He merely grunted and looked down at the newspaper. "Well, Señor Rivera, we should get the kitchen measured so you can tell me how much this will all cost me."

Miguel groaned and patted his stomach. "Much of the cost will be cabinets, unless you'd like to keep the ones you have. That, and labor."

Mr. Hernandez looked up and narrowed his eyes. "What if we do some of the labor ourselves to save money?"

"I think we can work something out." Miguel eyed the painted-over wood paneling in the kitchen. "We may need to hang drywall, depending on what's behind that paneling when we take it down. You and your family can always paint. But just remember, I might come into La Cocina and tell you how to cook," Miguel joked. He had subcontractors that he knew did good work. Amateurs sometimes spelled disaster.

At that, Mr. Hernandez tilted his head back and laughed.

"You are right, you are right. Let's get started. I want to make sure this is done right, and if I must stay out of the kitchen, I stay out." His voice sounded gruff, but Miguel caught a glimmer in the older man's eye.

"I'll run out to my truck and get my tape measure and notebook. Be right back." Miguel headed for the front of the house. He could hear Tommy talking to his parents about the new kitchen.

Miguel paused in the elegant entryway, lined with photos of the Hernandez family over the years. The caramel-colored walls made a nice contrast to the ceramic tile floor. He studied the tile more closely. Nope, that was travertine. Which meant the Hernandez family would spend money when they wanted to.

The last time he'd visited the family, things were different. They lived in a three-bedroom ranch house, a modest rental with an attached garage built in the 1960s. Then, once La Cocina took off, Juan Hernandez moved his family into something even better about eight years ago. Their own home.

Miguel swallowed hard. What he wouldn't give to have a legacy like that. Here he was, twenty-six. All he'd earned for himself were three years in prison, followed by rehab at New Life Center trying to be free of the drugs that he'd let seduce him. Mama now lived in Phoenix with his older, much more responsible sister and her family.

Yes, things were definitely different the last time he'd visited the Hernandez family in their home, especially for Tommy.

He ought to get moving, or Mr. Hernandez would

wonder if he'd chickened out and decided to drive home. Which, if given the choice a year ago, he probably would have.

Miguel flung open the front door and almost collided with something warm and solid.

Someone screamed.

❄

"What in the world are you doing here?" Gabriela clamped her hand over her mouth. She hadn't meant to scream while heading into her own home, and then she said the first thing that popped into her tired brain. Her feet hurt, she had a headache, and worse, somebody had parked their extended-cab pickup where she usually tucked her Mini-Cooper for the night. The older, but still shiny, red truck took up so much room in the driveway she'd been forced to park on the street.

And of course, literally coming face-to-face with Miguel Rivera had set her heart hammering in her chest. So *this* was the contractor Pop had mentioned? His unruly hair seemed as though he'd planned it that way. His dark-eyed gaze she didn't quite want to meet studied her with concern.

"Gabriela, I'm sorry. Didn't mean to make you jump like that." He shifted on his feet in the entryway and gestured, as if to signal he'd catch her if she tripped. "Uh, your dad invited me for dinner. To measure the kitchen."

She nodded. "Okay. Yeah. I just wasn't expecting to see you." Which really meant she couldn't avoid him anymore.

"You look tired. Was it a busy day?" He touched her arm. Pinpricks danced up her elbow, her shoulder, then shot down to her stomach. He was working out, and in lots better shape than the last time she'd really let herself take a good look at him. Amazing what taking care of oneself could do for a body.

"The usual." She tried to smile. "I actually got off a little early tonight for once. Aunt Celi's closing." As if she needed to explain.

"Well, uh, I'll let you go relax. I'm getting my measuring tape and notebook." Miguel sidled to one wall of the entryway, and Gabriela caught a whiff of his cologne as she passed.

She heard the door close behind her as she placed her keys on the entryway table then released her breath and leaned on the tabletop. Some things weren't hard, until you had to do them. The Lord knew she'd forgiven Miguel plenty more than seventy times seven, but the old feelings zinged through her once again, like Fourth of July bottle rockets. *Breathe in, breathe out.*

For a few seconds, she bowed her head and prayed for strength. When she rounded the corner of the family room that led into the kitchen and saw Tommy, she sent up a silent prayer again. He rolled his wheelchair back from the table and smiled at her.

"Gaby, you're home early." The lines around his eyes made him look older than twenty-four. But the light in his eyes spoke of the fighter that he was. "Aunt Celi chase you out?"

"Only because I let her. Did you save me anything to eat?" She went to get a glass of iced tea. They always had sweet tea in the fridge, year-round.

"Nope, of course not. You're on a diet." Tommy winked at

her and spun from side to side in his chair. "So Mama and Papa are taking the plunge and getting a new kitchen."

Gabriela put the tea pitcher on the counter and rummaged in the fridge for something to fill one of Mom's tortillas. Not all chefs cooked at home. If she knew that Mom didn't have something prepared on the stove, she'd have ordered takeout.

Her thoughts skittered back to Miguel, in their home, after all this time. Pop never talked about him, not even during the last few months when Miguel had started attending their church again after all these years.

"Did you hear what I said about the kitchen?" Tommy asked.

"Yes, about Mom and Pop taking the plunge. So where are they?" She glanced toward the kitchen entrance, then around the corner to their formal dining room.

"Mom's in the office, getting her kitchen idea folder. I think Pop's in the bathroom." Tommy turned in the direction of the family room. "Hang on a second. I want to show you something. I need my big sister's advice."

Aha. Gabriela found some leftover *carnita* meat in a storage container, plus some sliced American cheese. They'd run out of *queso fresco*, but the American cheese would do. She piled it all on a tortilla and stuck it in the microwave.

She heard the front door open, then Tommy and Miguel chatting. They both reentered the kitchen at the same time.

"That's amazing. You're quick in that thing, man," Miguel said.

"Built up lots of upper body strength." Tommy grinned, set a catalog on the kitchen table, then flexed his biceps. "See that? One day you can grow up to be strong like me."

The two men cracked up, and even Gabriela let herself chuckle. The power of true friendship, overcoming hurts of the past. She shook her head and watched the tortilla spinning inside the microwave.

She felt Miguel's gaze on her. Yes, everything had changed in their lives, and was continuing to change. "So, Tommy, what did you want to show me?"

"I'm planning to visit San Antonio Junior College after Thanksgiving, just to check it out. I was thinking about taking a class."

"Wow." She took her plate from the microwave, grabbed her tea, and joined the men at the table. "That's awesome. Do you know what you'd like to take?"

"I dunno." He shrugged, looking twelve again. "I like working with computers, and fixing them. I figure with Miguel here starting his own business, you finishing school, and even starting your own restaurant—"

"Restaurant?" Miguel asked.

"It's nothing official, really. Only an idea I've had." Gabriela glanced toward the family room. "The Market Square area gets a lot of traffic, and I've been thinking about opening a place nearby. Mexican upscale street food, with a twist. I went to visit my Abuela Hernandez last year in Mexico City, and took a side trip to Oaxaca. The flavors I found there are awesome. The only snag is, I haven't even mentioned the idea to Pop yet because—"

"Mentioned what to your papa?" Pop's voice boomed as he entered the kitchen.

"Did I miss something?" Mom was on his heels, clutching

her manila kitchen ideas folder to her chest.

"Um—" Gabriela began, trying not to squirm.

"I'm planning to start the spring semester at San Antonio Junior College, if I can get in," Tommy announced. As Pop thumped Miguel on the back, Tommy looked at Gabriela and mouthed, *You owe me.*

"M'ijo, that's wonderful." Mama set her folder on the table. "When did you decide this?"

"I've kinda been stuck here, wanted to get out more. Dr. Vickers says I should." Tommy's slow grin spread across his face.

Gabriela watched them. If only time could wind its hands backward, to a time when Tommy could walk, before the teenage insanity claimed him and he tore off after Miguel, his idol.

She chewed her tortilla-wrapped goodness. Normally Mama's cooking soothed her, as her voice often did even now, responding to Tommy's excitement about moving forward.

She thought about her parents, moving on and finally buying their dream kitchen, their home a reflection of decades of hard work in a country of endless dreams. She watched Miguel, now a professional contractor, talking to Pop as he measured the kitchen layout and made notes, listening to Pop's ideas.

"You see how we've had to cook around here?" Pop exclaimed, his voice echoing off the cabinets. "The refrigerator is all the way over—here. And the sink here. And the stove there. Makes no sense to walk all the way across the kitchen."

"Juan," Mama chided. "Your voice, it carries. Miguel is

right here with us."

"I see your problem, Señor Hernandez." Miguel made some notes. "We can move the refrigerator over here, where it should be."

"The walk-in pantry, too. My Rita wants a walk-in pantry. We don't have any room to store things. We misplace things and buy more than we need because we can't find what we look for." Pop waved his arms.

Miguel studied the rows of shelving near the door that led to the garage. "I think we can build something up here, not too large, and still leave room for you to access the garage."

"I don't know who designed this kitchen years ago, but it makes no sense." Pop shook his head. "We need to bring it to the present."

"Yes, I see."

But Gabriela didn't think he even saw her pop gesturing at the travesty of a poorly planned kitchen. Because Miguel's gaze held hers now, his eyes tender and a little sad. Somehow, a few of the bricks that she'd built up in the past years around her heart crumbled. She shivered in the warm kitchen. *Lord, everyone's moving forward. Everyone except me.*

Chapter 3

Gabriela cruised along South Saint Mary's Street with the top of her Mini-Cooper down on a surprisingly warm first of December day. What a beautiful day to have off, and she intended to use it for herself. A little dreaming and maybe a surprise for her family just in time for the Christmas season. With Thanksgiving behind them now, her surprise would be perfect timing.

She still hadn't fessed up to Mama and Pop about the whole restaurant idea after Tommy had to rescue her the other night. He probably didn't need to do much to save the situation, since Mama had been giddy about the idea of a new kitchen, and Pop enjoyed making her happy and telling Miguel how to go about demolition.

At last, here was Alamo City Restaurant Supply. The other night she'd stayed up way too late, writing out plans for La Cocina del Mercado menus, decor, and a list of connections in the industry she knew through Pop. She wrote down the names of young people from church who might make good servers. Ideas for local marketing. She'd said more than she'd intended the night Miguel had come to measure the kitchen.

Maybe she stayed up late working on a business plan to keep her mind off him. Those eyes of his, for one thing—and that beautiful hair. She couldn't help but stare when he walked into a room, which is why at church she'd taken to sitting more toward the front.

She pulled off the street and slipped into a narrow parking space that fit the Cooper just fine. Window-shopping, then maybe lunch, and then home again to start hanging the new Christmas lights she'd bought for the front of the house.

Once inside the store, the rows of stoves and stainless-steel countertops beckoned her like puppies in a pet store.

"May I help you, ma'am? Is there anything in particular you're looking for?" asked the salesman.

"I want to look at stoves, six-burner. Plus grill tops." She knew what they'd cost, but it didn't hurt to look and dream.

"Right this way." He led her to the new stoves. "If you need a quote, let me know."

"Of course, thanks." The clerk had brought her to the top-of-the-line equipment. Pop bought La Cocina with its old and borrowed equipment years ago. She wasn't above doing the same. Something about stainless steel drew her, the way a designer handbag drew a clothes diva over to a sales display.

She stood admiring a mid-grade stove with a center removable grill—a little too small for a restaurant stove, but something that would look nice in a home kitchen.

"Don't drool on the stainless steel," a voice said at her elbow.

Gabriela clutched the oven handle on the stove and laughed. "Miguel—hi." She smiled. "I'm doing some window-shopping. And this *is* a great stove."

He nodded. "That's a nice one. Your papa sent me here. Told me to look at the stoves." He held up his measuring tape. "I'm measuring to see what'll fit your parents' kitchen and stay within budget."

"If you buy something used or a floor model, Pop won't care." Her smile wouldn't go away. Pushing the past aside, part of her realized that seeing him here had turned her day from good to great. Not that she was falling in love or anything.

"I didn't think he would. If I find a model that fits, maybe they have a floor model he can get for a discount."

"It's—it's very sweet of you. I know Pop can be difficult, but he does like you." She looked down to see her hand on his jacket sleeve.

"He's a good man. I don't deserve the kindness, and I'm going to give him a kitchen that he and your mother will be proud of. In time for Christmas." Miguel pulled the tab on the measuring tape and stretched it across the top of the nearest stove.

"Did he faint when you gave him the estimate?"

"No, he turned sort of pale. Gave me a check for half of the amount. I only wanted a third up front, but he insisted on half." Miguel shrugged but smiled. "So, what's this about *you* starting your own restaurant?"

"I was saving up to buy my own house, but after spending

the summer at my *abuela's* in Mexico, I realized I want to stay in the kitchen and run my own business."

"Hmmm. . . Don't you pretty much run La Cocina now?"

"Some days, yes. But Pop won't vary the menu at all. I want to try some new things, and he stonewalls me. It's his business. Sí, Mama cooks some days, and me, and Pop cooks, too, plus we have a few sous-chefs. But Pop is king of La Cocina."

"Which is why he'll be proud if you open another restaurant."

"It's not that simple."

"Why not? Just sit him down in the office one day and tell him your plans."

"Because he'll tell me everything that could go wrong, how hard it is, and he'll probably tell me how he and Mama need my help at La Cocina." She bit her lip. If only she'd been another son, maybe Pop would think she could handle running a place all on her own. He'd practically passed out when she talked about moving out.

"Fine, be stubborn. But give him the chance to tell you no. What's the worst that could happen? He wouldn't fire you."

She laughed. "No, I don't think he'd do that."

They looked at each other for a moment. Then Gabriela fumbled with a cherry-red knob on the stove that caught her eye.

"This is the first time since—well—you haven't run the other way when you see me coming. Like at church." His gentle tone made her look up. "Even though I sort of snuck up on you today."

"I haven't run the other way."

"Yes, you have, Gaby. Even if you haven't used your feet."

"Miguel, we can't go back." Her voice caught in her throat. He used to call her Gaby, which got on her last nerve when they were younger.

"I know that. I know that as well as anyone. As well as Tommy does."

She'd never wanted to have this conversation with him, not in a restaurant supply store, not in La Cocina, not in her parents' kitchen. "I—don't know—"

"I want. . ." He ran his hand through his unruly hair. "I want us to be friends again. Can we start with that?"

Gabriela nodded. "Yes. Yes, we can."

"Good." Miguel smiled, his slow grin spreading. But his eyes were a little sad.

❊

He should've known better than to push Gabriela Hernandez. She could push back better than anyone. Friends, right.

Miguel had never wanted to kiss someone in a restaurant supply store before. Never wanted to kiss anyone besides Gabriela, although over his years of wandering he'd kissed a few women, and then some. But this morning, among the stainless steel, he wanted to take Gabriela in his arms right then and there.

All things new, the Bible promised. Who was he kidding, though? Sure, New Life Center had helped him kick the addiction, ignited a fire in his heart for serving God with his whole heart, but now that he was out in the "real world" again, the answers to dealing with those he'd betrayed and hurt in the past didn't come so easily.

The last time he'd talked to Brother Pete, one of New Life's pastors, Brother Pete told him that because the Hernandez family hired him and welcomed him into their home, healing had begun. Juan Hernandez didn't say that he'd forgiven Miguel, but he knew the elder Hernandez tried to live according to the Bible, and forgive.

He popped his Salvador CD into the truck's CD player and sang along as he rattled through downtown. A few of the streets were blocked off. He remembered the news said something about street repairs in that area. The detour sent him in the direction of the Hernandez's neighborhood. While at the restaurant supply store, Miguel realized he'd left his good tape measure at the Hernandez home and had planned to go by and pick it up. Now was as good a time as any. Maybe Tommy was home and they could go to the gym. Demolition didn't start on the Hernandez kitchen until Monday, and he was still waiting for a final quote on the cabinets. Once demolition began, Miguel's time would be completely devoted to the kitchen project.

He continued away from downtown and finally turned onto the street that led to Gaby's neighborhood. One day, he'd have a house in a neighborhood like this. To be able to look a man like Gaby's father in the eye. The fact that Miguel had been welcomed into their home and been entrusted with a five-figure deposit on the kitchen said a lot. Miguel appreciated Mr. Hernandez's trust.

There was the Hernandez house, a two-story home faced with limestone and an elegant stamped concrete driveway. A large truck was parked across the street, its side proudly proclaiming "Sheppard Christmas Lighting." Somebody was getting ready for Christmas.

But as he pulled in front of the Hernandez house, he saw Gaby on a ladder propped against the house, trying to hook some lights to the gutter. Unopened boxes of Christmas lights sat on the front steps in stacks.

He left the truck and glimpsed Gaby's expression as he approached. "Hey there," he called out.

"Hi, again. Are you here to take more measurements?" she asked, climbing down from the ladder.

"No. I forgot my good tape measure the other night, and thought I'd swing by to get it. I should have called, but I figured someone would be home."

"That would be me. Mom's at the restaurant, Tommy's at Nadine's."

"How's she doing? I haven't seen her in forever."

"Super. You know she's married, two adorable kids, and living in Universal City. Her husband's a lawyer."

"Wow, that's impressive." *What sort of profession would be good enough for the other daughter of Juan Hernandez?* He shoved the thought aside and gestured to the truck in the street. "Sheppard Christmas Lighting, huh?"

She shook her head. "Nope, not here." She laughed. "I stopped by Wal-Mart on the way home and bought some LED lights. We've got the old fat Christmas lights, but they're stuffed away somewhere, and nobody has really had the energy to put them up for a few years."

"So you're using your day off to put up lights?"

She shrugged. "We need a little Christmas now, like the song goes."

"If you want, I can give you a hand. It won't take long if we work on it together," he heard himself saying.

Gabriela opened up those soft-looking lips of hers and was just about to reply, when an approaching vehicle made them both look toward the street.

Chapter 4

G abriela froze at the sight of a gleaming silver Mustang, its passenger window gliding down. Travis from church, an air force officer stationed at Lackland. Here, at her house. Didn't people use phones anymore?

"Gaby," Travis said through the open window. "I didn't know you lived in this area of town." He turned off the engine, unbuckled, and left the car.

"Yes, I sure do." Gabriela felt Miguel's stare, and she had the distinct impression of two banty roosters facing off. Ridiculous. Travis had mentioned this past Sunday about getting together for coffee sometime.

"I'm house shopping." He grinned. The guy was good-looking, loved the Lord, seemed focused on his career, and had made her laugh more than once during Sunday school class. All pluses in her book of qualities she liked most in a man.

"Really?" Why he'd want to buy a house big enough for a

family was beyond her. But then she wanted to do the same thing, didn't she?

"I know what you're thinking. Why buy a huge house only for me? It's a good time to invest. After I'm eventually transferred, I can rent the place out." Travis had a bright smile. Then he glanced at Miguel. "Hi. Miguel, isn't it?"

Miguel approached him first, his hand extended. "That's right. Miguel Rivera."

"Good to meet you officially. I'm still getting to know people at church." The two men shook hands.

"Same here. I started attending again earlier this year," said Miguel. "It's nice to see how much it has grown. Lots of families."

This was definitely *not* how she'd imagined spending her day off. Here came Travis stepping closer to her, with his friendly blue eyes, boyish dimple, and short-trimmed hair. What a contrast with Miguel, who crossed his arms across his chest, his dark hair curling as if in defiance.

"I know we talked about getting coffee sometime," Travis said. "But how about lunch after the Sunday morning service? That is, unless you have plans with your family."

"I don't." She bit her lip. "But I'll have to check the restaurant schedule. I might be scheduled to work in the afternoon."

"All right. Let me know on Sunday." He smiled again, and Gabriela wasn't quite sure, but she thought she glimpsed Miguel's jaw tighten slightly. Then Travis was off, pulling away from the curb with a honk and a wave.

"Well, that was unexpected." She hadn't meant to say it out loud.

Miguel only grunted in response.

"Oh, your tape measure. C'mon inside. It's either on the hallway table or the kitchen countertop." She stepped over the boxes of LED lights and into the entryway.

"I still want to give you a hand with the lights, if you don't mind. That ladder could be tricky."

"So you think I can't handle stringing up Christmas lights by myself?"

"No—no, that's not what I meant. I mean, what if you fell off the ladder, or needed an extra pair of hands?"

She glanced at Miguel, and he flushed. There was the tape measure. They both reached for it, fingers tangling. Hers tingled, and she laughed.

"Oops. Sorry, I didn't mean to sound like I didn't really want you to stay." She rubbed her sleeves. "It's a 'Pop reaction.' He makes me want to show him I can do things without a man's help."

"I get it." Now his smile captivated her like Travis's hadn't. "Gabriela Hernandez, I don't think there's anything you can't do on your own."

"Thanks." She felt herself blushing at the words of praise from him. He admired her. "But I appreciate the extra hand hanging the lights."

They paused a moment, and she didn't know what to say to break the silence. They had that undeniable chemistry, like the old days. Except neither of them had ever stepped beyond glances, Miguel probably out of fear of her father, and her. . .? Until Tommy's accident, she didn't know why.

All she knew now was that her heart hammered in her chest, and she wanted to throw her arms around Miguel's neck and kiss him.

❄

Miguel wasn't about to stand down, not after the good-look-ing air force officer left. He'd seen Gaby's hesitation when Travis asked her out to lunch.

"Guess we'd better get those lights up." He held up his measuring tape. "But *this* is going in my truck first."

He left Gabriela in the entryway. That *something* had zapped him again, too, just like it had this morning at the store. But the zap of attraction wasn't enough to keep a rela-tionship going, not one that truly mattered. He knew that.

But Gaby deserved so much. A guy like Travis could probably literally give her the world, or show her most of it. And with Gaby's profession and culinary skills, any restau-rant in the world would be lucky to have her.

He quit his mental tailspin and tossed the measuring tape into his truck. *Loco*, the idea of having Gaby married off after one lunch invitation. By the time he reached the front of the house again, Gabriela had resumed her earlier position, up on the ladder and holding icicle lights. Her cheeks flushed, her lips red, she looked down at him.

Miguel reached for the end of the light string. "I'll feed this up to you." Mr. Air Force could have stayed to help, but he hadn't.

"Thanks." She slipped the light's wire into one of the gut-ter clips. "Pop and Tommy used to do this. It would take them all day to get the lights up. You'd think Tommy was getting a root canal, as much as he moaned and groaned about it."

"Funny. Sort of like, 'Russ, time to put up the lights.'"

Gaby nodded. "Sure, Pop was a regular Clark Griswold."

"I never told you how sorry I was about—everything. And now Tommy can't do this again. Hanging lights, I mean."

"I can picture him trying to wheel himself out here and hold the lights for Pop. But Pop would never ask him, not now." Gabriela's hand shook as she clipped another light to the gutter, and she paused. "I know you're sorry. You didn't plan for what happened."

"No, you're right; I didn't."

She blinked hard a few times then cleared her throat. "I can't throw stones at you. I can't dwell in the past. Not with the future rushing up to meet me now."

"I wanted to call, so many times, after the accident." Miguel fed more lights up to Gabriela. "But my lawyer told me it was a bad idea. Then when it was either more prison, or rehab through New Life Center, I knew it was a chance to start over. So I took it. Court orders."

Gabriela nodded. "I know. We—asked about you."

"Thanks." Now he felt his cheeks flame. "My mama didn't call me for a long time after I went to NLC. She thought it was another one of my tries to get clean. One more failure."

"But you're here now. You haven't failed. And we're—we're trying to go forward. You have friends, and you have the Lord. You're—you're not alone."

"Thanks." He repeated himself. So, she'd asked about him. Or, they had. If only he could claim her heart, a healed heart, and he could look at her without seeing the mess he'd helped cause for everyone. He should have never let Tommy start hanging out with him, going along with what he'd done. *Old things have become new. . .*

A car pulled into the driveway. Mrs. Hernandez, home again.

"M'ija, you're putting up lights." Her face lit up as her gaze flicked from her daughter to Miguel, then back again. "Your papa will be so happy. And you're working so well together."

Together. Sort of. Miguel looked up at Gabriela, and he couldn't read her face this time.

Chapter 5

Gabriela made sure she arrived at La Cocina early on Saturday morning. Most people didn't get to see the Riverwalk before the shops and restaurants opened. A handful of tourists ambled along the pathway, pausing every so often to take photos. A vendor was sweeping the walkway in front of his store as Gabriela passed. A cool breeze teased at her hair, and she pushed some of the stray locks away.

This morning at the house, she'd waved at Tommy as he left for his physical therapy appointment on the service van. He had a fire in his eyes.

"I'm going to walk again one day. I know I will."

"You're so brave, Tommy."

"Not brave. But I can't go back to being helpless. Even in this chair."

With that, he left, just as Miguel pulled up in his truck, and Gabriela scrambled for her own car.

She paused now at the water's edge and clutched her travel mug of coffee, warm to her fingers. One of the river taxis glided past, and Gabriela looked up in time to see a tourist point a camera at her and shoot. The taxi continued along under one of the stone arch bridges, toward La Villita and the amphitheater.

Christmas lights swung in the breeze. This morning they looked dull and listless, as if they weighed the branches down. But at night the Riverwalk glowed with the thousands of bulbs in the trees.

This Christmas Gaby wasn't feeling the joy of the season, even though she and Miguel had hung the lights on the house. Again, Christmas was coming, whether she was ready for it or not.

"You're thinking pretty deep thoughts, Chef Gaby," came a voice behind her. It belonged to Marcy, one of La Cocina's fixtures and one of their best waitresses.

"The lights look so dull this morning. I almost wish they could be on all the time." She smiled at the waitress. "Are you ready for Christmas?"

The woman returned the smile. "Ah, the usual question. Not yet, but I will be. My granddaughter is so excited about Christmas."

"How old is she now?"

"Six."

"Wow. I remember when she was born." Gabriela counted back the years. "She's at that perfect age when Christmas is still magical, special, and uncomplicated."

"Oh, it's complicated when they get a certain toy stuck in their head that they have to have." Marcy rolled her eyes.

"But, honey, Christmas can be special at any age." She laid a gentle hand on Gabriela's arm.

"It seems Christmas always reminds me of how much everything is changing." Gabriela glanced at her arm.

"The first Christmas was full of changes for Mary and Joseph, changes they certainly hadn't expected." Marcy's eyes sparkled.

"You're right." Gabriela shivered. "That's very true. I guess I've not bothered much with Christmas in a while. After my brother's accident, we spent time focusing on doctors and physical therapists, keeping the business running."

"Do you mind if I give you another slice of advice?"

"Ha! Of course not. Why stop now?" She grinned at the waitress.

"Just enjoy Christmas this year. Find something special and don't try to recapture what happened in Christmases long ago. Find something new."

"Okay, I'll try that. Thanks." Gabriela sipped her travel mug of coffee. "You're here early."

"So are you."

"We're having Las Posadas tonight at church, so I'm cutting out early. It used to be a sort of tradition that my family went to the pageant together. My sister and her kids are even coming from Universal City."

"That's a nice tradition."

"We haven't gone, all of us together, for a few years. I can't wait to see the sanctuary lined with luminaries and the entire stage set up like Bethlehem." She always felt sorry for Mary, traveling so far with a baby belly, and being turned away from inn after inn.

"It sounds like you're already on your way to finding something special for Christmas this year." Marcy glanced down at her watch. "Look at the time. I need to get in there and start rolling silverware before the boss docks my pay." She gave Gabriela a departing smile and trotted off into the restaurant.

Marcy had also arrived earlier than usual for her shift. Pop had mentioned he'd be scheduling her for a few extra hours during Christmas, as Marcy needed the extra money. Gabriela sighed. Pop had a giving heart. Which is probably why he'd chosen Miguel as their contractor.

She closed her eyes. For the past five days, she'd seen Miguel every morning. Today he'd met her at the garage door with her favorite latte. To make up for the mess in the kitchen, he said.

The day entered its flurry of activity, Gabriela surrendering to the flood of orders and going with the flow. Pop was at her side. On the line, they never talked about anything but the food.

Maybe she could somehow talk about her menu ideas.

"Hey, Pop." She spooned a ladle of molé sauce over a pair of chicken enchiladas.

"Yeah?" His hands moved as if they had a mind of their own, plating a series of tacos accompanied by beans and rice.

"I had this idea for a *torta*."

"La Cocina doesn't do *tortas*."

"Why not?"

"Because we don't do tortas."

"Aw, Pop. Think of it. A *bolillo*, spread with black bean

paste, covered with pork *carnita*, guacamole, and cheese. Then you grill on both sides."

He merely grunted. "Nah."

"Pop, we serve tacos." She nodded at the plate he put on the tray. "Even shrimp tacos, and you hate shrimp."

"But everybody likes tacos."

"Well, what if we add a torta for a daily special to see how people like it?"

"It's too expensive right now. We need to watch our food budget."

"Okay." She bit her lip and kept plating. Maybe she ought to warn Marcy not to offer a special molé *verde* sample dish, even though Gabriela bought the ingredients with her own money.

"Chef Gabriela, your mama wants you in the dining room," Marcy called through the pass-through.

"Tell her I'll be right there." Gabriela slid one more plate onto the counter. "Taco combo, fajitas for two. Table 26."

"Go ahead now," Pop said. "I can do the plates myself for a while."

"Okay." It seems she kept repeating herself to Pop. Keep agreeing, keep her ideas to herself. She washed her hands and left the kitchen.

A few diners smiled as she passed their tables, the mariachis playing their music at full volume, just like Pop wanted it.

"M'ija," Mama said as she reached the table. "Carmen Valdez from church said she wanted to talk to us today about Las Posadas. She sounded like it was pretty important."

Carmen was the drama director at their church, and a

friend of Mama's for years.

"What could Las Posadas have to do with us? Do you think she wants catering for the program tonight? It's late notice, but we could work something out."

"Here she comes."

Carmen bustled past Maria, the hostess, and up to their table.

"Oh, Rita, something terrible has happened." Carmen slid onto the chair across from Mama.

"What's wrong?"

"Megan's got strep throat. She can't be Mary." Carmen's ample frame made the chair groan. "I need a replacement for Mary, and now. Which is why I need your help. Well, not yours, exactly."

Mama glanced at Gabriela.

No, I couldn't possibly—

"Gabriela has never had the honor of playing Mary," Mama began.

"Now, Mama, I'm sure Mrs. Valdez has someone else in mind. Maybe Nadine could be Mary." *Because Mary was kind and gentle, a forgiving woman.* She didn't blink when her world was upended. Not like Gabriela, that was for sure.

"Why, if Gabriela played Mary, that would save me a lot of trouble and phone calls." Carmen assessed her, and this made Gabriela want to sit up straighter.

"I'm really not Mary material."

"Why not?" both older women chorused.

"You'll fit the costume." Carmen nodded. "We need you at the church by six thirty so we can go over how you're to sit on the donkey."

Donkey? That was right. They always used live animals.

"My Gabriela, as Mary. Nadine was Mary the Christmas she was eighteen, and now you get to be Mary. What an honor." Mama beamed.

"I'll be there early," Gaby said as she got up to leave. Maria had just seated three tables, one right after the other. Hector and the crew would be in the weeds, and Pop would be hollering if she didn't get herself to the kitchen.

Lord, I know You look at the heart. And You already know that I'm no Mary.

❄

Miguel's throat tightened as he slipped the thick woven tunic over his T-shirt and basketball shorts. The hair on his legs prickled in the chilly air of the choir room. He felt like he was twelve again, in awe of the chance to play Joseph, before he became old enough to make fun of Goody-Two-shoes guys who went to church and dressed up like Bible characters.

Megan, the young woman originally set to play Mary, had gotten sick suddenly, but they told him his Mary would be there soon.

A familiar voice sounded outside the door. "I don't have to say anything, do I?"

At the sound of the voice, Miguel definitely didn't feel twelve anymore, an age when girls were still gross.

In came Gabriela, his Mary, dressed in a flowing blue robe. With her head-covering and sandals, and natural sun-kissed skin tone, she almost could pass for a young Jewish woman. But her round brown eyes and full cheeks made the similarity end.

"Hey, Miguel. I didn't know you were in Las Posadas."

She blinked at him, her cheeks turning red.

"Matter of fact, I am. So you're the new Mary."

"Yes. It was sort of last minute. Mama and Carmen Valdez voted me in."

"So you came here, kicking and screaming."

"Not exactly." She laughed.

"You're not into acting or anything."

"No, I'd rather be cooking or running things from the sidelines." Gabriela glanced around the room. "So, Carmen said something about a donkey. Oh, and I'm with Joseph, too."

"That would be me. Joseph, I mean."

She laughed. "This should be interesting. How are you at handling donkeys?"

"I can manage. They had some livestock at the New Life Center. I got pretty good with the animals. I won't let anything happen to you. I promise." At his words, his throat caught. Talk about mangling things again.

"No, I'm sure you won't." Gabriela looked down at her sandaled feet.

"Makeup, we need makeup!" Mrs. Valdez bundled into the room. "Mary, why, your cheeks are flaming already. I doubt we'll need much blusher for you. Must be the handsome man here."

Now Miguel felt his own face flame. He dared not look at Gabriela, whose face Mrs. Valdez descended on with a makeup brush and eyeliner.

Why did he always get reminders of how badly he'd done at protecting people in the past, people like Tommy? He would definitely give Brother Pete a call tonight. How did people do it, rebuilding relationships with people they'd hurt in the past?

The room soon filled with characters from the town of Bethlehem, fellow church members talking and laughing. One of the wise men was Mr. Top Gun himself, who tried to shoot straight over to Gabriela but was intercepted by Mrs. Valdez.

"Crowns! We need our wise men to wear crowns. And get the treasure boxes, Steven, will you?" she called over her shoulder as she blocked Top Gun Travis from reaching Gabriela.

"So," Miguel ventured, "how was lunch the other day with Top Gun?"

"Top Gun? Oh, you mean Travis. I didn't go. I worked the afternoon shift and closed that night." She shrugged. "He's a great guy, but. . ." Gabriela gestured, her full sleeves swishing.

"I see." Miguel glanced over to see Mrs. Valdez trying to fix a crown to Travis's head.

"We should stick together," Gabriela said. "I know everyone will be coming out before us, but I still get nervous."

"Don't be nervous." He looked down at her. "Everyone will be looking at the new set. The whole thing's on rollers so the church can slide it into storage until next year."

"Did you build it?" Gabriela's voice held admiration.

"I had help." He hoped he'd didn't sound too proud of it, but the set was awesome.

"Oh, but it's beautiful. And the design is genius." She touched his arm, and he allowed himself to pat her hand.

She didn't pull away.

Chapter 6

Gabriela felt like she had cotton in her throat. She'd forgotten how warm and strong Miguel's hands were. Calloused, too, from hard work.

Voices in the room seemed to disappear. One of her friends passed, chatting and waving at her. Her voice sounded dull, as if from a distance or under water.

I didn't know you were Mary. How cool is that? Glad you made it into the program this year.

To which she mumbled something in response, as Miguel kept his hand over hers.

"Pregnant! You need to be pregnant!" Mrs. Valdez appeared in front of her. "Or at least look pregnant. Stand back, Joseph."

Mrs. Valdez held up a baby tummy form.

"I need to put that on? What happened to a pillow?" Gabriela asked.

"That's twentieth-century, m'ija. Lift up your robe. We

should have done this earlier, but I forgot the box in the car."

Miguel stood off to the side. Gabriela didn't dare look at him as Mrs. Valdez helped strap the baby tummy over Gabriela's shirt.

"There. That happened fast." Mrs. Valdez started laughing at her own joke as she went off. "Once everyone leaves, you two head to the front hallway to meet up with the animal handler."

Gabriela settled her robe over the belly form. Strange, it felt. She wanted to have a lot of kids, one day. Four, at least. That desire had taken a backseat to culinary school, college, and helping with Tommy the past few years, but now shifted to the front. Literally, for tonight. She put her hand down and felt the silicone under the robe. It sure felt real.

"Let's go find your ride." Miguel tugged on her sleeve.

The rest of the Bethlehem cast drifted from the choir room and through the rear entrance to the sanctuary platform. Gabriela could hear applause rippling outside.

She let Miguel lead her to the doorway that led to the hallway. Strains of "O Little Town of Bethlehem" filtered under each set of closed sanctuary doors as she passed. Mary. Maybe it wasn't such a big deal to some people, but she'd never acted a part in her life.

A donkey's bray made Gabriela pause.

"Don't worry. I've got you." Miguel took her hand. She clutched it.

They found the donkey and stood next to the animal, waiting. Mrs. Valdez magically appeared through one of the sanctuary doors. "There you are. Pastor's reading about the tradition of Las Posadas now. Once he's done, I'll send you in to make your journey."

"Do I have to actually ride the donkey? I heard that according to some historians, Mary likely walked to Bethlehem."

"It's part of the live Nativity. And here's your lines."

"Lines?" She looked at the piece of paper Mrs. Valdez gave her. Okay, she could read these lines. She hoped.

"It's only a few lines," Mrs. Valdez said. "You can even ad lib when necessary."

"Ad lib?"

Miguel was chuckling as he took the donkey's reins from the handler. "You're stressing out over nothing."

"Ha." She'd show him. "How do I get on?"

The handler put a small stool next to the donkey's left shoulder. "Just hop up on this, and sit sidesaddle. Your right leg hooks around here, your left foot sticks in this stirrup on the bottom. Peanut will take good care of you."

She would have much preferred sitting astride and wrapping her arms around the animal's neck for dear life.

"Here we go, Peanut." Gabriela hauled herself up onto the donkey, which didn't fall over once she'd settled onto the saddle. She felt tall, as she looked down slightly at Miguel.

"I won't let you fall." He squeezed her hand again.

"Thanks." She wrapped one hand around the saddle horn.

"Don't worry about the lines. Follow my lead."

She could trust him with Las Posadas, but not her whole heart—not just yet.

The door swung open, and Miguel led Peanut down the aisle. Luminaries flickered along each pew, then across the front of the stage. A guitar softly played "Silent Night" without accompaniment. The lone instrument echoed across the sanctuary filled with nearly five hundred people.

Five hundred people—all looking at us. Gabriela gripped Peanut's stubby mane with both hands, crumpling the card with her lines on it. The fake baby tummy made her feel lopsided, as if she were on the verge of toppling off and landing on poor Miguel.

"Have you any rooms?" Miguel asked at the first door.

"No, no room," was the reply, and the door closed.

Again, the scenario was repeated at the next house.

"We will find a room, my dear Mary," Miguel said to her.

Line—she had a line. She glanced at the tiny card.

"I know we will, my Joseph. I trust you, and I trust God to take care of us all." Her face flamed, and her hand shook. She didn't know if anyone could hear her voice, or her heart galloping away in her chest. If Peanut matched that stride, he'd win the Kentucky Derby. But then, that wasn't a race for donkeys. . .

Her thoughts drifted as Miguel led her to the next house, where again they were turned away. Molé. She had to find a way to convince Pop to let her switch up the menu a little. He hadn't changed it in years. Maybe she'd follow Hector's suggestion to introduce molé verde.

". . .isn't that right, Mary?" Miguel asked.

She froze and placed her left hand on Miguel's shoulder as Peanut sidestepped. Miguel slid his arm around her waist and stepped closer.

"I've got you," he whispered. "Peanut's not going anywhere, either."

"Thanks." She could hardly whisper back. "I messed

up my line. Sorry."

He released her and looked at the innkeeper. Their last stop. "Yes, I think the stable will be perfect for us." Then he glanced at Gabriela.

"Yes, that will do nicely." She nodded.

The stage lights went low, and only the luminaries lit the room as the stage shifted. Gabriela sat frozen on Peanut.

"Don't leave me." Not only did the donkey make her nervous, but she also didn't like sitting on a donkey in the dark, either. She felt six, not twenty-six.

"I won't." Miguel squeezed her hand.

"Okay, here comes the baby," a familiar voice said in the dark. Mrs. Valdez.

Gabriela managed to climb off the donkey and started unfastening the baby tummy from her waist.

Someone shuffled her and Miguel into the stable backdrop. The straw made her sneeze.

"Sit, m'ija." Mrs. Valdez guided her onto a cushioned chair. "You, too, Joseph."

Then a soft gurgling sound came closer. "Careful, Gabriela."

"Who's that?"

"It's me, Judith Glassberg. I've got my little Joshy here, lending him to the play."

A warm, soft bundle was placed in Gabriela's arms.

"I'll take good care of him." Something stirred inside Gabriela when the soft spotlights came on.

Judith's little Joshua had blond hair and blue eyes, which made the genetics improbable, but Gabriela didn't care, and neither did the audience, judging by the soft gasps that came up at the sight of a real baby portraying the Christ Child in Las Posadas.

Then Miguel knelt next to them, and brushed her head with his hand, and then touched Joshua's head. "God has provided for us this warm stable, this place of peace for the birth of the Prince of Peace."

She had a line but could barely breathe as she read the cue card taped to the manger. "In His wisdom, the Father has guided us to this moment. The journey has been hard, but we have been in the shadow of His unseen Hand."

A tear fell onto the flannel baby blanket. *Lord, the journey has been hard. Where are You guiding me this Christmas?*

G'night Miguel. See you later!" a friend called as they pulled out of a parking space.

Miguel waved. He scanned the cars in the parking lot. Gabriela had remained quiet for the rest of the evening, and had left him at the first opportunity. Something was going on with her.

He knew that resuming their friendship had been difficult for her. He understood that all too well. But this—this was something else. He stifled a yawn, unlocking his truck.

A lone figure by the nearest light pole caught his attention. Something about the way the guy leaned on the pole and watched him.

Then he started strolling in Miguel's direction. Miguel clenched his keys. Santos. He hadn't seen this dude in a few years.

"Hey, Rivera. What's up?" Santos extended his hand.

Miguel shook it.

"Not much. I've been busy, working."

"Good for you. I, uh, I've got something you might be interested in."

"Sorry, I don't think you do. Not anymore." Miguel crossed his arms across his chest, his back firmly set against the truck.

"You sure about that? Listen, I wouldn't ask you if I didn't need the money."

"What do you need? Are you hungry? Do you need food? Where are you living?"

"I don't need food. I need the money." Santos shifted from foot to foot.

"I can't just give you money, Santos. I'm sorry."

"You're acting like a rich church boy, Rivera." Santos took a step closer. His eyes glittered in the lights of the parking lot. "But I know better. I know what's inside there. You need what I have. And I need the money that you have."

Santos whirled on one foot and stalked off, away from the parking lot. Miguel climbed inside his truck, slammed the door, and locked it. He leaned back against the headrest.

"Lord, I knew this would happen. Seeing the Hernandez family again, everyone else I hurt—but now seeing Santos. . ." Miguel closed his eyes. "I know I was as hard up as Santos. I don't want those things anymore. I don't. I have You, my refuge, my strength."

He turned the ignition and listened to the music fill the cab of the truck. No one could hear him singing along in his slightly off-pitch rendition of "How Great Is Our God." That didn't matter.

He had his faith, his freedom, his business, and maybe even a chance with Gabriela, a chance he'd tossed away years ago and probably didn't deserve even now. A lot to be thankful for. A man would be insane to run back into slavery again.

❄

Gabriela's head swam with the events of the whole evening, from Miguel's obvious tenderness and care for her, to the words they said in front of everyone, to the sensation of holding Judith's sweet little bundle in her arms. She'd never felt so exposed in front of so many people before.

She sat in her car and wiped her eyes. Tommy had ridden with Mama and Pop, and her sister and brood had already cleared out. Time to go. Bone tired. She'd have to peel herself out of bed for work in the morning.

There was Miguel, standing beside his truck and talking to a guy who looked like he'd crawled out from under a rock. Whatever the conversation was about, Miguel didn't look too happy.

What if he's using again?

The thought darted through her brain, and she gripped the steering wheel tighter. The little bit of her heart that she'd opened to Miguel stung at the barb. She couldn't bear to hang on to that idea.

Part of her wanted to rip a U-turn in the parking lot, shoot back to Miguel, and beg him to tell her what was going on.

But users could be good liars. Tommy—and Miguel—had taught them all that. Tommy, even now, lived his life openly with accountability. Miguel, now that she'd let him in, well, they hadn't gotten that far for her to know yet. That pastor from the New Life Center seemed to help him a lot, though.

Love always believes the best.

She drove out of the parking lot and headed for home. Mama had promised to make her homemade hot chocolate, and the family joked about them standing around a hot plate in the garage. Everyone would remember the Las Posadas night they'd had hot chocolate in the garage.

This Christmas wouldn't be ruined, even though the kitchen was still in a shambles. Hopefully she could keep her heart intact as well.

Their home glowed with lights, along with several others in the neighborhood. Gabriela parked and followed the laughter to the garage.

"Nadine! You came over anyway." She hugged her sister. "I thought you were heading home."

"Mama said she didn't feel up to making hot chocolate, and the kids really wanted to help."

Her niece and nephew bounced around the garage. Someone had turned on the radio, and Christmas music echoed off the walls.

"Have you finished your shopping yet?" Nadine asked.

"No. I think I'm going to make special gourmet meal gift cards for everyone." Gabriela sighed. "So act surprised."

"Wow, I'll try to." Her sister sidled closer. "Speaking of surprises, you and Miguel looked pretty, um, cozy tonight."

"We were playing a married couple, you know."

"I think he didn't have to act very hard. He looked at you

as if you were the only woman on earth."

"That's a little dramatic."

"He's in love with you. I'm sure of it."

"Sometimes love isn't enough."

"Love endures all things; love never fails." Nadine stirred the chocolate in a saucepan on the hot plate.

"Sure, quote Scripture at me," Gabriela laughed. "I do care for him. If I didn't, all of *this* wouldn't hurt. He was a friend for a long time, until—"

"I know. But he's a better man now. We've all seen it. Even Tommy has."

But I've refused to. Nadine didn't need to say the words. Gabriela had been blind, willingly so. And then tonight her eyes were opened.

"I wonder if he's ever tempted to go back."

"Temptation isn't a sin," Nadine said.

"Of course not." Nadine sure knew how to deflect any of Gabriela's words. "But I'm afraid for him."

"Then pray for him, and be there for him."

Gabriela nodded. "I do, and I'll try to be."

Nadine looked toward the kitchen. "Papa's taking an awful long time."

"Where'd he go?"

"He went to check on Mami."

As if bidden by their conversation, Pop entered the garage, Mama following.

"Girls, I'm bringing Mama to the hospital."

Mama leaned in the doorway. "I—I don't feel very well."

Nadine dashed to meet her and touched Mama's cheek. "You're burning up."

"And I had to leave during the service tonight—I kept getting sick in the bathroom."

"Nadine, do you want to go with Pop, or stay here?" Gabriela asked. Mama must be really sick, if she wasn't arguing against Pop taking her to the ER.

"Mama, if you were sick, why didn't you say anything?"

"I didn't want to worry anybody. Tonight was special, and we were all together." Mama shivered.

Gabriela went to the living room and snatched a folded afghan from the back of Pop's favorite chair. She hurried back before they loaded into the car. "Here." She tucked it around Mama's shoulders.

"Thank you, m'ija." Now Mama's teeth were chattering.

"I'll be praying."

"*Tia* Gaby, is Abuela going to be okay?" her little niece, Hayley, asked.

"Yes, yes she will."

"Why don't you have a Christmas tree up yet?"

How to explain to a child why the Christmas tree wasn't up yet. "Your grandparents are pretty busy, with the restaurant and with working on the kitchen."

"Can we do something fun for Christmas tonight?"

Gabriela's first inclination was to cook something, but the kitchen consisted of a hot plate, a microwave, and a toaster oven. "We can make cookies."

"I want to play video games with Uncle Tommy," said Mark.

"Sure enough, dude." Tommy ruffled Mark's hair. "We'll let the ladies bake all of us some goodness." Off they went to the other end of the house.

Baking always took longer when Gaby's niece was involved, but soon Gabriela and Hayley had a batch of chocolate-chunk cookie dough that would bake, half a dozen at a time, in the toaster oven.

Hayley frowned, her light brown hair and tawny skin giving her an exotic look.

"What's wrong, m'ija?" Gabriela asked.

"My friend Brianna is mean. I told her a secret, and she went and told everyone in class, and they laugh at me every day." Hayley dropped a small mountain of dough onto the cookie sheet.

"Did she say she was sorry?"

Hayley nodded. "But it still hurts. Kids still laugh."

Even when someone said they were sorry, the hurt still stung. "I know it hurts. Someone hurt me like that, too, once."

"My Sunday school teacher says that Jesus wants us to forgive, because God forgives us."

"Your teacher is right." Gabriela tucked the first small tray of cookies into the oven.

"So I told Brianna I forgive her, but I can't stop thinking about it." Hayley stuck her finger in the bowl for a bite of dough.

"Well, does Brianna act like a friend to you now? Is she still mean?"

"She's not mean anymore. She gave me one of her new pencils, her favorite one. And she invited me to sleep over after school gets out for Christmas."

"I've been told that one day you wake up, and the hurt is a little bit less." Gabriela didn't know how much an eight-year-old would understand. She wasn't sure how well she understood the way healing and forgiveness worked together, either. "And then another day, it might hurt a little bit less. Not that you ever forget. But when you don't forgive, it continues to hurt you. It sounds like Brianna really is sorry."

"Yeah. Plus she told some of the kids to quit laughing at me." Hayley smiled. "Tia Gaby, can I lick the spoon when we're done?"

Gabriela laughed. "Of course you can." She might have been trying to help her niece, but repeating what she already knew helped her some, too. Maybe God knew she needed the reminder.

❅

Nadine didn't return until five in the morning. "Mama has the flu, and she's dehydrated, so they admitted her."

"Oh, Mami." Gabriela sat up straight on the love seat. "Where's Pop?" Hayley and Mark snored, sleeping feet to feet on the long couch across from her.

"He's staying with her. They're keeping her until the afternoon. I already called Tia Celi, and she was already planning to open for Pop for Sunday lunch."

"Good, good." Gabriela gestured to the pair of kids sleeping on the couch. "They were angels. We made some cookies you can take home."

"Thanks." Nadine gave her a hug. "I'm so tired."

"Will you be okay?"

"Yes. I'll put the kids to bed, then sleep for a while, then go get Mama and Papa at the hospital."

"I'll let Tommy know when he wakes up. I think he and Mark wore each other out on the video games."

She helped load her sister's children into the van then

went back inside. Her own eyelids drooped a little.

Gabriela paused in the kitchen. The new cabinets were hung, a dark maple. On Monday the granite countertops and island were being installed, and the electrician was coming Tuesday to install the pot lights that would run the perimeter of the kitchen. Nine days later, the kitchen would be done. After the kitchen, what then about Miguel?

She'd entered new territory, she knew. She could quote Scripture about forgiveness and say that she'd forgiven him long ago. Maybe the hurt at last had started to heal. She inhaled the aroma of the wood. Building something new. That's what they were doing, in more ways than one.

Chapter 7

Morning one of Gabriela's exile at home. Exile, because Pop insisted on her remaining at home while Mama recovered from her flu. Better Gaby than Pop: she could imagine Pop going stir-crazy at the house, thinking about the restaurant.

She addressed Christmas cards on behalf of the family after having a quick breakfast then popped the envelopes in the mailbox. Mama only wanted some toast and a banana, plus a cup of hot tea.

Miguel was the only one working in the kitchen so far. He was actually waiting on the electrician, and the slab of granite leaned against the wall where their table usually stood. His workers were due to arrive to help him install the countertop.

She hadn't talked to him much since the night of Las Posadas, its memory still fresh in her mind every day. Something had happened that night, and she wasn't exactly sure what. But the vulnerability still made her very aware of how she'd inadvertently exposed herself that night. If not in so many words, the fact that she'd put herself in a position to trust Miguel. Something she'd promised herself she wouldn't be quick to do. Not again.

Mama lay in bed, apologizing for being so weak. "And taking you away from what you love. You don't need to be here."

"Pop insists, and it's no trouble, because I love you, Mama. How many times did you take care of me and Tommy and Nadine when we were sick?" She held Mama's breakfast tray with an empty plate and empty teacup. "Don't worry. You rest and get better, okay?"

"Sí, m'ija." Mama gave her a salute. "I will."

Gabriela closed the bedroom door. Although her parents' master suite was at the opposite end of the house from the kitchen, she didn't want any construction noises to drift back to the room. Hopefully Mama would get some healing rest.

Miguel was measuring the countertop when she entered the kitchen. He smiled when he saw her.

"Hey, Miguel. You'll have help with that counter, I assume?"

"Sure will. The crew should be here any minute." Music echoed off the kitchen walls and new cabinets. Miguel reached for the volume on the radio. "Sorry. I don't want the music to keep your mom awake if she's trying to sleep."

"I think it's pretty quiet back there, but thanks."

"Oh." Miguel put the tape measure on the counter. "Come see what I installed in the pantry. Your mama's gonna love this."

He motioned toward the pantry, and Gabriela followed. "What did you do?"

They entered the small space. Big enough to hold more than one person, yet definitely way too tight for both of them. The door started closing shut behind her.

"Don't let the—" The latch clicked as the door slammed.

"—door shut." Miguel sighed.

"Why is that a problem?" Gabriela reached for the handle. It wouldn't budge. "Oh no."

"That's why." His voice sounded tired in the dark. "Here." He flipped a switch, and an overhead light came on.

"What's wrong with the handle?"

"The latch gets stuck. Either that, or there's a problem with the handle tumblers. I have it propped open. One of the little details I was going to worry about after the electricity was finished."

"You've got to be kidding me. Why didn't you say something?"

"I did."

"If we holler for Mama, I doubt she'll hear us, especially with the music. And Tommy's at the college, seeing an advisor today." She looked at him. "We can call someone to come to the house."

"Um, my cell phone is on the counter. What about yours?" Miguel looked sheepish.

"It's in my purse," she admitted.

"So, we're stuck until the crew gets here."

"I guess so." She bit her lip. "You might as well show me what you were talking about."

"See?" Miguel faced a trio of shelves. "I made stackable

racks, so she can see everything instead of having to move stuff around to see what's behind the stuff up front."

"Mama will love that."

"I only made a few of these. If she wants, I can put in a few more." He sat down on the floor. "Might as well sit and wait."

Gabriela did the same. "You're right." His cologne smelled good, and his hair looked just a touch damp and unruly. She glanced at the door. "Are the hinges on the outside or the inside?"

"Outside."

"That figures. Do you have a screwdriver in here? We could always take the door handle off and pop the latch."

Miguel shook his head. "Good idea, but no."

"Well, I tried." She couldn't help but smile at him. Butterflies turned into hummingbirds in her stomach.

"Someone will be here in a while." Miguel studied her, and she tried not to squirm. "So why are you trying so hard to get away from me?"

"I'm not."

"Ha. Right." His face darkened. "You know, the other night something happened with you and me. I could tell. And I know you could, too."

She wouldn't answer him, because she knew he was right.

"But it still comes down to Tommy. I can't say I'm sorry enough. I can't undo anything. If I could, I would."

"I know that." She fought to get the words out. "Tommy's turned around. And so are you. And I'm glad about that. . ."

"But?" His gaze bored into her.

"I should have stopped Tommy that night. I should have told him to stay home." Gabriela gritted her teeth. "But I was so angry and tired of trying to talk him into staying, into trying to help us stay a family without him running off, losing jobs, quitting jobs, spending all his money on drugs, breaking my parents' hearts."

"None of that is your fault."

"But he lied to us so many times. He was so convincing. So. . ."

"So?"

"So how do I know, how do any of us know he's not, and you're not, going back there again?" The words tasted bitter to her.

"You can't know. Because no matter how many times I tell you I won't go back to the old ways, that doesn't prove anything."

"Miguel. . .I know you can't. I. . ."

She moved toward him, and he closed the space between them. Then she was in his arms, and his lips were on hers. She held him tightly, allowing one hand to touch his face and the other that unruly hair. Tears burned her cheeks, tears she refused to let anyone ever see.

"*Te amo*," she whispered after the kiss ended.

"Te amo," came his deep reply. "Trust that, and trust God, my sweet Gaby."

"I'm afraid."

"I know you believe in me, and your family does, too." He held her at arm's length and looked into her eyes. "Don't blame yourself about Tommy. He always knew right from wrong. Sure, he looked up to me. But that night, running from the police, God showed mercy on us both. By letting Tommy live after he fell off that roof. By letting me hit rock bottom. That changes a man, and a man's got to decide if he's going to make the break once and for all. And I have."

"The other night, after Las Posadas? Who was that man at your truck? The scruffy guy?"

"Santos. He was trying to sell, and I told him I wasn't buying. He said he needed money, but when I offered to buy him something to eat, he said that wasn't what he wanted."

"Do you think he'll come around again?"

"I dunno. If he does, I'll give him the same answer."

"Good." Then she smiled at him. "I wanted to stop the other night when I saw him, and ask you then."

"Well, I'm glad you did now." He pulled her close again, and she leaned on him. "I sure hope someone gets here soon."

"Me, too." She gave a soft giggle.

"So, tell me more about your restaurant. Did you say you found a building near El Mercado?"

"I'm still looking. Downtown property is expensive, so I'll probably have to rent for a long while." She shifted to sit cross-legged across from Miguel.

He cleared his throat. "Have you talked to your papa about your restaurant?"

She shook her head. "We've been busy. And now with Mama getting sick. Maybe after New Year's."

"If it's your dream, you should talk to him. He's your papa. If he encouraged me in what I'm doing, I know he'll support you, his daughter."

"It's not that simple."

"Why not?"

"He might be encouraging, but he's got old ideas about women running things. Sure, he'll let me run the kitchen sometimes, but I'm not the head chef." She sighed. "I don't want to cause a family drama by upsetting the status quo."

"But this is something you really want, isn't it? You're not causing family drama by wanting to open your own restaurant."

"Maybe not—maybe I will talk to him. It won't hurt. But I'm not holding my breath. I could show him the plan I wrote up."

"So you made a plan?"

"I even made a menu." At this, her face glowed. "Homemade soups, tortas, enchiladas, *carnitas*, and a whole list of tacos with fillings Pop wouldn't dream of using. I already tried asking about adding tortas to the menu, and he wouldn't budge."

"Promise me something?"

"What's that?"

"Promise me you'll tell him your ideas." Miguel touched her shoulder. "You deserve to have that dream come true."

"Okay, then. I promise." She smiled at him. "But enough about my dream. What about *your* ideas for Rivera Remodeling? Where are you planning to go with it?"

"I want to help families make their homes better places to live for a fair price, without giving up quality. That's important to me."

"Maybe you can help me design my restaurant. Your woodworking skills are awesome, and I know you have a good sense of how space is supposed to flow."

"I don't know much about restaurant design."

"We can learn together. I know what works, and chances are I'll have to lease a building that needs remodeling. So I'll need a remodeler. Which you are." With that, she shifted to lean against a cabinet.

He took her hand and kissed it. "It's a deal."

The house phone started to ring.

Gabriela shifted to her knees and pushed on the door. "Unbelievable. If Mama isn't awake already, she will be now with the phone ringing. I don't know if anyone turned the ringer off in the back of the house."

She thought she heard the scuff of slippers on the unfinished floor. "Mama! Is that you?"

"M'ija? Where are you?"

"We're stuck in the pantry." Gabriela stood.

"Oh, my." The sound of slippered feet came closer. "Is this locked?"

"No, Mrs. Hernandez." Miguel joined Gabriela at the door. "The catch is stuck. If you jiggle the outside handle, it might pop and open."

The handle wiggled on the inside. "It doesn't seem to want to open."

"Get a butter knife and stick it where the catch inserts."

"I'll be right back." She padded off, probably to the garage and their makeshift kitchen.

"We'll be out of here soon," Miguel murmured and squeezed Gabriela's hand. "I have a lot of work to do. But it was nice being trapped with you for a little while."

"I thought so, too." She placed a hand on the door. "I didn't realize till now how angry I still am at Tommy, and you helped me see that. Plus—"

"Here I am," came Mama's voice at the door. "I think if I stick the knife here and twist the handle, then—"

The door popped open, and the sudden daylight made Gabriela squint.

"Thank you, thank you. But I'm sorry the phone woke you up."

Mama waved her hands. "Don't worry. It was your papa, saying he is coming home to check on me. The restaurant is slow right now, so he's leaving Hector in charge."

Gabriela tried not to frown, and then Miguel caught her eye. "Now's your chance, Gaby."

"Chance for what?" asked Mama.

"I sort of wanted to talk to Pop about some business ideas. But it's been hard to get a chance to talk to him lately."

"I know. It's been a busy time of year for us all." Mama sighed. "Let's wait in the living room."

Miguel said, "I have a kitchen to work on, and an electrician to call."

Gabriela helped Mama to the living room. "Here, you rest, and I'll get some lunch for you and Pop."

"I only want some tea."

"All right, then." Gabriela went to the garage and tried to put something together. Some tamales that Nadine had made would be perfect for Pop. She tucked them into the microwave and went to fetch her business idea folder.

Pop finally arrived, and she brought him his lunch while Mama sipped her tea.

"My two ladies of the house, how are you?"

"I'm feeling much better, even though I'm tired." Mama

smiled at Pop, and Gabriela saw the love pass between them, even after more than thirty years of marriage.

"Pop, I know you don't have long, but there was something I wanted to talk to you and Mama about." Gabriela clutched her folder.

"What is it? What's that you're holding?" Papa asked between bites of tamale.

"What would you say about me *not* moving out?" She paused for their reaction.

"M'ija, this will always be your home, and as long as you want to live here, we're happy to have you." Mama's expression was full of questions.

"I—I have some ideas." She opened the folder. "I wasn't sure what you'd think about it, and I tried to talk to you about a few of the smaller ideas, Pop."

"The tortas?" Pop frowned. "I thought I already said I didn't want to change the menu."

"Um, actually, I was thinking of something bigger than changing the menu. I—" She sensed Miguel's presence in the doorway. "I want to open La Cocina del Mercado."

"Another restaurant?" Pop placed his plate on the coffee table, stood, and started pacing the room. "It's risky, especially now."

"Going into business is always risky. You knew the risks when you bought the first La Cocina." Gabriela sat up straighter on the love seat. "And here you are."

"Yes, here I am." Pop stopped at the fireplace mantel. Someone had draped it with artificial pine garland. Who had, Gabriela didn't know. Tommy?

"I have some money saved, the money I was going to use

as down payment for my house. It's not enough for a restaurant, but if I could find some backers, I can get started—"

"But why at El Mercado?"

"It's a popular area, but it's far enough from the Riverwalk that it wouldn't compete with your La Cocina. I want to do upscale street food."

"Let me see your plan, and if I think it's a good idea, I'll match what you've saved."

Gabriela's hands shook as she handed Pop the folder. "You would do that for me?"

"You are my daughter; of course I would. What wouldn't I do for you?" Pop's eyebrows shot to the top of his forehead. "Is this what you have been trying to tell me about for the past few weeks?"

She nodded. "There was never time."

"We should have made time." Pop sat down and snatched one of the tamales with his free hand and balanced the open folder on his lap.

"Pop, do you like the idea?"

"M'ija, the kitchen at La Cocina is crowded. I'm not ready to retire, and you're ready to run your own restaurant. Too many chefs in the kitchen, as the saying goes, and there can only be one head chef." Pop paged through the folder, nodding. "I'm not promising I'll back the idea. We may need to do some refining. Many things to think about when opening a restaurant. But this is nice, very nice."

"Oh, gracias, Papi." She shot from the love seat, managed not to trip over the coffee table, and hugged him. "And I already have a contractor, when the time comes."

"Now why does that not surprise me?" Pop said in her ear.

❄

Someone had been digging in his trash can. Miguel paused outside his apartment. Maybe it was a kid, or someone wandering by looking for who knows what. He caught a whiff of old coffee grounds combined with the contents of leftover take-out, and wrinkled his nose.

He clamped the lid down more securely and glanced around. The other residents' trash cans sat undisturbed by their back doors. Maybe he was being a little suspicious, but he knew some people would stoop to anything. Identity theft happened too frequently.

As soon as he entered his apartment, his phone started ringing. "Rivera Remodeling."

"Brother Miguel! How are you?"

"I'm fine, Brother Pete." He tossed his keys onto the counter.

"So how's that kitchen remodel going?"

"Great, even with a few delays I think we'll still be done next week, as promised."

"You sound like something's on your mind."

"Yes, and no." He sank onto his lumpy living room chair. "Last Sunday night, after church, someone found me from my old days."

"How did that go? Did you have a hard time?"

"Not as much as I thought I would. It was Santos. He wanted to sell me some product, but I told him no."

"Good, good for you. Praise God. But there's more to it than that, right?"

"There's this woman. . . ."

"Ah, I see," said Brother Pete. "Is she someone you recently met?"

"No, I've known her since I was a teenager. In fact, her brother and I used to run around together—back then. He's—he's in a wheelchair partly because of me. There was some bad blood between me and his family, for a long time."

"Is she still angry at you?"

"I—no, she's not." Miguel swallowed hard at the recollection of what happened in the pantry. "If anything, I think we're, well—we're friends, maybe more."

"Take your time, Brother. You don't have to love her to make up for what happened."

"It's not like that. Gaby is a giving, caring person. Would do anything for her family."

"She likes to rescue people, doesn't she?"

"She does like to help people."

"Give it time. Make sure she's not trying to rescue you and mistaking that for love."

"I don't need rescuing. I'm not the man I was, but I know I'm a work in progress, like they say. She accepts me in spite of the past, and maybe, one day, we'll have a future."

"Good. That's good to hear you say that. I'll be praying for you both."

"Thanks, Bro. Thanks."

He ended the call and spent the rest of the evening rattling around his apartment. The pot lights were functioning in the Hernandez kitchen, plus the granite was installed and the new sink. The backsplash and tile floors were next. Christmas was coming, and he had a promise to fulfill.

Brother Pete's words came back to him. He meant well, and Miguel knew him enough to trust his words. Gaby, a rescuer? She always defended the weak and the underdog.

Was that him? A weak underdog? He thought of Top Gun Travis from church, who'd probably never gotten a speeding ticket. Not that there was much of a comparison between him and the air force officer, but he shouldn't put himself down.

Because Gabriela had chosen him. If she'd really wanted to be with Travis, then she would be. And she hadn't been locked in a pantry with the man, either. He was proud of her, standing up for herself and talking to her papa tonight.

Miguel took the latest receipts and started adding them to his expense list. And he smiled the whole time.

Chapter 8

Christmas crept closer, and Gabriela lived up to her promise to Nadine. She made gift certificates for her family, good for one gourmet meal during the next year. She made one for Miguel, too. Maybe it wasn't the most personal of gifts, but he was a man, and he definitely liked to eat.

In fact, she thought she'd surprise him with an early present by making dinner and bringing it to his apartment tonight. She put together a fresh molé verde, with beans and rice on the side, and headed toward his place. He'd already left for the day, and said something about having a quiet night at home. He looked quizzical when she asked if he planned to be there.

She found his apartment complex, a simple group of buildings in a row, each with a pair of parking places in front. His red truck was close to his apartment's front door.

Marcy was right. This Christmas had turned out to be

something new, different, and she loved it so far. She'd heard it said before that Christmas was really about God reaching out to man, and offering ultimate reconciliation. No more walls. She liked the sound of that. It looked like the same was happening for her and Miguel. Humming, she carried the insulated dish up the sidewalk to his front door then paused. Yellow police tape blocked her path. What on earth?

Did she have the right place? There was his truck, and she double-checked the address she'd written on an index card. She stared at the yellow tape.

Then his neighbor's door opened, and an elderly Mexican woman peeked through the crack. "Señorita, you look for Miguel?"

"Sí, sí." Gabriela switched to Spanish, and the neighbor told her everything she knew.

No, he wasn't there. Yes, the police came and took him. No, she wasn't sure why he was arrested. All she knew was they'd asked if he was Miguel Rivera, and when he said yes, they showed him a piece of paper and pushed inside the apartment. They made him sit in the squad car for a long time, while some of them were inside his house. Drugs, maybe, the woman wondered.

"Gracias, Señora." Gabriela's breath came in short gasps. Miguel, arrested? No way. Had that Santos guy come back and caused trouble somehow? She hugged the casserole dish and trudged to her car.

What to tell Mama and Pop?

She tucked the casserole onto the front seat next to her. Last week, she'd been locked in the pantry with Miguel, and she'd wanted nothing more than to get away—at first. But now?

Oh, Lord, be with Miguel. I don't know what's going on, but You do. This can't be another disappointment. It can't be true.

❄

It figured. His past had been dragged out again. Miguel sat in an investigation room in one of the San Antonio Police Department's precincts. Outside the thick glass window that faced the office, someone's tabletop Christmas tree sparkled, looking out of place in the serious setting.

His head ached. "Yes, I am Miguel Rivera. No, I did not purchase those items. I didn't write those checks, either. That's not my signature."

Detective Dominguez of the SAPD looked across the table at him through narrow eyes. "Miguel Rivera went to Electronics Haven, purchased over three grand of audio and video equipment using this checking account last week. Here's the signature on the merchant copies of the receipts. Then yesterday he hit up a men's clothing store and later bought himself a sweet little MacBook Air."

"Detective, I don't want to give you a hard time. But I'm not saying anything more until I talk to a lawyer." Miguel knew the system could eat up both the innocent and the guilty, and all those in between, like him.

"Do you want to call anyone?"

"*Sí*, I do." Miguel swallowed hard. He thought he'd been done asking for help in situations like this. Brother Pete would listen to him. But maybe someone else could really help him.

He dialed the number on the precinct telephone. Not his sister. He'd tired of the disappointment and wariness in her voice, although she'd been happy to hear about his project at the Hernandez home.

"Señor Hernandez?"

"*Sí*—Miguel? Why are you calling from the police? What has happened?"

"I've been arrested, but I didn't do it. They've got the wrong man, but they won't listen to me."

"I believe you. My Nadine is married to a lawyer. I will see what he can do."

"Please, pray for me. And tell Gabriela to keep believing in me."

"I will. I will. Should I have Bryan call this number?"

"Yes. Someone will be able to tell him what to do."

Detective Dominguez stood. "Okay, Rivera. Time's up. Your lawyer can get here in the morning."

"Señor Hernandez, I need to go. But please, pray for me."

"I will, I will."

Miguel hung up the phone. He didn't want to let the receiver go, his lifeline to the outside.

"Up you go." The detective took his elbow and helped him to his feet.

Miguel knew the drill. Don't fight. Don't struggle. Go along and keep your mouth closed. He clenched his jaw and refused to hang his head low. No weakness. No fear. *God, You knew this would happen. Deliver me. Help me be strong.*

Gabriela would know about this soon, if she didn't already. He should have called her, to explain, to see if she could help. But her papa—his opinion mattered.

❉

"So they're saying Miguel wrote a bunch of hot checks?" Gabriela hugged her cup of coffee. The night had been long, but she was glad the entire family had rallied around Miguel.

Bryan, her brother-in-law, sighed. "Yes." He'd spent several hours at the precinct.

"But he couldn't have. Don't they have security camera footage in those electronics stores?"

"They do, and it shows a Hispanic man, about Miguel's height and age, entering the store."

"I know he didn't. He couldn't have." Gabriela sat down and rubbed her arms. "Besides, didn't the store realize it was someone else and not Miguel?"

"They have those electronic point-of-sale terminals where you sign the screen. They didn't bother to check the man's ID, or if they did, not very carefully." Bryan accepted the cup of coffee Mama offered him. "Thanks."

"I sure hope he didn't do it." Tommy frowned. "I know he's different, way different than he used to be. In a good way."

Gabriela dared not voice her thoughts. Liars could be convincing, and look you in the eye and tell you they had stock in Enron for sale. But if Miguel was telling the truth, and she knew he was—

"What if there is another Miguel Rivera? I mean, it's not a common name, but it wouldn't surprise me if another Miguel Rivera did this." Gabriela paced the room. "Can you find that man? Another Miguel Rivera with a record? And prints. Don't they check for prints in that store?"

Bryan smiled. "Yes, that's a distinct possibility. Prints take a while to confirm. A store has many surfaces touched by customers, and with the DA likely seeing this as an open-and-shut case, I doubt they'll agree to investigating too deeply."

"How much is bond?" Gabriela didn't care about her restaurant at this moment.

"M'ija, I already offered," Pop said. "Tomorrow morning he goes before the judge to be arraigned."

"It's wrong. It's wrong."

"Gabriela, sit down," Mama said. "You'll make yourself sick."

"And what will this do to his business reputation?" Gabriela sank onto the empty spot on the love seat. "This will be in the news."

"He can explain once he's exonerated," Bryan replied.

"Pop, I want to go with you in the morning."

"No, I need you to open La Cocina."

She opened her mouth to protest, but it was true. *Someone* needed to open tomorrow. Pop would keep his temper tomorrow, and she wasn't so sure about herself.

"You're right."

The family gathering wound down, and at last Gabriela retreated to her room.

Chapter 9

Miguel stared at the concrete wall. He'd forgotten how bad places like this smelled. Not that it was filthy, but the air in the cell felt heavy, like a thick blanket. He was lumped in with a bunch of other guys. Two of them kept cussing a blue streak until the warden threatened to throw them both in a solitary confinement room. Yeah, he'd been there once.

And he'd been guilty. He deserved what he'd gotten. Maybe he deserved this. Whatever the reason, he felt the old shame creeping back in like the scent of rotten egg.

This time, it was different. He had plenty of people outside who believed him. If only he'd called Gaby. To hear her voice, even if the news he brought wasn't good. He wished they'd let him keep his cell phone, so he could listen to her voice mail over and over again.

Calling her father, though, had made him face his fear. He didn't want the man to think he was hiding what had happened. Better to tell him straight out than let him hear about it in the news, or hear it from an upset Gaby.

Somehow the night that seemed to last a lifetime ended, and with the morning came a bottle of water and a breakfast sandwich. If only he had coffee, but that would be a luxury in here.

He hoped to see the judge early. But maybe he should hope to go later, depending on what Bryan, Gaby's brother-in-law, could help him with. This had to be a horrible, horrible mistake.

Trouble was, once you'd been on the wrong side of the law and branded as "bad," the system wouldn't listen to any protests.

Another eternity went by, and one by one the other occupants left the cell for their respective arraignments. Then it came down to him and one of the late-night cussers. The man sat on his bunk, glaring at the world, which at that moment included Miguel.

"Rivera," barked the warden. "Your *lawyer*'s here." The guy said the word as if he were referring to a dirty sock found in the corner.

He was handcuffed and escorted to an interrogation room, where Bryan Gillespie sat waiting for him.

Bryan gave him a confident smile. "Thanks to Gabriela, I think I've figured out your problem. If all goes well, you'll be out of here by lunchtime."

"You're optimistic." He wanted out, too, but he was a realist. But wait. . .*Gabriela* waited for him. She believed in him.

Bryan continued, "I read about a case like this once. It's truly a case of mistaken identity. You're Miguel Rivera, and

Miguel Rivera *did* write a bunch of hot checks. But it's not you. I'm thinking they need to do another check on the Miguel Rivera they hauled in."

"So you're saying since I'm the guy with the bigger rap sheet, they picked me first."

Bryan nodded. "Not only that. I think you're taller than the guy in that video. Plus, he looks older than you."

"You could tell?"

"I went to the electronics store to view the video. You're at least five-eleven. This guy was no more than five-eight at the most. If they'd taken a little more time, they would realize you're not the right Miguel Rivera."

Miguel grinned then suddenly realized one glaring fact. "I'm not expecting to make bail."

"I'm going to ask the judge to release you. You're not a flight risk, and once they realize their mistake, the charges will be dropped."

Before long Miguel was whisked before Judge Guzman. The clock above the judge's head read a few minutes past eleven thirty.

Miguel couldn't help but see the judge's black robe and feel as if judgment loomed ahead. But he wouldn't allow himself to think that way. He kept his head up. Bryan's presence beside him reminded him he had people on his side.

"Miguel Rivera," called the judge.

Miguel and Bryan rose.

"Your Honor," Bryan said, "I move that all charges against Mr. Rivera be dropped. With a little more attention to detail, I can show you that the wrong Miguel Rivera is in this court-room."

"Is that so?" asked Judge Guzman. Dark spectacles perched on the edge of his nose as he read the charges and evidence. "Explain. Because this isn't Mr. Rivera's first incidence of running against the law."

"You're correct." Bryan then explained, a hundred times better than Miguel could've, about the mistaken identity. "I also ask that he be released on his own recognizance pending the verification of everything I've said."

"Really?" Judge Guzman sighed.

Then an officer burst into the room. "Excuse me, Judge. I have some new information regarding the Rivera case."

❄

Gabriela stole a few seconds at the edge of La Cocina's patio and observed the sight she loved. The Riverwalk brimmed with tourists tonight, and a light wind moved the tree branches, making the strands of Christmas lights swing. A river taxi containing a small brass band drifted by, and strains of "Joy to the World" mingled with the laughter and chatter of those enjoying a night out on the river. After a long day on her feet, Gabriela wasn't sure if the merriment could drag her spirits up very much.

Then someone caught Gabriela's attention. A young woman with blond hair in a short choppy cut dashed past the restaurant. A tear glittered on her cheek.

Gabriela knew that feeling. Her heart ached for Miguel. Why hadn't she heard anything from him? Pop didn't say much when he came to work, other than it would be best for Miguel to explain himself.

A guy about her age soon passed, his stride determined, his jaw set. He had the look of someone frantically searching, the look of a man in love.

"Ecko, I love you!" he called out.

Gabriela hoped he found the one he was searching for. The mariachi band was going full throttle tonight and didn't match her mood at all. Feliz Navidad. Right.

I'm whining again, Lord, and I'm sorry. I need to trust You, and Miguel.

"Chef," a diner waved at her. "Might we speak to you for a moment?"

Gabriela turned away from the patio and approached the table. Tonight she hadn't been able to lose herself in the food as she usually did. Hopefully this tableside request didn't mean bad news. "Yes, of course."

"This is one of the finest meals we've had in San Antonio." An older, slightly balding gentleman and his wife sat across from each other, their plates empty. "We come to San Antonio several times a year, for business and pleasure, and haven't eaten here until tonight."

"Thank you very much."

The couple held hands across the table, and a lump lodged itself in Gabriela's throat. Love was everywhere tonight.

"I'll be recommending this establishment to a friend of mine who's a New York food critic. They're supposed to be doing a Texas restaurant tour, and I'll suggest this to them."

"Thank you again." Gabriela smiled. Pop would be proud. But a New York critic? The idea distracted her from Miguel for about five seconds. "I'll have your waitress bring by a dessert sampling plate, if you'd like. With our compliments."

"That would be lovely," said the wife. "Especially if you have anything chocolate."

"I think we can definitely do chocolate." She liked this lady. "I'll let your waitress know."

Where'd Marcy go off to? She thought Marcy had zoomed behind her a few seconds ago, so she headed toward the kitchen.

The kitchen aroma struck her again. Pop was in his zone, plating and barking orders, where she needed to be.

"Marcy?" she called out.

"Yes, Chef?" Marcy emerged from the linens room with a small stack of towels. "Sorry, I needed to get a few towels. A minor crisis at the Riverwalk."

The woman fairly glowed.

"What did I miss?"

"Oh, it's so romantic." Marcy beamed and dashed a tear away. "I need to run. I'll tell you soon. Love is in the air, Chef."

"If you say so." Gabriela cleared her throat. "Bring a dessert sampler to Seventeen. It's on the house, too."

"Will do." Marcy bundled the towels on one hip and pulled out her order pad. Then she looked over Gabriela's shoulder and froze.

Gabriela turned. There stood Miguel, his hair damp and unruly. Crazy man, he'd catch a cold.

"Miguel!" She threw her arms around him. "Why didn't you call? What happened? I was so worried." He smelled wonderful, and she didn't want to let him go.

His arms went around her. "I can explain."

Pop growled. "The kitchen's crowded. Go, get out of here." But his eyes sparkled, and he dashed the back of his arm against his eyes.

"We should listen to him." Miguel released her from his arms but still held her hand. "Let's go for a walk. Like Marcy said, love is in the air."

They passed through the dining room, and at the table closest to La Cocina's Riverwalk entrance, Gabriela saw the blond woman, no longer sad, seated next to the man who'd been calling for Ecko. He was soaked wet to the skin, but the grin on his face told Gabriela he didn't feel the cold one bit. The blond gently touched his face. Then her eyes locked with Gabriela's. She smiled a knowing smile then turned her gaze back to her man.

Once outside, Gabriela shivered, and Miguel slipped his arm around her and held her against his side. "Better?"

"Much. The cold felt good at first after being in that kitchen all day." She could get used to being by his side. In fact, it felt like a place she belonged.

"I told your dad I'd explain." Miguel paused at a stone bench tucked underneath a palm tree. They both sat down, and Gabriela leaned on him. "I meant to come earlier, but once I got home and showered, I thought I'd lie down for a few minutes. Next thing I knew, it was nighttime."

"I knew they had the wrong guy." She watched the lights dance in the trees. *Lord, if this is a dream, never let me wake up.*

"That's what Bryan found out. The other Miguel Rivera struck again, writing more bad checks. And that was the night of Las Posadas."

"So the police ran a check again, and hauled the other guy in."

"That's right."

Gabriela turned to face him. "Well, you're here now."

"Yes, I am." He kissed the top of her head. "Last night was the longest night of my life. But knowing you and your family were on my side, that I had the Lord, too—I hung on."

"I have to admit that when I went to your apartment and saw the police tape, and talked to your neighbor, I was a little frantic."

"Did you wonder if. . ."

Gabriela nodded, and looked down at her hands. "For a few seconds. Especially after seeing Santos. But then I made myself stop and think. You've come so far that you wouldn't do something like that. You're not that man anymore."

At that, Miguel stood and pulled Gabriela to her feet. "So what kind of man am I?"

His hands felt warm, holding hers. She realized for the first time her face was probably greasy and her hands stained from working with food. But the dizzying feeling she'd had that day when they were locked in the pantry came back.

"You're not street smart, but street wise. You know you're not perfect, and you know how to receive grace. You're a carpenter after the Carpenter's heart. And I never want to let you go, ever again." She bit her lip and looked into his eyes. "And. . ."

"And?" Miguel leaned closer.

"Call me shallow, but you have the most gorgeous hair." She touched the curls that barely ruffled in the breeze.

He pulled her close so their foreheads touched. "My love, I never want to let you go. I didn't plan this. I don't have a ring or anything. All I know is I love you, and I want to spend this Christmas with you, and every Christmas after this."

Gabriela's heart soared among the Christmas lights as she said, "Every Christmas, always. Feliz Navidad."

Just before he kissed her, Miguel replied, "Feliz Navidad."

LYNETTE SOWELL works as a medical transcriptionist for a large HMO. But that's her day job. In her "spare" time, she loves to spin adventures for the characters who emerge from story ideas in her head. She hopes to spread the truth of God's love and person while taking readers on an entertaining journey. Lynette is a Massachusetts transplant, who makes her home in central Texas. She loves to read, travel, spend time with her family, and likes to eat Mexican food whenever she can. You can find out more about Lynette on Facebook or www.lynettesowell.com

REMEMBER THE ALAMO

by Kathleen Y'Barbo

Dedication

To Beth, Lynettte, and Martha.
Viva San Antonio!

Chapter 1

"Nothing is impossible with God."

LUKE 1:37

*"Happiness often sneaks in through a
door you didn't know you left open."*

John Barrymore

Los Angeles, California

W hat do you mean we have no Davy Crockett?"
Sienna Montalvo held her breath and prayed
the executive producer of the most talked-about
film of the year would not call on her to answer the question.
While the prize role of the defender of the Alamo had gone
to John Wayne some fifty years ago, the role in the updated
version was not yet as strongly cast.

Or rather, it wasn't anymore.

This time Art Kelton's attention was squarely focused on Sienna. "Who told Brent Campbell the schedule gave him no time off for Christmas?"

All eyes turned toward Sienna as heat flamed her face. It was common knowledge that to work with Art Kelton meant to keep to a strict code of silence about everything related to his movies. When she signed the confidentiality agreement with the production company, she'd never expected those who must be kept in the dark would include the actors themselves.

"Anyone?"

This time, Mr. Kelton looked right at her.

"I—I—I might have mentioned it." She turned her attention to the pages on the conference table in front of her. Nowhere in the perfectionist producer's minute-by-minute agenda did she see this topic on the schedule.

Not that she could have read it if it were there. The words blurred as tears threatened.

After splitting the silence with a few choice words, Art Kelton drew in a deep breath and released it with gusto. "Why in the world would you tell an Academy Award–winning actor he would be required to work during the Christmas holidays?"

"He asked," was a poor defense, but Sienna lifted her gaze to meet his icy stare as she offered it.

"And you told him?" Mr. Kelton's busy gray brows rose. "Someone please explain to Miss. . ."

"Montalvo," she offered. "Sienna Montalvo. I'm your new—"

"Does it matter?" He peered over glasses that dangled

precariously at the end of his rather prominent nose.

"No," came out barely above a whisper.

"No," Mr. Kelton echoed. He made a great fuss of taking his seat at the head of the table then adjusting the stack of papers before him until they were exactly square with the edge of the table. Finally he leaned back against the chair and let his hands fall into his lap.

"Our new Production Assistant has obviously not been instructed on protocol on the set. Would someone educate her?" He shook his head. "No, let's say it together on three."

While the producer counted, Sienna braved a look across the table to Regina Barlow, the casting director who should be catching the heat on this debacle. Was that a sympathetic look she spied before the director looked away?

"Always ask Art," the group said in unison.

Sienna nodded. "Absolutely," she said.

"So when the talent comes to you, Miss. . ."

"Montalvo," Sienna said.

"Right. When the talent comes to you for information of any kind, except perhaps the whereabouts of the john, what will you tell them?"

"Ask Art?"

"Miss. . ."

This time Sienna didn't bother to help. Instead, she kept her mouth shut and her gaze intently focused on the Los Angeles skyline outside the window.

"Montalvo," the casting director offered.

"Miss *Montalvo*," the legendary producer said. "We are in the business of filming a remake of *The Alamo* that would make John Wayne proud. We are not filming an episode of

Jeopardy. Thus, there is no need to phrase your responses in the form of a question."

"Yes sir," Sienna managed as she made a vain attempt at not withering under his glare.

"Now shall we all put our heads together and see if we can't figure out how to undo the damage Miss Montalvo has done? Who here knows how we can get a box office draw who will work for peanuts during Christmas?"

A shaky hand went up at the far end of the table. "How much money are we talking, Art?"

"Take what we were going to pay Campbell and subtract what we've already spent on promoting the fact we had last year's big action hero playing next year's war hero." He shrugged. "Anything left goes to the next guy."

Sienna shrunk farther into her chair.

Mr. Kelton glanced at his Rolex and frowned then, to Sienna's relief, went on to the next item on his agenda. While the others debated the finer points of budgets and schedules, Sienna could only wonder why she'd ever thought herself worthy of taking a seat among them.

She kept a brave face throughout the rest of the meeting, only dissolving into tears when she returned to the tiny cubicle she called her first real Hollywood office. As she fell into her chair and swiveled to face the wall, it was all Sienna could do not to crumple up today's meeting agenda and throw it at her newly framed diploma.

"USC School of Cinematic Arts with honors," she grumbled under her breath as she reached into her desk. "What does it matter when I'll never live this down?"

"It got you in the door." Sienna whirled around to see

Regina Barlow leaning against the door frame, arms crossed. "Now that you're in, it's up to you not to get thrown out of the building."

A toss and the agenda landed in the trash. "I think it's too late for that," she said. "Between the short notice, the reduced salary, and the fact whoever takes this part will be on location during the holidays, I'd say it's an impossible task."

Regina pointed to the frame just below Sienna's diploma. It was a gift from her sister, who had hand-writtten in calligraphy, embellished with curlicues and glitz, the Montalvo family motto: *Nothing is impossible with God.*

With a half smile, Sienna shrugged. "Busted. It's just that I can't imagine how anyone would—" No need to say the rest. "I know," she added, "leave it to prayer."

"Exactly." The casting director grinned. "Though you're from San Antonio. If you happened to know some handsome Texas cowboy who could play a decent Davy Crockett and doesn't mind spending Christmas with a bunch of movie types, that would be great, too."

"Davy Crockett was from Tennessee."

Regina rolled her eyes. "You know what I mean, Sienna."

"Yes," Sienna said, "and I know the perfect man for the part, but he's the last person I'd recommend."

"And yet he was on the original short list for the film." Regina shrugged. "I assume you're thinking of Joe Ramirez."

Fresh hurt swept over her as she recalled the headlines the press had created in those dark days after their highly publicized breakup. The Ramirez Reject. No Mo Joe.

There were more, but she was blessedly unable to recall them now.

Sienna shook off the image of her face staring back from a half dozen gossip rags at the grocery checkout. Some days it felt like yesterday. "Don't you read the gossip columns, Regina?" she said. "He and I are old news."

"Last I heard he was still on the market and looking good as ever. You sure there's not something still simmering between you?"

She wasn't. "Yeah," Sienna said. "Sure as I'll ever be."

Regina shrugged. "Then you won't mind that I already recommended him for the part."

Chapter 2

Near Brackettville, Texas

Joe Ramirez reined in his horse and sat back in the saddle. Far as the eye could see lay God's handiwork, from the low scrub along the canyon walls to the lush green valley and the West Nueces River below. And above, though the sun beat down relentlessly now, tonight there would be a thousand stars and a moon bright enough to light the Texas night.

If The General were here, the two of them might have ridden off into the canyon like a pair of nineteenth-century cowboys and slept in bedrolls beside a campfire and told jokes until the first one gave up and started snoring. But it was October, and Dad was in his swim trunks trying to master the art of diving off Cayman Brac while Mom read a novel under an umbrella on the beach in front of their condo. Or at least that's what the plans were when Joe talked to The General over Skype last night.

He thought of his soldier father, a man so intimidating

even his wife called him The General. And yet also a man who loved the Lord and had passed that on to his only child. As relentless in retirement as he had been during his globe-trotting military career, Hector Ramirez was now commanding an army of one—his wife—and on occasion, Joe.

Reaching into the saddlebag, Joe snatched up his mp3 player. Loaded with a month's worth of Spanish lessons, he had figured to catch up on the research his agent assured him was necessary to play next year's part of a lifetime. The great irony in being cast as the explorer Hernando Cortez was that, although his family tree had roots in both Spain and Mexico, thanks to his own rootless existence as an army brat, he spoke not a word of Spanish beyond what was required to order a decent meal at the local taqueria.

The idea of learning while he rode had some appeal, until Joe gave it a try and failed miserably at the endeavor. Instead, he turned his mare toward the latest place he called home, a rock and timber structure perched on the side of a canyon. According to local legend—and his agent, Gabe Chandler, who'd arranged the rental—the home was built to house some of the movie folk who gathered to film *The Alamo* back in the 50s.

Alice, the woman who came to clean and bring groceries every Monday, could tick off a list longer than her arm of all the stars whose dirty socks and soiled coffee cups she'd washed while visiting this place. Though Joe wasn't sure he believed the tales, he did choose the north-facing bedroom at the far end of the house because Alice swore that was his hero John Wayne's favorite.

Leaving his boots on the back porch, Joe poured a glass of

sweet tea—another of Alice's specialties—and found a shady spot on the deck to return to his studies. When his phone rang, Joe spied the name of his agent on the caller ID and answered it with a hearty, "*Bueno*."

"Very funny, kid," Gabe Chandler said. "Guess that means you're taking these Spanish lessons seriously."

"I am." Joe lifted the glass of tea and took a long drink then set the glass back on the table. "So what's new, Gabe?"

A long pause. "Understand I'm passing this on only as a favor to a friend." Another pause. "Kelton's looking for an actor on short notice. Money's lousy, and Kelton's demanding his actors work Christmas. And you know he's always got some crazy initiation stunt he pulls on them before the talent starts work. Last time it was a ropes course. Can you feature it, Joe? A bunch of Hollywood millionaires swinging through the Costa Rican jungle like Tarzan."

"Wait," Joe said. "Kelton? *The* Kelton? Tell me the terms again."

"Lousy money, work Christmas, crazy director."

Joe sat up a little straighter. He had plenty of money, and with parents who were less likely each year to land in a place where he could join them, the idea of Christmas on a movie set beat any other plans he might have.

And as for crazy, he lived in Hollywood. Out there crazy was relative. And a ropes course through the jungle sounded like a grand time.

"Tell me more. What's it about? Can you get me a copy of the script?"

"You know I'm sworn to secrecy, Joe. I can't give you any details until you sign the agreement. I'm not even supposed to know them myself. Thank goodness Art's craziness extends to my wife's lasagna. We had him over to dinner last night, and he spilled his guts. Not literally, of course, but he did let me in on a problem he's got—other than indigestion, which is a nasty thing at his age."

"Focus, Gabe."

"Yes, well, you weren't there. The man was positively belching up his—"

"Gabe, really."

"All right. He said his casting director put you at the top of the short list. I told him I might have an opening for you to do this. Emphasis on *might*."

"He wants me to sign on for the movie but won't show me the script?"

"Yep. That's standard procedure for an Art Kelton film these days." Gabe paused. "Everyone is sworn to secrecy until the movie's in the can."

Joe chuckled in disbelief. "With all due respect, Gabe, how can anyone, even the great Art Kelton, expect an actor to go into a movie blind? Just a few pages are all I need."

"Can't do that." Another long pause. "But I don't guess it would hurt if you figured it out."

Joe rose to peel off his shirt and use it to wipe the perspiration on his brow. "Let me get this straight. He told you? Because he likes your wife's lasagna?"

"Hey now, the wife makes a fabulous vegetable lasagna. Makes her pasta from scratch. Art, he's got a bit of a cholesterol problem and—"

"Gabe! Stick with me here. What's the movie about?"

"All right," his agent said. "Tell me where you're staying nowadays."

The attempt at sidetracking the conversation irritated Joe. Still, he figured not to rock the boat until he had the answers he needed. "You know where I'm staying. That place in Brackettville your buddy who worked on the original screen version of—" A thought dawned, and he put it together with a few stray rumors he'd heard pass between locals at the diner where he ate most of his breakfasts. "*The Alamo*. Kelton's remaking it."

"I can neither confirm nor deny this," was his agent's coy response.

"Which part?" Not that any of them would be bad.

"Joe, you know I can't—"

"All right," Joe interrupted, "but can I get a hint?"

His agent chuckled. "You still sleeping in that same bedroom you told me about?"

John Wayne.

Joe set the phone down and lifted his eyes heavenward. Forget next year's movie. This was the part of a lifetime, and only the Lord could have made this possible. He let out a whoop that sent the barn cat scurrying back under the deck.

"I take it that's a yes," Gabe said when Joe picked up the phone once more.

"Yes, that's a yes," Joe said. "When do I start, and how do I get a copy of the script?"

"Before you go saying yes for sure, there's one more thing you might need to know." He made Joe wait before continuing. "Kelton's got himself a new PA. Mentioned her by name at dinner, and let me tell you Kelton's not one to do that. This gal graduated first in her class at USC film school, and the talk is she's going to make one fine director or producer someday. He's thinking of offering her a mentorship, though right now she's got him madder than a hornet. The name sounded familiar, so I did a little research."

Joe only half listened. His mind was already tumbling forward to the day he'd get his hands on that script. "Is that so?" he offered when silence fell between them.

"You didn't hear a word I said, did you, Joey?"

Joey. The name still sent his mind tumbling back to the woman who'd insisted on calling him that since high school despite his protests to the contrary. An ornery gal, that one. Just one reason he'd been unable to forget her.

Another was the way it ended. Seven months and five days ago. Not that he was counting.

"Joe?"

He cleared his throat and shoved the thoughts back where they belonged. "You were telling me about the woman Kelton's thinking of mentoring. I'm guessing she's going to be on location. Are you warning me to keep away?" He paused. "Because you know I've mended my ways."

Ways that had cost him the only woman he ever loved, though to be fair their breakup was as much her fault as his. If Sienna hadn't given him an ultimatum, he might have gotten his stubborn up and chosen not to listen to his publicist.

As he thought about it, Joe cringed. The blame lay completely at his feet, which was why the publicist was gone and so was Joe's attitude—mostly.

His agent chuckled. "Considering past history, it's probably better you don't know ahead of time anyway."

"Yeah, Gabe, whatever. Just get me the script and make it official."

"Done," he said. "I'll overnight the script. Plan on being in

San Antonio the first week of November to seal the deal."

"San Antonio? What happened to Costa Rica and the ropes course?"

"Kelton'll be in town checking on progress at the location site. Makes more sense than having you fly out to LA, and this way you can see where the movie's going to be filmed."

A circling hawk caught Joe's attention, and he watched it swoop down out of sight into the canyon below. "Kelton's not renovating the original site here in Brackettville? I figured with his attention to detail that would be his plan."

"You're partly right," Gabe said. "Only the historians he hired to authenticate the original movie set suggested some changes, so he's building from scratch."

"From scratch?" Joe laughed. "As in creating a whole new Alamo?"

"That's the idea, kid. Now go celebrate, and I'll take care of the details."

Joe's first call was to The General, where he left a message. Then he went inside and poured another glass of sweet tea and reached for the remote. Thinking better of it, Joe snatched up the well-worn deck of playing cards and dealt a hand of solitaire.

"The life of a Hollywood star," he said as he turned over the first card. "King of hearts." He laughed. "Hardly, but I am going to be Davy Crockett, and that's almost as good."

And by the time Joe's boots landed at the front entrance of San Antonio's Hotel Valencia Riverwalk, Joe had his lines memorized. Most of them, anyway.

Gabe's last e-mail had indicated someone from the film crew would be picking him up in the morning to take him to the site, so Joe stowed his gear then turned on the television to check the football scores while he dealt a hand of solitaire. Somewhere between commercials, he fell asleep fully dressed and did not awaken until his phone alerted him to the impending arrival of the studio's limo.

He reached for the remote to shut off the television then rose to take a quick shower and shave. By the time room service brought breakfast, Joe had dressed and stepped into his boots. When the call came that the car had arrived, Joe grabbed his sunglasses and room key and then paused to give thanks one more time for the opportunity that had taken him—but not God—by surprise.

"Give me the good sense and grace to live up to the part." Joe reached for the doorknob. "And let me be a light that shines toward You."

The studio's car was waiting when he stepped out into the unseasonably warm November dawn. Though the sun shone over downtown San Antonio, the ache in his knee—a high school football injury that predicted weather more accurately than the weather service—told him rain was on the way.

Slipping on his shades, Joe moved toward the limo. Whatever the cause for this meeting, or rather, whatever type of initiation awaited him, Joe knew he could handle it. He climbed in and leaned back against the seat, closing his eyes.

"Good morning."

That voice. His heart jolted and his eyes flew open. It could only be—

Joe nearly lost his sunglasses trying to get them off. The woman before him was sleek and well put together, a dark-haired beauty he'd more than once likened to dynamite in a tiny package. Her briefcase matched her boots and her eyes—all deep coffee-colored brown.

He swallowed hard. "Sienna?"

Her lips turned up in a slow smile. Without pausing, she reached her hand toward his. "Welcome to San Antonio, Joey."

Chapter 3

A full week of practice still had not prepared her for this moment.

Sienna called upon her limited training as a high school drama club actress to keep her breathing even and measured and her tone light and unaffected by the man sitting so close their knees almost touched. The fact he looked as flustered as she felt gave Sienna enough courage to offer a smile even as she wished to rub her palms against her jeans to rid herself of the feel of his touch.

Joe appeared to be completely unaffected by her presence, or at least he showed nothing of any feelings to the contrary. Sienna leaned back against the soft leather of the limo's backward-facing seat and tried not to take offense. Of course the man who broke her heart would move on and feel little or nothing for her.

Why had she expected anything different?

"Your hair's longer," the object of her thoughts said. "Still wearing it up, though."

That's it? Seven months and eight days of total silence, of headlines proclaiming her Joey's reject, and the best Joe Ramirez could manage was a comment about the length of her hair?

Sienna resisted the urge to tug at her ponytail and instead let out a long breath as she watched Joe put his dark shades back in place. The better to hide his emotions, she decided. For anything Joe Ramirez felt was easily discernable in those caramel-colored eyes.

"Yes, well, I trust you've settled in comfortably at the Valencia." Too formal and yet the only thing she could think to say.

"Do you now?" His grin was slow, familiar. She had to look away. "Not sure how you did it, but I'm glad you found me."

On this she couldn't help but stare. Did the man actually think she had gone hunting for him?

"Actually you've got Regina in casting to thank for that," Sienna said.

He seemed confused by her statement then shook it off and leaned forward to place his palms over her hands. "I should have expected you'd have connections. Makes sense you'd use them to locate me." Before she could respond, Joey slid across the gap between them to settle himself beside her. As he stretched out, he also had the audacity to reach behind her to gather her close. "So, all's forgiven."

Forgiven? She leaned away and focused on his face. Slowly the shades came down and his gaze collided with hers. While she felt the impact down to her toes, Sienna did her best to keep her expression neutral.

Joe reached to trace the line of her jaw with his finger. "You don't know how many times I wanted to call you," he said as her heart softened.

"And yet you didn't." *For seven months and eight days.*

She felt his hand brush her shoulder then slide down her arm in a loose embrace. "I was an idiot," he said in a hoarse whisper.

Ignoring the butterflies in her stomach, Sienna swallowed hard and managed to say, "Well that's true."

His chuckle grazed her ears a second before his arm drew her close. "Did you arrange this?"

Had the man lost his mind? Did it matter who recommended him for the stupid part? She almost laid the blame on the casting director, but allowing him to think she might have had something to do with it just a moment longer was far too much fun.

"You can blame the casting director," she repeated.

Joey leaned back against the seat and shook his head. "Well, you're here now, and we can pick up where we left off."

"Pick up where we left off?" Sienna frowned. "Joey, I don't have any idea what you're talking about. We're both here for the same reason, and it has nothing to do with the fact you walked out on me seven months ago."

"Seven months and eight days," he said as he lifted a dark brow. "And it was *you* who ended things."

Her breath caught, preventing Sienna from the sharp comment on the tip of her tongue. "When you chose her over me—" That's all she could manage for she refused to cry in front of Joey.

"Sienna, honey, you know that's not completely true."

And it wasn't, though she'd rather not admit it. Joey Ramirez had been perfectly happy to continue their relationship as if he hadn't broken her heart by allowing the press to believe he'd left her for his costar. That he'd tried to convince her it was "just business" made things even worse.

So, technically, when Sienna put her foot down and decided there would only be one woman in Joey's life, she'd set in motion the series of events that caused the demise of their romance.

"Joey, *honey*," Sienna said as she inched backward until her shoulders touched the door. "You know that's not how it happened. If you'd decided not to take that publicist's advice and make people think—"

"Why are we talking about this?" He grabbed for his shades and fitted them back in place. "You're in the business. Don't pretend you don't know how things work. I was doing what was best for both of us."

Anger and surprise blended to render Sienna speechless. When she could manage it, she shook her head. "Are you seriously going to try to continue to defend your choice to allow the press to believe you were carrying on with your costar while we were in a committed relationship?"

There it was. The question she'd never asked, though it had crawled around inside her heart for seven months and eight days.

His sigh was long and audible. "Sienna, honey—"

"Don't." She reached over to rap her knuckles on the glass that separated them from the driver. When there was no immediate response from up front, she knocked again.

"Look," Joey said as he once again removed his sunglasses. "How did we get off track? All that matters is that you're back." He closed the distance between them. "*We're* back."

And then he kissed her.

✳

Sienna was back.

This tugged at the edges of his mind even as his lips found hers. All the stupid, prideful things he'd done and all the words he'd left unsaid were gone. Forgiven. All the nasty headlines in the gossip mags forgotten.

And even though she seemed determined to make him suffer a little more before she completely forgave him, Sienna was back.

The whir of the glass moving behind him caused Joe to cut short what might have been a much longer kiss. No sense allowing any part of this reunion to be played out on a public stage.

This time around it was him and Sienna. No one else. No more listening to bad advice from his publicists or making decisions based on what would get him his next film then claiming he was thinking of the both of them.

"Fresh start, babe. This time we're fifty-fifty," Joe whispered against her ear as he righted himself. "We come first. Everything else second."

He only had a moment to notice the stunned expression Sienna wore before he turned to face the driver. Indeed, he'd felt it, too. Just like no time and bad feelings had come between them.

"Thought someone knocked." The driver winked at Joe.

"Looks like you got everything under control back here though." When Joe made it clear he did not see the humor in the man's remark, the guy had the decency to turn around. "Couple minutes and we'll be on our way," he said as he gripped the wheel, his knuckles white. "Just waiting for Mr. Kelton."

Joe said nothing, nor did he blink.

"Right," the driver continued. "I'll just close the glass now unless there's anything else I can do for you," he said as he peered at Joe through the rearview mirror.

"We're fine," Joe said then beamed at the double meaning.

We're fine.

And until Art Kelton arrived, they were free to repeat that kiss. He reached for Sienna to do just that, and she slipped under his arm to land on the seat across from him.

Chapter 4

"Oh, I see," he said with a grin. "Is that how you're going to be? Well, I suppose you've earned a little hard-to-get. Just remember, though. *You* came after *me*."

Sienna scrubbed at her lips with the back of her hand and narrowed her eyes, giving him a look that would stop a sane man in his tracks. But she was his again, and that fact alone meant sanity was tossed out the window in favor of more happiness than he'd expected he could feel.

Thank You, Lord. You heard my prayers. Sienna is back.

"Never assume what you just did was okay. Do you understand, Joe Ramirez?"

"I'm sorry." He leaned back and pretended to get comfortable then, a second later, dove across the aisle to land beside Sienna. This time she held him at arm's length. "Stop it this instant."

He froze. Where was the Sienna who'd tracked him

down, shown up in his limo, and practically begged him to come back? Well maybe not begged, but she did go to a lot of effort to land across from him in a studio car.

Joe decided to take a softer approach. "Come on, honey," he said as he reached for her hand then watched her move farther out of reach. While he understood her need to make him crawl just a bit, there would be time for that later. "It's been seven months. I know we can't catch up in one day, but can't a guy at least get one more quick kiss before you have to leave? Then we can talk about who did what."

She crossed her arms in front of her and glared. "I'm not going anywhere."

And neither was his bid to settle this before Art Kelton arrived, for the man was now heading toward them. When the producer paused to take a call, Joe returned his attention to Sienna.

"Look, we really need to talk about this, but here and now's not the time or the place." He reached for the doorknob on the opposite side from where Kelton would be entering the vehicle and gave it a tug. "Let's continue this over dinner tonight. You obviously know where I'm staying. I can meet you in the lobby or pick you up. Are you at your dad's house?"

Sienna didn't move a muscle, and yet Joe had no question about how she felt. "Look," she said with more than a little disdain, "my name may not be on the marquee, but I'm just as important to this film as you, Joe Ramirez."

"Wait." Joe moved back to a spot across from Sienna. Only then did he recall the love of his life had arrived in his limo with a briefcase, which now rested at her feet. Two and two became four as he began to logic out a scenario he hoped was dead wrong.

"Why are you here, Sienna?"

Her eyes narrowed. "I'm working just like you."

"You mean you didn't track me down and hide out in my limo so you could convince me to get back together with you?"

Her laugh held no trace of humor. "Why would I want to do that?"

Because I love you refused to come out. *Because you forgave me* sounded so pitiful he refused to say it.

So he just stared. And then the door opened, and Art Kelton climbed inside.

"Looks like the gang's all here." Kelton gestured to the door Joe had opened. "You bailing on me already, son?"

Giving the handle a yank, Joe slammed the door then looked past the producer to Sienna Montalvo. "I wouldn't think of it, Mr. Kelton."

"Good." He nodded toward Sienna. "Have you met Miss Montalvo?"

"We're acquainted," Joe said. "Known each other for years, actually."

Sienna remained silent.

If he noticed the tension between them, the producer gave no indication. "Excellent," he said as he tapped on the glass and waited until it slid down. "Get this heap in motion. The morning's half gone, and I've got a movie to make." Kelton turned his attention to Joe. "You're the talent so you get a pass right now. Don't make any plans for the rest of the day, though. And I'll need your cell phone."

"But what if I. . ."

When he paused, Kelton frowned at Sienna. "Get Regina on the phone. Looks like she's sent me talent who doesn't want to play by Art's rules."

Joe suppressed a sigh and handed over his cell. "Anything else?"

"That'll do it unless you've got any other contraband on you."

This must be the initiation. "Contraband?" Joe asked. "What would that be?"

The producer gave Joe a cursory glance over the top of his glasses. "GPS, portable televisions, or any food or plant items?"

Joe shrugged. "Nope."

"All right then. You," he said to Sienna, "get ready to take some notes."

As the limo blended into drive-time traffic, Joe studied Sienna from behind his shades. Before they reached the freeway, she was on her second page of hand-written notes and had reached down to retrieve her phone from her briefcase.

Kelton was legendary for his schedules, and Sienna seemed to be the person currently charged with keeping the movie on track. When she finished entering details on her phone's calendar, she tucked it back into her briefcase.

All of this activity kept her from speaking to Joe or even acknowledging his existence, for that matter. It also gave Joe time to study her.

Of all the stupid decisions he'd made, listening to Gabe and his publicist had been the stupidest of them all. The woman who'd come between him and Sienna was long gone, enjoying a decent acting career after being seen with the likes of him on the red carpet and in several dozen staged and regrettable paparazzi photographs.

But the woman he truly wanted to walk that red carpet with—and any other carpet—was right here. And all he could do was make stupid assumptions and kiss her when she obviously did not want him to.

Though to be fair, she did not protest until *after* the kiss, which told Joe she might not have minded it as much as she let on. He'd certainly not make that mistake again, however.

No kissing Sienna Montalvo until she was good and ready.

Another glance and he caught her staring. From the look on her face, he'd have a long wait before he was invited close enough to kiss her.

Crossing his arms over his chest, Joe made himself comfortable. When the limo lurched to a halt, he roused himself from a light sleep and prepared to greet the sun.

Instead, he found it had begun to rain.

Looking down at the snakeskin boots he'd worn for the occasion, Joe prayed he would not be following Art Kelton and his assistant out into the drizzle. And yet the moment he hesitated, Kelton shouted his name and out he went.

Mud ran in brown rivers on either side of the wooden planks that formed the makeshift sidewalk leading to the back of the set. Sienna held the umbrella with one hand while the briefcase dangled from the opposite shoulder. Kelton strode ahead as if he were immune to weather of any sort.

"Ramirez, follow me," he called just before disappearing into the gap between two large piles of what appeared to be tarp-covered lumber. And then he bellowed, "Miss Montalvo, front and center. Now."

Chapter 5

Caring whether his favorite pair of boots got ruined came second to looking like a rookie on Kelton's film set, so Joe squared his shoulders and lengthened his stride. When he emerged on the other side of the lumber, he found Kelton waiting for him.

And so was a replica of the Alamo, so startling in its attention to detail that it took Joe's breath away. He ignored the mud and the wacky producer to get a closer look.

It took two tries to get past the collection of rocks and debris that blocked the path to the gates, but he managed it, though he'd most certainly ruined the suit he'd bought for the meeting. He ran his hands over the limestone and grinned.

Looking up at the edifice, a chill rose. If he closed his eyes, Joe could almost hear the sound of McGregor's bagpipe as he entertained those mustered behind the walls, could nearly smell the powder as it was loaded into the muskets while the invading army marched toward them.

Joe only opened his eyes when the sound of applause reached him. There he found Art Kelton staring at him with great interest, and so was Sienna.

"Bravo, Crockett," Kelton said. "You saw it, didn't you? That's exactly what I expected of a defender of the Alamo." He gestured to the eastern end of the clearing. "You'll find appropriate clothes over there. Go change." The producer strode away, and Sienna and her umbrella followed a step behind.

Joe watched them disappear behind the set then turned to spot what appeared to be a hunter's shack a few hundred yards away. With rainwater sliding down his spine and weighing down his boots, he gladly headed in that direction. With every step his thoughts churned.

Sienna was back. And yet she really wasn't—not yet.

The waterworks stopped at the porch then took up again where a hole in the roof allowed the rain to pour into an overflowing rusty bucket. Joe sloshed past to yank open the door.

Expecting some sort of production office, he found the shack—and it truly was a shack—had likely not been used since last year's hunting season. The production company's use of the land seemed to have kept anyone from stepping inside for some time. The woodstove had collected more dust than firewood, and the gun rack was empty of any weapons, though the trio of deer heads attested to the fact someone had done some shooting. A table leaned precariously to the right, two of its legs seemingly having fallen down through an unstable floorboard.

In the opposite corner, an iron bed frame had been

stripped of its mattress, and a set of clothes had been placed across the springs. Joe recognized the shirt and trousers as an exact replica of the clothes used in the previous Alamo movie. And the coonskin cap was unmistakable.

Gabe must have sent ahead his measurements because the costume fit him perfectly, right down to the leather workman's boots. While they weren't anything to compare with the custom snakeskin pair he'd worn for the last time, this pair would certainly withstand a walk down a muddy road.

They were put to the test when Joe stepped onto the makeshift street and looked in both directions. The rain had slowed to something less than a decent drizzle, and there was no need for an umbrella—not that Davy Crockett would have carried one.

Still, owing to the fact the clothes were the property of the studio, Joe left the distinctive Crockett fur hat back in the shack. Eventually he'd have to wear it, but now was not the time.

And it wasn't just because of the rain. Outside of participating in an actual movie scene, he felt like a fool wearing the back end of a stuffed coon on his head.

Joe got three steps away from the porch then stopped in his tracks. If rumors were true, Kelton could very well send him packing for not following directions. And the directions were to put on the costume.

Including the coonskin cap.

Suppressing the urge to mutter under his breath, Joe stormed back into the shack and jerked up the hat then stepped out onto the porch. Neither Sienna nor Art Kelton were anywhere to be found, so Joe headed off toward the last place he'd seen them.

At least the rain had stopped, though the promise of more hung heavy in the clouds. His boots hit the sidewalk, and he picked up his pace. Joe emerged onto the other side of the set just in time to watch the limo speed away.

❊

The temptation to let Joey believe he was alone kept Sienna from speaking up immediately. Instead she watched him stare off in the direction of where the limo had gone, his back straight and his shoulders broad.

From her spot beneath the tarp protecting the pile of lumber, Sienna couldn't see his face, but there was no doubt the former man of her dreams had realized the nightmare situation he was now in.

Mr. Kelton might not see the experience as that, but to Sienna it was nothing more than glorified hazing. Which is why, despite her better judgment, she asked that she be left on set should anything go awry.

The other actors had one another, she'd argued. Leaving Joey out here alone was a plan fraught with more dangerous endings than any writer or insurance carrier could craft.

Better she finally convinced the producer to leave the talent to suffer under her temporary supervision than to wander about the set until such a time as the limo returned.

And it always returned. For though Mr. Kelton was an odd man, he was not stupid. He might put his players through their paces, but the ultimate goal was to come in under budget and worthy of winning not only the box office draw but also awards.

It was a goal Art Kelton always achieved.

Someday Sienna hoped to do the same. But for now, she was a lowly PA on a Kelton film who was assigned to keep tabs on the talent. Talent who had stormed past her without bothering to look up and see her.

Oh but she saw him. What was it about Joey Ramirez that set her heart fluttering, even when he was wearing a slightly soggy coonskin cap? She touched her lips and thought about the misunderstanding in the limo. How many times had she considered chasing the fool man down and demanding he give their love another chance?

Exactly twice—once on her birthday, which truly didn't count as it was one of those dumb milestone years, and again when Regina informed her Joey was their new John Wayne—was the truthful answer, and neither time did she allow herself the humiliation.

She was fine. Would be fine, Sienna corrected, once she got Joey Ramirez out of her heart. And the only way to do that was to be as professional as possible. Starting with forgetting what happened in the limo and moving forward as coworkers on a movie set.

"Going somewhere?" she called.

Chapter 6

S ienna? Is that you?" Joey's boot heels rang out on the
sidewalk as he came barging back through the opening
where, once filming began, Santa Ana's troops would
do the same. And likely be wearing the same expression.

"It's me." She took a deep breath and steeled her courage even as she renewed her resolve to guard her heart. "Up
here."

He turned her direction. "What are you doing up there?
And where's the car?"

"It's dry up here." Sienna gestured to the tarp. "And the
car's taking Mr. Kelton back into town."

Joey appeared to be sizing up the situation. Time to head
off any further misunderstandings between them.

"So we're alone?" Joey asked before she could speak, his
expression unreadable.

"For now." Sienna looked past him to where the sky had
begun to darken again. "Before you start thinking I had

something to do with this, I didn't. Leaving the talent on set is part of Mr. Kelton's plan to acquaint them with their characters. The rest of the actors were subject to the same thing."

"That explains why I'm here." He easily joined her atop the lumber. "But why are you here?"

Several answers came to mind. "I felt sorry for you having to be here alone. The others were left in a group," was the most neutral of them.

Stretching his legs out in front of him, Joey shrugged. "Thanks but I don't need your sympathy."

Well that did it. "I see." She rose to her knees and yanked the briefcase from beneath the tarp. Upending it, Sienna found the package and thrust it at Joey. "Here's your homework, then. Study it. There will be a test."

Scrambling off the lumber, Sienna pulled the briefcase after her then adjusted her pride before storming away. *I'll just call the driver and tell him I need to be picked up immediately after he delivers Mr. Kelton.*

"Walking back to town?" Joey called, though he made no move to follow.

"I just might," she said as she picked her way around the muddy puddles to reach the gravel road. "And Mr. Kelton's serious about that test. Expect him to quiz you on the way back to the hotel."

"When's that going to be?" he called.

Sienna ignored him to keep walking, though the loose gravel that had been poured as a parking spot for the contractors' trucks made for slow going. With each step her certainty that her prayers had led her to this place waned. In its place was a huge question that began with, "Lord, what in the world am I doing here?"

"Sienna, wait," Joey said as his footsteps crunched on the gravel.

She picked up her pace and paid for the decision by losing her footing. The hand that caught her released her just as quickly.

"Be careful," Joey said when she turned to look at him. "Your boots aren't made for walking."

"Neither are yours." She gave him a cursory glance. "Wardrobe will have half your salary if you ruin any of that. I suggest you get out of the weather before you have to write the studio a check."

His chuckle was a low rumble. "Honey, I didn't take this gig for the money," he said. "And likely you didn't, either."

Her traitorous heart jolted. Despite his behavior in the limo, had he known she was working this film? Was that his reason for taking the part?

She braved a look at his face. "Then why?" Sienna dared ask even as she hoped she knew the answer.

A shrug was his quick response. "Who wouldn't want to work with Art Kelton? And you know what a John Wayne fan I am."

Of course. It had nothing to do with her. "Well then," she said with her best professional tone, "you've got some work to do there. Study hard, Mr. Wayne, so you can be prepared when the troops return. Or should I say, Mr. Crockett?"

"You're really leaving?"

"My job here is done." Sienna reached to shake his hand then took a step back and pulled the folding umbrella out of her briefcase to open it. "Good luck, Joey. I'll see you at the round table reading at the end of the month."

Sienna set out walking, this time taking care not to slide about as she reached into her pocket for her cell phone. The last thing she needed was for Joey to rescue her again.

"End of the month?" he said. "But—"

She paused to glance over her shoulder. There he stood in all his nineteenth-century frontiersman glory, a coonskin cap on his head and a studio packet under his arm.

"But what?" Sienna said.

He appeared to want to say something. Perhaps to ask her to stay. And then he held out the packet. "Thanks."

Thanks?

She took a deep breath and let it out slowly. "You're welcome, Joey," she called as she reached the dirt road and turned toward the highway some three miles east.

"Are you really walking?" trailed after her.

Sienna's response was to hold up her cell phone. "Calling the driver to tell him to hurry back." Only when she punched in the numbers to call the driver to return for her did she realize her phone had no service.

Three tries and another quarter-mile down the road, Sienna slowed her frantic pace. The terrain here was flat, but still she hoped she might come upon some higher elevation that would allow her to make the call. Instead, the only things that seemed to be elevating were her irritation and her blood pressure.

So Sienna continued to walk, her right arm in the air and her attention equally divided between the uneven ground under her feet and the bars—or lack of them—on her phone.

With every step came a prayer that the Lord, who had no such issues with lack of service, would hear her and come to the rescue.

Up ahead the dark clouds were gathering, and there was no mistaking she'd be walking into a rainstorm if she continued in that direction. The wind had already picked up, and the slow sprinkling of raindrops had turned into a drizzle. Soon the drizzle would be a downpour.

Sienna paused to gauge how far she'd walked. *Not nearly far enough.*

San Antonio was thirty minutes away by car and an eternity away on foot. At some point she might find a Good Samaritan to rescue her, but the old saying about speaking to strangers would surely prevent her from climbing into a vehicle with one of them.

And so Sienna was left with two choices: keep walking and take her chances or turn around and find shelter on the movie set.

"Lord, not my will but Yours. And I *know* Yours is to get me out of here."

Once again she punched the numbers for the car, and again the call refused to complete. Resisting the urge to throw the gadget hard as she could at the nearest rock, she decided to take it apart and put it back together.

Sienna juggled her umbrella to tuck the handle between her chin and shoulder then turned the phone over to remove the battery. Counting to twenty, she put it all back together. When the display came alive, she said one last quick prayer before hitting redial.

Nothing.

"This absolutely *cannot* be happening." She stabbed the button again.

Still nothing.

While she stared at the display, a gust of wind blew past and tore the umbrella away from her. Scrambling to stuff the phone into the briefcase dangling from her shoulder, Sienna did her best to give chase, though the umbrella bounced end over end against rocks and cacti and the gnarled trunks of several mesquite trees before she snagged the handle.

Looking down at her mud-splattered jeans and soggy boots, Sienna's decision was made. Marching back to the Alamo had not been in her plans, but there simply was no alternative.

So she held the briefcase close against her side and grabbed tighter to the umbrella's now soggy handle as she slogged her way back down the once-dusty road. With each step the dark clouds seemed to close in until Sienna felt as if she might be swallowed up in the impending storm.

By the time Art Kelton's version of the Alamo came into view, she could have shouted for joy. She didn't however, for that might alert Joey to the fact she'd returned.

And that was the last thing she intended to do. As soon as the weather cleared and her cell phone found a tower, she intended to find her way back to San Antonio and forget this day ever happened.

Until then, however, Sienna could only pray that she'd make it inside the shack before the bottom fell out of the clouds that seemed to be following her.

Chapter 7

The tarp atop the pile of lumber flapped wildly in the breeze as Sienna passed by. It appeared the ramshackle building at the edge of the property would be the only dry place, so she made her way toward it. With each step she prayed Joey would not be waiting for her.

Had she a choice, Sienna might have taken her time arriving at the only solid roof within a half mile. Unfortunately, lightning zagged across the sky, and the drizzle became a torrent. With it the temperature began to drop noticeably.

Mud made the going slow, and the wind swooped beneath her umbrella to turn it inside out. She battled and won, but by the time the umbrella was back in place, she hardly had any use for it.

Reaching the porch was half the battle, though the gaps in the roof dumped rainwater on her as she raced past. Finally, Sienna reached the door and gave it a tug.

As she stepped inside, a match flamed, and Sienna turned

toward it. The flash blinded her for a moment, but the warm yellow light allowed her focus to return soon enough to see Joey blowing out the match.

"Thought you left." He gave the match a shake then tossed it into the sink as he sank onto one of the two stools nearby. "Change your mind?"

"Not exactly." Lightning crashed outside, and she squealed then immediately felt like an idiot. "As you can see, the weather's not exactly cooperating."

"So, you don't have a ride?" He shrugged. "I find it hard to believe no one in that interesting family of yours was willing to make the drive, rain or not."

It figured that topic would eventually be brought up. "Leave my family out of this."

When he snorted, Sienna debated the response she longed to give then thought better of it. Giving her umbrella a shake, she left it on the porch and stepped fully inside. The door swung closed but stopped a few inches shy of completing the process.

All the better, Sienna decided. If Joey didn't wipe the smug look off his face, she might need to make a quick exit. And with the door already partly open, she'd be that much ahead of the game.

While standing near the exit had some appeal, she wandered toward him as much to avoid the gray shadows that held who knows what sort of vermin as to find the only place in the shack where she could sit.

Joey gestured to the packet on the table in front of him. "Haven't opened this yet, but I'm guessing it's the script."

Sienna set her briefcase down then considered the

condition of the floor and snatched it back up to placed it on the table. "Not exactly." She removed her phone from her pocket and sat it atop her briefcase.

His eyes scanned the screen of her phone. "No service, I see."

When Joey lifted his gaze to meet her stare, Sienna nearly lost her balance. What was it about that man that made her want to throw caution and good sense to the wind and fall in love again? Even when she'd promised herself she wouldn't.

"So," Joey said, "I assume you're Kelton's right-hand man. Or rather woman." He paused and seemed amused with his cleverness.

"I'm his PA on this film," she said.

"One more chance to tell me the truth. Did you arrange this?"

"This as in what's happening right now or this as in you working on the same film with me?"

He lifted a dark brow. "Both." Before she could respond, he set her phone aside and hauled her briefcase toward him. "You don't have a weapon in here, do you? I know we didn't part on the best terms but—"

"I've told you the truth. I'm thrilled to be working with Mr. Kelton, and as for today, he did this with the other actors. You can check with them once everyone's on set together."

"Oh, I plan to." He paused. "Now about the fact you took sympathy on me. Sorry, but that seems a little coincidental, don't you think?"

Sienna made a grab for the briefcase, but he held it out of reach. "Don't be ridiculous, Joey. I've long since moved on."

Even as she spoke the words, she longed to truly believe them. Instead, Sienna thought of his embrace. Of his hurried kiss in the car. And of how good, for just that moment, being in his arms once again felt.

"Really?" He gave her a sideways look. "Who's the lucky guy?"

"None of your business." She gestured to the packet with the studio logo. "Open it."

With what appeared to be reluctance, Joey slid the briefcase back toward her. This time Sienna sat it on the floor heedless of what sort of insect or rodent might crawl up from the gaping hole nearby. She also discreetly pocketed her cell phone with a prayer it would somehow lock on to a signal once the weather improved.

The crinkle of paper caught Sienna's attention, as did Joey's laughter. "What is this?" he asked as he removed a box from the paper and opened it. "It looks like lunch."

Sienna shrugged. "The others only got a script. I figured you'd already have your part memorized by now. That's why I included the deck of cards. For playing solitaire."

"You know me well," he said then looked away.

An awkward silence fell between them, broken only by the sound of the awful weather now raging outside. Sienna rose and walked toward the door as Joey repacked the sandwich and chips into the box.

"I listened to the wrong people," he said. "But so did you, Sienna. I'm not nearly as awful as your father believes, and your sister never did like me."

"Papa was right," she said under her breath as she recalled his warning that choosing work over relationship was the way to a broken heart. What she'd never tell Joey was that her father was equally troubled by both of them and not just Joey.

"Maybe so, but your aunts always liked me. All but Vi. Or was it Consuela?"

Sienna turned to face him. "Look, Joey. It appears you and I are both stuck here. That doesn't mean I want to talk about old times." She returned to look out the door. "Or bad memories," she added. "So talk about the weather, the Spurs, or whatever else you can think of but I refuse to say another word about us." A pause. "Or to listen to any either. Understood?"

"Yeah," she heard him say as the thunder rolled past and shook more than just the door frame she was holding. "So honestly, what's the point of this?" He moved across the floor, heavy footsteps that ceased in a spot just behind her. "What do you suppose Kelton intends for me to get out of this?"

Swallowing hard, Sienna glanced over her shoulder. With the lamplight behind him, Joey's face was in shadows, his expression unreadable.

"His intention with the other actors was to build camaraderie and to give them an idea of what it would have been like to depend on one another."

His chuckle was soft, distinct. "Boot camp for Alamo defenders?"

"Something like that," she said. "He figured you should experience what the others had. I convinced him you probably deserved some company as no one else was forced to be alone."

"Cozy," he said, his tone neutral.

Irritation rose. "Actually, I had hoped to enlist someone else for the job. I think Mr. Kelton's still upset with me over the other Davy Crockett quitting."

A curt nod and Joey made his way back to the table and the circle of lamplight. "How long were the others left to fend for themselves?"

Sienna frowned. "Overnight."

"Overnight?" Joe shook his head. "You've got to be kidding."

"No," she said slowly, "I'm serious. However, the arrangement was for me to call the driver and have him come back for me as soon as I felt the least bit uncomfortable out here with you. Thus, your initiation into the defenders of the Alamo club might have been much shorter than the others."

"Because you were in a hurry to leave?"

"Yeah," she said as she sank carefully onto the nearest stool. "Guess that's not going to happen now."

Joe leaned back against the sink and crossed his arms over his chest. "Surely there's a default time for the car to return. In what, a few hours?"

"Honestly, I never really paid much attention to that part of the briefing."

Dark brows rose. "What do you mean?"

"I knew I'd be calling so I didn't—" She shrugged as she looked out the dust-covered windows to where the rain poured down in sheets. "What does it matter? Surely Mr. Kelton wouldn't leave us out here for long in this storm."

"That's brilliant logic, Sienna," Joey said. "Except for the fact there are at least two miles of dirt road between us and a highway. With this kind of rain, I guarantee that's nothing but mud now. How do you figure that limo's going to come back for us?"

A flash of lightning illuminated the shadows. "Slowly?" was her only response.

"Sienna." His voice was soft but firm. "Just one more time so I understand. You neither planned this nor expected to be abandoned here with me?"

"Of course not," she said quickly. "I'd have to be an idiot to want to. . ." Her voice trailed off when she took note of the disappointment on his face. "To break Mr. Kelton's rule."

Joey gave her a sideways look. "Which is?"

"No romance on the film set," she said.

"I see." He reached for the packet and pulled out the deck of cards. "Want to play gin rummy, or do I have to resort to solitaire?"

Chapter 8

B y the time the car returned—this time a four-wheel-drive Jeep station wagon—Joe had almost decided he could be friends with Sienna Montalvo. After all, he'd known her well before braces and acne cream had been replaced with scripts and movie openings.

And this acting thing was all her fault anyway.

Making the change from vagabond army brat to a kid with a house and a yard and, for the first time ever, a dog, hadn't been enough trauma for him. No, he'd gone and fallen in love, too.

With Sienna Montalvo, the pretty girl with the big smile and the plans to become a famous Hollywood director once she left San Antonio.

The General advised Joe to figure out what interested Sienna and find a way to get her attention through being part of that interest. He could still remember the look of surprise on his father's face when he came home to tell him the star of the Freshman Drama Club's fall production was Joe Ramirez.

"What's so funny?" Sienna nudged him with her elbow. "Still gloating about beating me at gin rummy?"

He swiveled to see the whole of her, and his smile broadened, though it had nothing to do with winning at card games. "Actually, I was thinking about Miss Harrison's drama class. Ninth grade, I believe it was."

Sienna laughed even as she shook her head. "Oh no, whatever for?"

"Oh, I don't know. Guess I was wondering how I got where I am today. Best I can recall, it began with that stupid class. Who would have thought I'd be making movies? Surely not Miss Harrison. I think she predicted more of a jailhouse scene for me. As in me ending up in jail or dead in a ditch somewhere."

"Oh please, Joey. You're a wonderful actor *despite* Miss Harrison. As I recall you spent almost as much time in detention because of your behavior in that class than you ever actually spent participating in the class."

"I did not." He laughed. "Every time I did something wrong, she put me up on the stage and made me recite something or act out a scene. That woman really didn't like me."

"You're probably right." When she reached to touch his sleeve, Joe resisted the urge to place his hand over hers. "Though you'd never know this to hear Miss Harrison speak of you now."

"Oh yeah?"

"Yeah." Sienna pushed a strand of ebony hair back and smiled. "Britny was elected president of the Thespian Society and is quite a little actress, if I do say so myself."

"Britny? Your sister's little girl? I know it's only been seven months since we. . ." He paused, jolted at the sudden reminder of their breakup. "That is, it surely hasn't been that long since I've seen her. Last Christmas she was still playing soccer with the boys, for goodness' sake."

"Oh she still plays soccer," Sienna said, "only now she plays on the freshman team. They took district in the girls' division this year." She paused. "But, oh, Joey, for all that she's good on the soccer field, she's simply *amazing* up on that stage. You should have seen her in *Fiddler on the Roof*. I cried, and I'm only the auntie."

"What does your sister think of this?"

Sienna shrugged. "You know how Dina is."

"So she's not thrilled that her daughter might get mixed up with those awful Hollywood types?"

"Joey." A warning attached to a name. "We're talking about Dina and Britny, not Dina and you."

He let out a long breath. "Yes, of course," Joe said. "Sorry. It's just that—"

"That my family hasn't exactly been welcoming of actors?" Sienna met his stare. "Trust me, Joey, it's just *you* they don't like."

"Comforting," he said as he noticed the twinkle in her eye. "But you're teasing me, Sienna. I like that, even though you know there is more than a little truth in what you're saying."

"I think you'd be surprised," Sienna said as the Jeep turned off the freeway and made its way down the ramp toward downtown. "Of all my family, I think Dina actually came closest to being your ally. Auntie Vi, Auntie Consuela, and Auntie Dolores, not so much, though they seemed to change their minds after that last movie of yours. And Papa? Well, let's not even talk about him."

Joe reached over to snag her wrist. "Let's do talk about your papa," he said softly.

Sienna swung her gaze to collide with his. "He was right, and that's all I intend to say about my father."

"Yeah, he was." He released her and sat back against the seat. "I'm sure he's glad his little girl's home."

"Actually I haven't been home yet. Mr. Kelton scheduled production meetings all day yesterday, and I knew we were leaving early this morning, so I stayed at the hotel."

Under the same roof as me.

Joe pushed away the thought and forced a grin. "Does your father know that?"

A smile touched the corners of her mouth. "He would not be pleased if he knew I was so close to his casa and didn't call," she said. "But I'm making up for it tonight."

"A Montalvo family fiesta?"

Joe had attended his share, and they were among his favorite memories. Nowhere had he felt so included as under the Montalvo roof, at least until news of their breakup. He briefly considered skipping his dinner with Art Kelton to crash the party and make a grand gesture of contrition to try and win back Sienna's heart.

Likely he'd have to get past her older sister Dina and the three aunties to even reach the door. And if he managed that, he'd be certain to find Mr. Montalvo on the porch cleaning his shotgun or sharpening his best hunting knife.

For a man of less than huge stature, Jorge Montalvo always made a big impression.

The car jolted to a halt in front of the Hotel Valencia, and Joe lost any opportunity to continue the conversation. As the door opened, he reached for Sienna one last time. Capturing her hand, Joe tried to make up his mind what to do next.

Other than grovel, which was what he'd truly wanted to do most of the afternoon.

"It's been an interesting day, Sienna." He released her to let his best acting skills carry him through the exit he planned. "I look forward to working with you."

Without looking back to see her expression, Joe grabbed his coonskin hat and what was left of his heart and climbed out of the Jeep only to trip over his own feet. By the time he regained his dignity and found his footing, the car and the woman he knew he'd never stopped loving were heading toward the highway.

✻

Sienna leaned back against the seat and groaned. Today had been a complete disaster. What happened to the scenario where she left him with his sandwich and cards and high-tailed it back to San Antonio? Had her cell phone worked, she might have been forced to spend an hour alone with Joey at most. Instead, the driver waited three hours to return.

"Why do You do all these things, Lord?" she whispered, thankful for the headphones in the driver's ears. *You know how I feel about Joey Ramirez. He broke my heart! Turned me into the Ramirez Reject!*

And yet she'd felt like anything but a reject today. From his first misunderstood attempt at a kiss to his admission that he'd wanted to make the first move toward reconciliation, he'd almost been the old Joey.

The man she loved.

Past tense.

Nothing is impossible with God.

"Joey Ramirez is impossible. Can't You do something about that, God? Please?"

Sienna let her complaint stew until the Jeep turned off the highway toward the neighborhood that had once been all she knew of the world. Before college, before the years of paying her dues and working her way up to becoming Art Kelton's PA, she had simply been her father's Sissy.

Every time Sienna spied the rambling frame cottage with the patch of grass and climbing roses in the front and the garage apartment out back, she felt ten years old again. A check of her watch told her that Papa's sisters, Auntie Vi, Auntie Consuela, and Auntie Dolores, would likely be competing with Papa to create whatever feast had been chosen for tonight's menu.

She leaned forward to reach for her briefcase and spied the wet lump of folded clothing on the floor. Joey had forgotten the clothes he'd worn this morning.

Tempted to tell the driver to turn around and head back to the Hotel Valencia, Sienna instead waited until the car pulled to a halt in front of her home to climb out and point to the ruined suit and soggy boots. "Mr. Ramirez has forgotten his clothes. Would you run them back to the hotel? Might be a good idea to have the valet send them to the hotel laundry rather than delivering them as they are now." She reached into her briefcase and wrote down an address. "Not sure if the boots can be salvaged, but I know a great place near the Mercado that might be willing to try."

As the Jeep departed, Sienna watched longingly. Choosing the chaos of a Montalvo family meal over a night in a fabulous hotel had seemed like a great idea at the time. But with the sound of a Spurs game drifting toward her through the remains of this afternoon's thunderstorm, Sienna was no longer sure of her decision. Then all three aunts and her niece poured out of the front door heedless of the rain.

"Where did he go?" Aunt Dolores called.

"Who?" Sienna called as she determined not to be disappointed that she wasn't getting the grand reception she'd hoped.

"Joe," Auntie Vi said. "That boy, he's our special guest tonight, no?"

Sienna shouldered her briefcase then reached for the handle of her rolling suitcase. "No," she said as she darted through the raindrops toward the porch. "I thought the three of you were mad at him."

"Let's not be unpleasant. Didn't you tell him I was making my special menudo tonight?" Aunt Consuela whined. "Every good boy whose mama raised him right loves a spicy bowl of menudo."

Auntie Vi added her opinion of Auntie Conseula's cooking skills in loud and emphatic Spanish while Britny merely rolled her eyes and stormed back inside. "Figures I'd come over to this loony bin for nothing," the teenager muttered.

Sienna pressed past the disappointed women and swiped her feet on the mat before stepping inside. There the salsa music blared, competing with a Spurs basketball game currently in overtime on Papa's giant flat-screen television.

Dina's husband, Ernie, waved from one end of the recliner sofa. Resplendent in Spurs gear from his hat to his flip-flops, he balanced a plate overflowing with the bounty of the aunties' cooking.

"Hey, Sissy," he called as she hauled her suitcase and her soggy self around his outstretched feet. "Could you grab me a soda and some of that *queso* while you're up? And throw a couple peppers on the side."

"What kind of welcome is that?" her sister Dina called from the kitchen. "Shame on you, Ernie!"

Sienna left her bags where she'd stopped and turned her back on her brother-in-law without comment. Around the corner in the kitchen, she found her sister Dina, older by a decade, standing at the counter with mascara running down her tear-stained face and landing in dark puddles on her glitzed and rhinestoned blouse.

"Dina!" Sienna rushed to her side. "What's happened?"

Her sister gestured with the knife in her hand while reaching past Sienna for a handful of tissue to dab at her eyes. "Onions, you goof."

"Oh." She began to laugh, and Dina joined her.

The chaos that was the trio of aunties who lived upstairs came rolling in along with a loud complaint from Ernie about missing someone's three-point shot. It all combined with the salsa music blaring on the radio in the windowsill to welcome Sienna home to her favorite place on earth.

And then the back door flew open and Papa stormed in, silencing the symphony of females without saying a word. He would have made a wonderful director, her papa, for never had she seen a man whose ability to control the entire room with a glance or a lift of his dark brow was so finely honed.

Papa said it came from his years in the Marine Corps. Sienna suspected he'd been born with it. If Mama weren't watching from heaven, she would likely have agreed.

"Where is he?" her father demanded as the crowd parted and Jorge Montalvo took center stage. He turned his attention and his open arms to Sienna. "Baby girl," he called as if welcoming her back from a hard day at kindergarten.

She flew into his embrace and rested against his shoulder. He smelled of Brylcreem and Brut, a heady combination that was distinctly her father.

"Welcome home, Sissy," he whispered against her ear before holding her at arm's length. "Now where is that man? That—" He paused as if to consider his words then dove into a less than flattering set of adjectives in Spanish.

"He's not here," Sienna said.

Papa surprised her by looking disappointed. "Then I suppose I can put away the shotgun I was cleaning on the back porch."

Only when Pap finally began to grin did Sienna decide her father had to be teasing. At least she hoped so.

Chapter 9

Between the music and the food and assembled crowd, Sienna not only lost track of where she'd put her phone, but she lost the thing altogether. By the time she found it wedged between the cushions of the sofa where she'd endured the Spurs' heartbreaking loss to the Rockets in overtime then later downed two slices of Auntie Dolores' *tres leches* cake, she'd missed four calls and was in danger of missing a fifth.

"Hello," she shouted over the sound of the video game blaring on the television.

"Miss Montalvo?" she thought she heard.

"Yes." Sienna climbed over the obstacle course of people and furniture to slip to the quietest spot she could find: the only bathroom in the house. "Yes this is Sienna. Who's speaking?"

"Art Kelton."

Sienna slammed the door and turned the lock. "Oh, I'm

so sorry, Mr. Kelton."

"Did I interrupt something? A street festival or riot of some sort?"

She sank onto the only horizontal surface in the room, the toilet seat. "No," she said. "That's just my family. They're a bit—" What was the word? "Boisterous."

Someone knocked. She ignored it.

"All right then," he said, "get ready to take some notes on tomorrow's agenda."

"Notes?" Panic slammed her as she opened the nearest drawer and began digging through its varied contents. "I, that is, well—"

Three toothbrushes, a handful of cotton balls, and a bottle of aspirin later, she found what had to be one of the aunties' red lip liner. "Go ahead," she managed as she cradled the phone between her ear and shoulder and rose to prepare to write on the bathroom mirror.

Another knock. Again Sienna ignored it as the producer barked instructions on the other end of the phone.

"Investor meeting. Got it," she repeated as the tip broke on the lip pencil. At the same moment, the knocking became an incessant banging. "I'm sorry." Sienna reached for the bar of Ivory soap on the edge of the sink and touched the corner to the mirror. "Did you say Mi Tierra?"

"Excellent restaurant, Miss Montalvo," Mr. Keller said, "but our chief investor prefers La Cocina del Rio. Do you know the place?"

"Yes, I know it. There's a nice roof patio with a view of the Riverwalk."

"Call them and book the patio then."

"Absolutely, sir. And just to be sure there's a private place should the weather not cooperate, I'll have Mr. Hernandez save us a nice section on the second floor in the back." A *thud*, much like the sound of a body slamming against the door caused Sienna to jump. "What time again?"

"Time to get out of the bathroom, Sissy," her brother-in-law shouted from the other side of the door. "Unless you want to be the one doing the mopping."

Sienna thought she heard laughter on the other end of the line, but the pounding on the door combined with the pounding of her heart prevented her from knowing for sure. She dropped the soap into the sink and stormed toward the door. Opening it to give her brother-in-law her sternest look.

Unfortunately, Ernie barreled past without meeting her stare just as a cheer went up from the video game competitors in the living room. The bathroom door slammed behind her, and Sienna dropped the phone. Scrambling after it, she managed to hear Mr. Kelton call her name.

"I'm here now," she said as loudly as she could.

"Forget it, Miss Montalvo," the producer said. "I'll send an e-mail."

As the line went dead, Sienna could only hope her career hadn't ended with that call. She'd missed half of what Mr. Kelton said, and who knows how much she'd misheard? *At least I have my notes.*

The door lurched open and, after locating pen and paper, Sienna slid back inside to transcribe the writing she'd left on the mirror.

Only the mirror had been wiped clean, the evidence of

which was smeared on the hand towel beside the sink.

"Don't thank me," Ernie called. "But you really left a mess in there, Sissy."

"No!" Sienna sank onto the side of the tub and sat the phone on the tile between her feet then buried her head in her hands. "I'm sunk."

Her phone jangled and clattered against the tile, indicating an e-mail had come through. She picked it up and clicked the icon to read Mr. Kelton's note.

I'm from a big family, too, so you're forgiven this one time. Enjoy your night off. Tomorrow you'll be working, so you'll stay at the hotel. The car will come for you at 4, so you can do whatever it is women do in order to get ready for an important dinner. Meet in lobby for dinner at 8:30.

Yes, sir. Thank you for understanding, she typed then paused when she head another e-mail come through.

Clicking over to her inbox, she saw Mr. Kelton had sent it. *I had wardrobe send over a few outfits for you to choose from. You'll find them in your room when you arrive tomorrow.*

Sienna breathed a sigh of relief. For now she had a reprieve, and not just because someone had finally turned off the television.

"Thank You, Lord," she whispered as she trudged back to the kitchen to join her family for coffee and conversation. "Your grace is beyond my understanding. Now if You could just do something about Joey Ramirez."

While the Lord seemed to be remaining silent on Joey, every member of her family managed to state an opinion on him and what she should do in regard to the man. The aunties were divided two against one with Vi and Consuela for taking him back and Dolores solidly against it. Dina wanted to catch him alone and explain to him in detail why he was no longer fit to lick the bottom of Sienna's shoe, and Ernie offered tips on how to win him back.

At the far end of the table, Papa sipped his coffee and kept silent. He was, however, listening to all the others and formulating his own opinion. Whether he might share it was anyone's guess.

"You know, Aunt Sissy," Britny said in her characteristically dramatic way, "you should be glad he still wants you. You're not getting any younger, and that last woman he dated was blond."

Well that did it.

Papa's coffee cup hit the saucer with enough strength to slosh the black liquid in a pool on the white tablecloth. All talking ceased.

"Sienna, may I see you outside?"

Though the request was phrased as a question, it was no question at all. Not when it came from Papa.

Sienna pushed back from the table and rose. Dina met her gaze and rolled her eyes then turned to Britny. "Come on, Miss Dating Expert. The dishes await. And while you're washing and drying, you can begin praying I will forget that you called my *younger* sister old."

The teenager's complaints of antique houses and no dishwashers followed Sienna outside, as did Dina's swift response for her to mind her words. *Mind your words.* How many times had Mama said that exact thing to Sienna? Almost as many times as she told Sienna to guard her heart.

Sadly she'd always had trouble doing both.

The old swing creaked as her father made himself comfortable. Sienna settled beside him and inhaled deeply of the rain-drenched earth. The night air held the promise of a chill, and she gathered her arms around her waist. Papa must have noticed, for he wrapped his arm around her to hold her close. Together they watched the first stars appear, their silence a comfortable language that spoke volumes.

Papa reached across the gap between them to grasp Sienna's hand. "Sissy girl, how many times have you and I sat like this?"

"Too many to count." She chuckled and squeezed his strong fingers.

He returned the gesture. "Now tell me what happened with the Ramirez boy."

Only her father would refer to an Academy Award nominee for supporting actor as "the Ramirez boy."

"Today?"

"No." Her father lifted a dark brow then shook his head. "You loved him."

"Yes," she said softly to cover her surprise, "I did."

"Maybe still do?" He only let the question hang between them for a second before waving away any expectation of an answer. "I know he and I have had our differences, but Joe, he seemed like a good man. Took good care of you. What happened? How did he become this man who broke your heart?"

Sienna blinked back sudden and surprising tears. "All the times we talked, you never asked."

"You're grown, Sissy, much as I hate to admit it. A father, he tries to respect that even when. . ." He squeezed her hand once more before crossing his arms over his chest. "But I'm asking you now."

"I guess it all came down to what was important to him, Papa." Sienna paused to collect her thoughts. "It all started with the premiere of his last movie. I guess I wasn't A-list enough for his agent and publicist." As she spoke the words, pain hit as if it had happened yesterday. "So he went with his costar as his date. I wasn't invited."

"Honey, I'm sorry," he said. "And I agree he used poor judgment. But that seems like a poor reason to leave the man you love." One dark brow rose with a silent question.

"I gave him an ultimatum. Her or me." Saying it aloud made her cringe. And yet so much had led up to that moment. Somewhere between San Antonio and Hollywood, she and Joey had made their careers a priority over their relationship. Work had become an excused absence for any occasion, special or not.

And until she saw the man she loved walking down the red carpet with a stranger, it hadn't bothered Sienna in the least.

Her father let out a long breath and leaned forward to rest his elbows on his knees. "So you feel he chose her."

He chose work. But then so did I.

"He *did* choose her," Sienna said, as much to convince Papa as to convince herself. "I told him if he took that woman to the premiere, we were through." She shrugged. "So what could I do?"

Again silence fell between them. Sienna blinked back tears as the disappointment welled up. Disappointment that was completely directed at herself.

"What you *could* have done no longer matters. Nothing is impossible with God." Papa gave Sienna a sideways look. "So the real question is, what will you do now?"

What will I do now?

Papa's question chased Sienna as she enjoyed the rest of her time with the family. He was a wise man, her father, and one not given to lecture. The aunties, however, had entertained her with suggestions that alternated between how to get even and how to get him back. Even Dina had weighed in, deciding that Joey deserved to suffer a bit, but he also needed to return to his place at the Thanksgiving table.

She'd ignored them all—politely of course—though Dina's comment about Thanksgiving had Sienna wondering how she would break the news that she would be missing another family holiday due to work. Much as she'd love to watch Papa carve the turkey and the aunties bustle about for days making three dozen side dishes and desserts, the production schedule and meetings just wouldn't allow for the time away.

At least she'd be home for Christmas.

Chapter 10

Already there were signs that Thanksgiving was just around the corner. Joe had promised to make a cameo in the Caymans for Mom's traditional turkey dinner and The General's advice, though the movie schedule would require him to fly back to Texas the next morning.

At least he'd be in San Antonio for Christmas. By then there would be a plan to fix what was broken between him and Sienna.

Joe stepped out of the car in front of La Cocina del Rio, signed autographs for a trio of tourists, then shrugged into his jacket and slid his phone into his pocket. As he'd done several times since yesterday, Joe punched in Sienna's phone number then looked up at the roof patio of the tri-level restaurant and hit CANCEL.

Even if she took his call—which she might, considering the cordial ending to their unusual day yesterday—what reason would he give for calling? The truth was Joe missed her every single day since he'd made his stupid mistake.

But even an idiot like him knew that wasn't something you tell a woman over the phone. Nor over a business meeting, though Joe decided if given the chance tonight, he'd surely try.

"Good evening, Mr. Ramirez," the hostess said. "Come this way. Most of your group has already arrived."

"Thank you, Miss. . ."

"Maria," she supplied as she led him toward the stairs.

When he emerged onto the rooftop deck, the sun was setting on the Riverwalk and sending threads of gold through Sienna's dark hair. She'd fashioned it into a severe knot at the nape of her neck that his fingers itched to release, and she wore a dress of deep emerald green that almost made him forget why he was there.

The rest of the crowd, the typical mix of business folk and artsy types, milled about or stood at the rail taking in the view while a quartet of mariachi added a soundtrack to the festivities. The river did look spectacular from this vantage point, but Joe only had eyes for Sienna.

"There's my star." Art Kelton grasped him by the shoulder and grinned. "I understand you and my assistant braved a downpour yesterday."

"We did, sir," he said. "Though I must commend Miss Montalvo. Not only did she provide a delicious lunch, but she also was quite entertaining."

The producer seemed to ponder the statement a moment. "I see." Another pause, presumably to find Sienna in the crowd, though how anyone could miss her was beyond Joe's understanding. "The purpose was for you to get an idea for what it might have been like for Crockett. Entertaining was not the goal."

Joe found Sienna looking his direction and winked. When she offered him her back, he turned his attention to the producer and shrugged. "I beg to differ, sir. You see, I've done a little research on this, and during the siege Colonel Crockett and Sergeant John McGregor took turns entertaining with fiddle and bagpipes. McGregor, as you might guess, was the bagpiper."

Kelton's snort told Joe he held little interest in the topic. "Go and meet the investors," he said. "Money always enjoys mingling with talent." And then he gestured for Sienna to join them. She responded immediately by extricating herself from the conversation then moved toward them.

He couldn't help but let his gaze slide the length of her. And as pretty as she was on the outside, Sienna Montalvo was drop-dead gorgeous inside as well. Only a fool would have let her go.

And right now Joe felt like the biggest fool on the planet.

"You look lovely," he said when she was close enough to hear.

"Stick close to Ramirez tonight, Miss Montalvo," the producer said. "Be sure he knows the names of everyone here before they introduce themselves. Got it?"

"Got it," she said.

"And let's keep the entertaining to a minimum, shall we?"

"Got it," Joe echoed as he watched Kelton maneuver himself around the chairs and into an animated conversation with a half dozen men in the center of the patio. When he returned his attention to Sienna, he found her staring.

"What is he talking about?"

He considered answering but found his ability to string his thoughts together compromised by looking into Sienna's eyes. Instead, he stared past her at Kelton, who seemed to be having a grand time.

"Who are they?" Joe asked, though he truly didn't care. When she easily rattled off the names, he laughed. "No wonder he's keeping you as his assistant. You're good at this sort of thing."

Sienna looked less than thrilled. "Not everyone can be a star, Joey. Now let's go show you off," she said in what Joe recognized as her most sarcastic tone.

Joe played along as Sienna hauled him from one investor to another, never failing to smile or say just the right thing. Just when he figured they'd run out of people to meet, Sienna would guide him toward another. Finally, after a full two hours of smiling, his jaws hurt.

"Come on," Joe said as he grasped Sienna by the elbow. "I've got to get out of here, and you're going with me."

She shook her head. "I can't. Unlike you, I'm working tonight."

"Sienna, honey, I've just done some of the best acting of my life tonight." He nodded toward Art Kelton. "Now watch me perform the grand finale."

❄

Sienna watched Joey capture the producer's attention as he slid into the group of men from Tennessee. The largest of the groups of investors, the businessmen all had roots in the

Nashville music scene. Any question as to why they would want to be associated with a remake of a John Wayne movie would be put to rest tomorrow when the performers on the soundtrack of *The Alamo* were announced.

And of course, plans for a tour to coincide with the opening were also in the works. She sighed. This part of moviemaking—the business deals and incentive packages—was her least favorite. The real fun would come on December 1 when filming began.

Joey broke away from the group to join her. Linking arms, he turned her toward the exit. "Shall we?"

Sienna stalled. "What? No. I can't leave. I told you I'm working."

He nodded. "Yes, actually, you are. And I asked for Mr. Kelton to give you a special assignment."

"Which is?"

Reaching into his pocket, Joey palmed a deck of cards. "Gin rummy?"

She slipped from his grasp and shook her head then walked over to the edge of the terrace. Here the view of the river was exquisite. Though the air held a chill and the ring around the moon portended more rain, the night sky was clear and dotted with stars so bright that even the lights of San Antonio could not dim them.

Her former flame joined her at the rail, edging just close enough for discomfort. "Was it something I said?" he whispered. "No, wait, it was something I did."

"You're insufferable!"

Joey leaned into her line of sight. "And that's what you love about me."

"Loved," she said. "Emphasis on past tense."

But as Sienna spoke the words, she knew nothing could be further from the truth. Hot tears sprung to her eyes, and she blinked them back as she held on tight to the rail. The Riverwalk blurred and the sound of the mariachi faded as a lone guitar began to play.

She knew this tune and so did Joey. "Besame Mucho." Their song. Or, it had been.

If Joey noticed, he didn't let on. Instead, he reached to press his hand atop hers.

Besame mucho—"kiss me a lot."

Sienna stood very still, her effort concentrated on not falling apart or, worse, into Joey's arms. And then he leaned over again, this time to wrap his arm around her waist. Had she the strength, Sienna might have removed herself from his embrace.

But all strength had fled by the chorus. And then Joey began to sing. The words were soft, just enough for her alone to hear. Gradually, he turned Sienna toward him.

"Forgive me," he said as their gazes collided. "Please," was a ragged breath that landed in the gap between them. "I was so stupid. A real idiot." Joey paused. "You could disagree, you know."

"I wouldn't think of it," she managed, half laughing. "Go on."

"Idiot." He leaned closer. "A fool." Closer still. "Eight months and two days. I've been miserable."

Eight months and two days? So he had been counting, too.

"You didn't look miserable in those pictures." The tears had begun to fall in earnest now, and Sienna could only hope

Mr. Kelton and the investors were too busy making deals to notice. "And there were plenty of poses. Dozens. Surely if there was one ounce of regret in you, Joey Ramirez, you would have shown it at some point, but when you were with her and—"

Words ceased when Joey kissed her.

Chapter 11

Was that applause? Sienna's world righted itself, though it took more than a moment for her to realize she still stood on the roof deck of La Cocina del Rio. A second later, she breathed a sigh of relief that the clapping was for the singer, a well-known country music performer, and not the other entertainment, namely their all-too-public kiss.

"I still love you, Sienna," Joey whispered against her ear.

"It's been eight months," she said as she slipped under his arm and took a step back. "Eight months and you—"

"Eight months and two days," he interjected, "and I've been miserable every minute of it."

"I doubt that." She turned to walk away and Joey followed, which made Sienna irritated and thrilled in equal measure. Much as she wanted to believe him, too much had happened to let it go so easily. "I hear Playa del Carmen in spring is quite nice. At least it looked that way when you and she were lounging on the beach."

"Now wait just a minute." Joey grasped her elbow and hauled her back against him. His eyes narrowed. "That was a complete setup. The production company flew the two of us and thirty of our closest coworkers in for a fun afternoon of shooting fake photos of us. It was awful."

Tanned skin, blond hair, and a yellow bikini came to mind. So did the two of them on a Jet Ski. And in a hammock strung between two palm trees. "Yeah, Joey, I'm sure it was just horrible. You poor thing."

His almost defiant look went soft. "Look," he said gently, "I told you. I'm an idiot. I said yes to the wrong people, but I've learned my lesson. I won't let that happen again."

Joey's words struck something deep inside, and Sienna turned to point a finger at his chest. "I'm determined not to say yes to the wrong people, either. Or, in this case, the wrong person."

"You can trust me."

You can trust me.

"How can I know that for sure, Joey?" When he had no immediate response, she gathered her purse and hurried to the ladies' room to repair her makeup. "The Ramirez Reject indeed," Sienna muttered. "Well not anymore."

She took her time in the hopes when she finally returned to the patio Joey might be gone. Instead she found him waiting just outside the door, arms crossed over his chest. The music had returned to a lively salsa number, and a few of the guests were trying their hand at the piñata that Sienna had ordered especially for the occasion. Inside the likeness of a fiery-red jalapeño pepper were gifts from several elite San

Antonio establishments, all chosen to convey the flair of the city and wrapped to withstand a pounding.

If only her heart were so protected. Sienna felt Joey press his palm against her back and shuddered.

"Cold?" He had his jacket off and around her shoulders before she could protest.

Warmth enveloped her, as did the spicy scent of patchouli that was his favorite fragrance. If only she could turn the clock back. Back not just to before that awful premiere and the faux romance that followed, but back further to the day she stopped appreciating what she had in Joey Ramirez.

"All right, Sienna," he said. "How do we get past this?"

Art Kelton signaled for Sienna to join him, and she nodded. "Excuse me, but work calls."

Joey moved between her and the producer. "No."

"No?" She shook her head. "Have you lost your mind? Go back to playing Hollywood heartthrob, and I'll go be Mr. Kelton's PA. That's why we're here tonight, remember?"

"That might be why you're here, but I asked to be invited."

"What?" Sienna looked past Joey to nod once again at Mr. Kelton. "Why would you do that? These things are hopelessly boring most of the time."

"Because I knew you were going to be here." He reached to cradle her jaw with his hand. "I guess Kelton will toss me off the film for romancing his PA, but I don't care." Joey chuckled. "My agent is ready to kill me, and the new publicist is probably going to quit, but I figure Letterman and Leno and all those morning talk show hosts will survive if I don't do their shows this week."

Mr. Kelton gestured for her again and Sienna frowned. "But you chose me?"

He nodded. "Funny how easy it was. Guess it's because I love you." He leaned closer. "Did you hear me, Sienna? I. Love. You."

The producer had ceased attempting to get her attention and was now storming her way with a less than pleased look. At the same time, the Nashville singer emerged from the men's room.

Joey shook his hand then introduced him to Sienna. "I'm trying to convince her to take me back," he said.

"How's that going?" the singer asked, his attention purely on Sienna.

"Not so well."

"Even after I played 'Besame Mucho'?" He winked at Sienna. "You're tougher than he thought."

So Joey discussed her with this man? Odd. And yet interesting. And more than a little flattering.

"Well look at that, Joe," the singer said. "I believe she's coming around, though if I were you I'd learn how to sing that song just in case. Being an actor's fine and good, but the ladies love a singer, you know."

Joey grinned. "Why don't we take a stroll down to the river and talk about this, Sienna? Just the two of us," he added. "And maybe I'll give that singing thing a try."

"Maybe," was all Sienna could say before her boss closed in on them.

"Miss Montalvo, what is the problem?" the producer demanded soon as he was within earshot. "Grab your pen and paper. I've got some ideas, and I need you to write them down before I forget."

Joey said nothing, but his disappointment was obvious.

Sienna paused. "Actually, Mr. Kelton, I've got a situation here that needs handling."

"Excuse me, sir," the singer said. "But I was wondering if I might have a moment of your time. My agent's been begging me to consider that bit part you offered in this movie, but I wasn't much interested until the record hit number one. Now I'm thinking, after some serious conversation with a group of your investors, as a tie-in to the movie we might. . ."

And somehow, a moment later, the singer and the producer were walking away.

"He's good," Joey said. "And not just at singing."

"You had him play 'Besame Mucho'." She paused to gather her wits. "And you came here instead of going on Letterman."

Joey moved quickly to wrap his arms around her. "Leno," he said. "Letterman would have been tomorrow. Leno's West Coast, but Letterman's in New York and that's—"

"Joey."

He looked down at her, caramel eyes full of what she recognized as love. "Yes?"

"Shut up and kiss me, would you?"

Chapter 12

December 23,
San Antonio

Two weeks into filming, Mr. Kelton relented and gave the crew a full week off. Although Sienna enjoyed watching Joey act, she couldn't wait to see how he performed in front of her family. For though he had been in Texas all this time, Kelton's talent was not allowed off the set, and he'd not yet seen her family.

Before Sienna could unbuckle her seat belt, her family came pouring out of the house. While Britny and the aunties pressed forward toward the driveway, Dina held back to watch from the porch. Joey endured hugs, kisses, and at least one pinched cheek before Consuela, Vi, and Dolores finally let the poor man go.

Sienna reached for her niece, who looked strangely shy. If she was in awe of Joey, he'd cure her of it soon enough.

"Britny, honey," she said as they headed for the porch, "are you ready for tonight?"

"I'm a little nervous," she admitted. "But I think I'm ready."

Joey fell into step with them. "All the big stars get nervous."

"Really?" Britny's eyes widened. "Even you?"

He laughed. "Yeah, even me." And then his face went serious. "Hello, Mr. Montalvo." Joey moved ahead of them to reach out in an attempt to shake Papa's hand.

For a moment, Sienna thought her father might not take it. He surprised her by greeting Joey like a long-lost friend.

And then, to her further surprise, the two of them walked off together speaking Spanish. "Joey," Sienna called, "could I talk to you a moment?"

"Sure, honey," he said. "Mind if I catch up with your dad for a few minutes first?"

She watched the men head toward the back door and then shook her head when they disappeared outside. Dina came to stand beside her. "What do you make of that, Dina?"

"Don't try and figure it out," she said. "They're guys. My guess is they're talking football."

A peek out the window and her sister yanked her back. "Don't you dare go spying on them. Leave them be, and come help me get ready to start the tamales."

Reluctantly, Sienna joined Dina and the aunties in what had become a Christmas tradition. Though most of their friends had turkey and dressing for the holiday meal, the Montalvos had always preferred traditional tamales and queso.

Working with a recipe that required neither measurements nor instructions, the aunties supervised while Dina, Sienna, and even Britny did the work of chopping the meat, mixing the masa, and preparing the tamales. When the husks were filled and the tamales steamed, Sienna took a glass of sweet tea to the table and joined the ladies of the Montalvo house in conversation.

Only then did she realize Papa and Joey were still outside.

"Don't you wonder what they're talking about?" Auntie Vi asked.

"I think he's asking for her hand in marriage," Auntie Consuela said.

"Do people still do that?" This from Britny who rolled her eyes then jammed the earphones from her iPod in place.

Auntie Dolores moved to the window and peered out the blinds. "You've got to come see this."

By the time Sienna got her turn at the window, the other ladies were staring at her. "What?" she said as she lifted the blind and saw there were now three men on the porch, and one of them looked suspiciously like—

"The General?"

✻

Sienna burst through the door and landed in The General's arms. "It's so good to see you," she said. "Where's Mrs. Ramirez?"

Joe laughed. "You'll see her tonight at the play. She's back at the hotel getting ready."

"She's coming to Britny's play?" Sienna looked to her father. "What's going on here, Papa?"

Jorge Montalvo merely shook his head. "It's Christmas, Sissy. Don't ask so many questions."

The General shrugged. "Joe's far too modest to tell you, honey, but he's being honored tonight."

"Honored?" She looked to Joey. "What kind of honor?"

Leave it to The General to deflect the question. "Remember that drama teacher?"

"She's not—" Sienna laughed. "You're being honored by the Thespian Society?"

Joe thought fast. "Thespian of the Year," was the best he could come up with.

"Wait a minute," she said. "You have to be in high school to get that honor."

"Give poor Miss Harrison a break. She's righting a wrong. She knows I should have won that award instead of Buck Batson." He paused to give her a hug. "Actually, it's a surprise, so if you see her beforehand, don't mention it."

What he wouldn't tell her is the surprise was about to be on Sienna.

Leaving her to hitch a ride back to the hotel with his father was not what he felt like doing, but if Joe spent another minute with Sienna, he'd never be able to keep quiet.

"She's good for you," The General said.

Joe reached across the seat to clasp his father by the shoulder. "Yeah, she is," he admitted.

His father gave Joe a sideways look. "You'd best treat her right."

"Or I'll have you and the United States Army to answer to?"

The General laughed. "Hardly. I was thinking of a much

bigger threat: Jorge and the Montalvo women."

✳

Sienna followed Dina and her husband down the dimly lit aisle of the high school auditorium. "Still smells like moth-balls," she commented as she took her seat and settled in.

Dina giggled. "This place never changes."

"So, did Britny get over her nerves?"

Her sister launched into a story about her daughter's afternoon preparing for her role that had Sienna laughing aloud. When Papa joined them and gave them a look, the laughter increased. His attention was diverted, however, when The General and Mrs. Ramirez slid into place at the far end of the row.

Joe sank into the seat beside Sienna and gave her a quick kiss on the cheek. "Just like old times," he said.

"Well, sort of," Sienna admitted. "Except for the fact you were delayed a full fifteen minutes by autograph seekers."

"Sweetheart, I've always had my fans, but you are the president of my fan club." He laughed at his own joke while Dina groaned.

As the curtain rose, the aunties came hurrying up the aisle to take the last three seats in the row. "The gang's all here," Dina said. "This should be fun."

A brief medley of Christmas tunes courtesy of the high school honors orchestra prevented Miss Harrison from speaking immediately. Instead, she remained at the microphone, her posture impeccable, until the last cowbell was struck.

"Welcome to the Thespian Society's annual Christmas show. As you know, this is a time when our best and brightest shine."

And shine they did, though Sienna decided Britny's monologue was the best of all. And that was speaking from the point of view of a professional, not her aunt.

"Be right back," Joey said after Britny had finished.

By the time Miss Harrison reappeared on the stage, Sienna was beginning to wonder where Joey went. Surely there weren't that many people looking to have a photograph with the guy. Then she remembered his comment about the surprise award.

Likely that's where he'd gone.

"And now for our grand finale." Miss Harrison cleared her throat. "Please welcome to the stage one of our school's more famed alumni."

Sienna craned her neck to see if she could spy Joey.

"Miss Sienna Montalvo."

A cheer went up from the family as Dina poked her arm and Papa looked over to beam at her. "Go on up, Sissy," he said.

She shook her head. "What's going on, Papa?"

"Just go," he said. "And remember nothing's impossible with God."

Sienna pondered Papa's words as she made her way onto the stage. Though Miss Harrison thrust a microphone into her hand, Sienna kept silent.

"For those of you who don't know, Sienna was once a student of mine." She paused. "And now she's in Hollywood making movies. Isn't that something?"

The smattering of applause was accompanied by loud hoots and hollering from the Montalvo row. Leave it to her family—

"And so, given the fact she's been quite an asset to our drama department, we thought it appropriate to honor her with a plaque." Another round of applause that Miss Harrison brought to an end with a wave of her hands. "So, in order to accomplish this, I've asked a special friend of Sienna's and of this school's to do the honors."

Sienna looked off to stage left and saw Joey standing there. He waved and pointed to what was obviously the plaque that Miss Harrison was so excited about.

"Without any further ado, may I present the Academy Award nominee and alumnus of our fair school, Mr. Joe Ramirez."

Joey's round of applause lasted much longer than hers, giving him time to whisper a quick "I love you" in her ear.

"Did you know about this?" she responded, and he answered with a wink.

When the applause ended, Joey walked to the edge of the stage and pointed down at the orchestra. On his cue, the string section struck up the first chords of "Besame Mucho."

"What are you doing?" she mouthed to Joey when he glanced over his shoulder to meet her stare.

Rather than answering, he walked over and took the microphone from her hand.

And then he began to sing.

In flawless Spanish.

Somewhere around the second stanza, Sienna's tears had begun to fall. By the time Joey had finished, she'd cried off her makeup and generally made a fool of herself.

"*Gracias*," Joey said. "And now for the award." He turned to the audience and gestured to the plaque under his arms.

"Since we've made Miss Montalvo stand there and do nothing, I'm going to have her read the inscription. What do you think?"

When the cheers subsided, Joe slid his arm around Sienna's waist then handed her the plaque. "Go ahead and read it, sweetheart."

"To be or not to be?" Sienna began to giggle.

"Go on," Joey said. "Read the fine print."

Sienna squinted to read the words beneath the quote. "My wife?" She shook her head.

Joey released her. "Start over at the beginning."

She lifted the plaque again. "To be or not to be my wife. That is the question."

And then it hit her.

Wife.

"Joey?" She found him kneeling before her. "Joey, this isn't from the school."

Laughter rose from the audience.

"Sienna Montalvo, will you marry me and live happily ever after?"

Of course, when she found her voice, Sienna said yes.

Bestselling author Kathleen Y'Barbo has written more than 30 books. More than 950,000 copies of her works are in print, and her books have been translated into several languages, including German and Dutch. A tenth-generation Texan, Kathleen lives near Houston.

A Letter to Our Readers

Dear Readers:

In order that we might better contribute to your reading enjoyment, we would appreciate you taking a few minutes to respond to the following questions. When completed, please return to the following: Fiction Editor, Barbour Publishing, Inc., P.O. Box 719, Uhrichsville, OH 44683.

1. Did you enjoy reading *A Riverwalk Christmas* by Elizabeth Goddard, Martha Rodgers, Lynette Sowell, and Kathleen Y'Barbo?
   ❑ Very much. I would like to see more books like this.
   ❑ Moderately—I would have enjoyed it more if _____
   _____
   _____

2. What influenced your decision to purchase this book?
   (Check those that apply.)
   ❑ Cover   ❑ Back cover copy   ❑ Title   ❑ Price
   ❑ Friends   ❑ Publicity   ❑ Other

3. Which story was your favorite?
   ❑ *Riverside Serenade*   ❑ *Lights of Love*
   ❑ *Key to Her Heart*   ❑ *Remember the Alamo*

4. Please check your age range:
   ❑ Under 18   ❑ 18–24   ❑ 25–34
   ❑ 35–45   ❑ 46–55   ❑ Over 55

5. How many hours per week do you read? _____

Name _____

Occupation _____

Address _____

City _____ State _____ Zip _____

E-mail _____

CHRISTMAS MAIL-ORDER BRIDES

FOUR-IN-ONE-COLLECTION

When marriage arrives by mail-order—and just in time for Christmas—the results are unpredictable. Can true love grow after an awkward start?

Historic, paperback, 352 pages, 5⅜" x 8"